She lif... in acceptance

In all her life Dana had enjoyed few pleasures so much that she'd dreamed of repeating them. The thrill of amusement-park roller coasters had diminished in direct proportion to her age and successively higher levels of daring. Funnel cakes, those batter-fried swirls of sweetness sold at tourist traps around the country, had won first prize with her taste buds. She'd begged, wheedled or bought one at every opportunity since. The problem was that she couldn't quite recapture the first delicious sensation. Roller-coaster rides and funnel cakes never measured up to the pleasure she recalled, and so she'd come to the reluctant conclusion that memory endowed first-time experiences with a charm that could not be duplicated. She'd lived by that assumption, too—until this very moment, when Rick had kissed her and shot her theory to pieces.

ABOUT THE AUTHOR

Karen Toller Whittenburg credits her love of reading with inspiring her writing career. She enjoys fiction in every form, but romance continues to hold a special place for her. As a teenager she spent long, lovely hours with Emilie Loring's heroines, falling in love with every hero and participating in every adventure. It's no wonder she always dreamed of being a romance writer. Karen loves the challenge of creating characters and stories to capture those hours of romance and adventure for her own readers. She lives in Oklahoma and divides her time between writing and running a household, both full-time and fulfilling careers.

Books by Karen Toller Whittenburg

HARLEQUIN AMERICAN ROMANCE
197–SUMMER CHARADE
249–A MATCHED SET

Don't miss any of our special offers. Write to us at the following address for information on our newest releases.

Harlequin Reader Service
901 Fuhrmann Blvd., P.O. Box 1397, Buffalo, NY 14240
Canadian address: P.O. Box 603,
Fort Erie, Ont. L2A 5X3

Peppermint Kisses
Karen Toller Whittenburg

Harlequin Books

TORONTO • NEW YORK • LONDON
AMSTERDAM • PARIS • SYDNEY • HAMBURG
STOCKHOLM • ATHENS • TOKYO • MILAN

For my daughter, Jill,
who sweetens so many hours of my life

Published May 1989

First printing March 1989

ISBN 0-373-16294-4

Chapter One

"This place has gone to hell in a handmade basket!" Hezekiah Brown cranked down the pickup window and leaned out, as if he expected the flashing motel signs and wall-to-wall traffic to fade like a mirage upon closer inspection.

It was dead-center July and the heat was just this side of unbearable, but Rick reached across the dash and shut off the air-conditioning. No point in trying to cool the great outdoors of the Ozarks. Even less point in asking his old friend to roll up the window.

"This is progress, Ki." Rick downshifted to slow the truck to a three-mile-an-hour crawl along the main drag of Branson. "You knew it was coming when you left, and you've been gone a long time."

"Nothing shoulda changed this much in ten years. Tarnation! This used to be a nice, quiet little tourist town." Hezekiah loosened his necktie with an impatient jerk and flipped it free of the white collar. He worked the top button of his shirt with stubby fingers and mounting frustration. "Damn shirt collars! Can't wait to get out of these duds and into some overalls."

Rick resisted the impulse to suggest that the overalls probably wouldn't fit any better. No matter what he wore, Ki Brown looked as uncomfortable as a mule in a sunbonnet. The checkered beret he now sported did have a certain panache, but it would have looked better on a tall, thin Englishman. Hezekiah was short and tended toward the stout, muscular build of his mountain-men ancestors. He was somewhere around retirement age and the nearest thing to a father Rick had ever known.

"Ten years haven't changed you much, have they?" Rick said lightly. "You'll find most of the year-round residents haven't changed, either. Why, once we get to the intersection and head away from town, you'll be able to turn your ear to the wind and hear the echo of all the rumors that've been circulating about you. If Mrs. Dartney has asked once, she's asked a hundred times when you were coming home." Rick lifted a playful eyebrow. "She still has the hots for you, Pop."

"That old widow woman has the hots for any man who can stand upright without a prop." Ki managed to pry open the top two buttons of his shirt, then let his arm rest half in, half out of the rolled-down window. "And don't call me Pop, Sonny Boy. I can't have folks thinkin' I'm old enough to have a lunk of a son like you. It'd scare off the women."

Rick laughed. "You're rich enough now to have your pick of women. Nothing short of dynamite will scare them off."

"Is that what they're saying?" Ki turned cynical blue eyes to Rick. "That I'm rich enough to do whatever I want?"

"That's the way I hear it."

"And is that what you think, Rick?"

A slow affectionate grin tipped the corners of Rick's mouth. "I think you've always done whatever you wanted, Ki."

The older man emitted a gruff rumble of good humor. "That I have. And there's not been a day I've lived to regret, either."

Rick pushed back the brim of his Stetson with his thumb. "Then you're a lucky man."

"Hmmph." Ki turned his attention back to the panorama of No Vacancy signs and the endless ebb of bumper-to-bumper traffic. "I'm a crusty old son of a gun, Rick, and I wish I'd done some things differently." He rubbed his hand across the stubbly new growth of beard on his chin. "I have no regrets, mind you, but lookin' back, I see a couple of rainbows I shoulda caught hold of."

The traffic began to move and Rick made his turn on the yellow light at the intersection. "Most folks aren't going to see it that way, you know. You were raised dirt-poor, educated by the skin of your pants, and with nothing but a handful of dollars and a whale of a lot of determination you built a multimillion-dollar industry in a short ten years. Why, you and your partner, Henry, started with a sweet tooth apiece and ended up as the owners of London Country Candies, a gourmet candy company touted throughout Europe as the royal family of sweets. Most folks are gonna say you got lucky, Ki. Hoot 'n' holler lucky."

Hezekiah laughed at that. "They'll be right."

Rick didn't believe it for a second. Ki had worked hard and if Lady Luck had smiled on his efforts . . . well, that just meant there was still justice in the world. "I'm glad you decided to come home, Ki. Even after all this time, the home place seems lonesome without you."

"There're remedies for that, Rick. A smart boy woulda figured it out afore now and gotten himself hitched to a sweet young peach of a gal."

"You've done fine without a woman in your life, Ki."

"I've done all right without a wife, boy. That's not the same as doin' fine without a woman." Ki slid a careful glance to Rick. "And I hope you know there is a difference."

Rick eased down on the gas pedal. The road curved up and away from the hubbub of downtown Branson and the truck picked up speed. "Well, I'm doing fine on my own. The house hasn't been that lonesome."

Ki breathed in a mouthful of mountain air and released it in a satisfied huff. "You know why I haven't been back till now, Rick?" He didn't wait for an answer. "I knew once I breathed the fragrance of these hills again, I wouldn't be able to leave."

Rick understood. He loved his birthplace, the history of family and friends that was his birthright. "Why *did* you come back, Ki? I was surprised when you called and asked me to pick you up at the airport in Springfield."

"I'll probably surprise a lot of people, but I've got my reasons. For now let's just say I'm investigatin' a rumor." Ki turned his gaze to the countryside and Rick let the subject drop.

The truck took the first curve of a tree-shaded bend. "Up ahead," Rick said. "You'll notice the log-cabin facade of the Ausbrook Confectionery. It, too, has changed some since the last time you saw it."

Ki greeted this information with a disgruntled snort. "Old Maggie Jane is still at it, huh? I kinda hoped she'd have got her comeuppance by now."

"Not a charitable thought, Ki. Margaret Ausbrook has done a lot for this town and not, I might add, at the expense of the area. You won't see any flashing neon signs around here."

"I'm sure the skunks and other wild critters appreciate it."

Rick frowned. He knew, as everyone in the area knew, of the long-standing feud between Margaret Burton Ausbrook and Hezekiah Brown. But he didn't know why the passing of the years and the attainment of success on both sides hadn't softened the bad feelings. "A lot of folks appreciate how she's tried to blend business and nature into an agreeable setting for both. You're just letting personal feelings interfere with your judgment."

"Darn right I am." Ki narrowed his eyes and leaned forward to eyeball the upcoming bend in the road. "I learned all about personal feelings the hard way. From old Maggie Jane, herself. I'm surprised to hear you defend her, Rick, considering how she sent you packin' the minute you set eyes on her daughter."

"It wasn't quite that way, Ki." Rick shifted on the bench seat. He hadn't thought about Dana in some time. These days he tried not to think about her at all, which was a little like trying not to think about pink elephants. "Margaret Ausbrook only precipitated the breakup. I would have come to my senses sooner or later, anyway."

"Maybe you would. Maybe you wouldn't. The point is, you'll never know for sure."

A valid argument, Rick conceded silently, although he still preferred to believe his own good judgment would have surfaced . . . eventually. Ten years ago, he'd made a fool of himself over Dana Ausbrook, but he chose to look at it as a valuable lesson learned. One he wouldn't need to repeat. "The point is," he said, striving for conviction, "it doesn't make any difference."

"Hmm," was Ki's only reply.

The truck came out of the curve, bringing the confectionery into view. It was a log cabin cleverly disguising the small but modern factory behind it. Rick had always thought it a quaint, cozy building, filled with wonderful, sweet smells, although he hadn't been inside it in years. He'd met Margaret Ausbrook on occasion, usually at social functions about town, but polite as she was and as friendly as he tried to be, there was still an underscoring of tension between them. Past history. It didn't make any difference, but neither one of them had quite forgotten it, either.

"What's goin' on?" Ki asked, his voice grumpy still. "Or does she always keep the place decked out like a peacock on the strut?"

It wasn't quite an accurate description, although there were dozens of brightly colored balloons festooning the entire front of the building. A banner, lettered in peppermint strips of red and white, streamed from twin chimney to twin chimney, proclaiming Welcome! to one and all. Cars nearly filled the parking area out front, and Rick recognized Lathan Williams, the local newspaperman, standing beside his car, camera in hand, talking to another man with a video camera. A number of people stood outside as if waiting for the doors to open, but the truck was past the building before Rick could make out any other familiar faces.

"What do you suppose . . . ?" Ki shifted in his seat, putting his head out the open window, trying to see in retrospect what had passed so quickly from physical view. "Turn around," he commanded.

Rick didn't need a second suggestion and slowed the truck for a U-turn. "Do you think she'll let us in?" he asked.

For the first time during the afternoon, genuine mischief sparked in Hezekiah's sharp, blue eyes. "I'd love to see her try to stop me." He looked slyly at Rick.

"Now, you I don't know about. Probably depends on whether or not the daughter is in the crowd."

"That's hardly likely, Ki. If Dana visits the area—and I've heard she does pay an obligatory visit to her mother every summer—she comes in like the fog and leaves in the dead of night. I haven't seen her since—" he didn't want to remember the last time he'd seen Dana Ausbrook "—a long time. Ten years, I guess." He shrugged. "Not that it matters. Margaret probably won't even let you on the parking lot, anyway."

"Now, that's an interesting thought, isn't it?"

The idea that Dana might be at the confectionery was of far more interest to Rick...which irritated him no end. To think that after all this time, his pulse rate still jumped at the mere thought of seeing her. And she wouldn't be there. She'd made no bones about disliking the candy factory. He'd heard her say many times over that she'd die before she'd work there. Of course, she'd been very young then, but in the last ten years Rick had yet to meet anyone half as stubborn as Dana Ausbrook.

"I don't see her anywhere," Ki said, reclaiming Rick's attention. "Looks like we'll get to surprise old Margaret."

It was hard to imagine how anyone could surprise Margaret, but Rick figured if anyone could do it, Ki would be the one. Rick glanced at his companion just in time to catch the glimmer of a wickedly eager smile. Whatever was going on at the candy factory, it was nothing compared to what would happen if the Burton-Brown feud flared again. And Rick had a sudden idea that, despite what he'd said about investigating a rumor, Ki had come home to reopen some old, personal feelings. If he had, it might just prove to be the best entertainment to come along in some time.

As Granny Varnell often said, "Fun is fun, but for real entertainment it takes a happenin'—like the day Ezra Midnight's moonshine still blew sky-high or the time the circuit preacher lost his dentures only to have the Widow Talbott bring them to the church on Sunday morning and drop them into the offering plate." Nope, Rick thought, there hadn't been a genuine "happenin'" in these hills for years.

"All right," he said as he parked the truck and pulled on the brake. "Let's see what's going on here."

Ki was already out of the pickup, hiking up the waistline of his slacks and adjusting his suspenders. He cocked the checkered beret at a jaunty angle on his balding head and his mouth slid into a laughing grin. "Yeah," he said. "Let's go see."

THE MACHINERY CLICKED into gear with a muffled hum that echoed through the plant like burgeoning amusement. This was it. There was no chance of escape, no last minute reprieve. Dana knew her fate, finally, was at hand. She turned from the office window overlooking the factory below.

"This really isn't necessary, Margaret," she said to her mother. "A couple of paragraphs buried somewhere in the business pages would have accomplished the same thing."

Margaret kept writing. She didn't look up.

Dana sighed. "I can see the headlines now. Peppermint Prodigal Returns or Bonbon Heiress to Sweeten Profits. Do you suppose they'll print any of my credentials or will they tout this as a case of pure and simple nepotism?"

"What difference does it make what they print? You have enough college degrees to overqualify you for almost any job this side of the Atlantic. And I'd have hired you even if you'd only finished high school." Margaret signed her name with a flourish and reached for her smoldering cigarette without lifting her eyes from the paper on her desk.

Dana watched the effortless movement in awed disgust. She hated to see her mother smoke cigarette after cigarette, but there was a certain fascination in the unconscious precision of motion involved. "Do you know how many of those things you've had in the past thirty minutes?"

"I've had several things during the past thirty minutes, Dana." Margaret placed her pen upright in its black and brass stand and breathed out a puff of smoke. "None of which has been the pleasure of your company." Brown eyes, a match to Dana's own, focused over the top of an innocuous pair of half-lens glasses. "You are as nervous and jumpy as a cricket on a skillet. Anyone would think you were afraid to face a handful of friendly faces and a couple of camera flashes. This meeting with the press is nothing more than a way of introducing you to the local residents."

Dana edged down onto the plush, tapestried arm of a wingback chair and returned Margaret's open regard. "It's nothing more than publicity, Margaret. You know it, I know it, and they—" she tossed her head toward the doorway and the waiting crowd outside "—know it. You introduced me to the local residents ten minutes after I was born and they haven't forgotten me. Let's not cloud the issue."

Margaret smiled slowly and eased into gentle laughter. "I adore you, Dana. If you weren't my daughter, I'd adopt you."

"A rash statement, Margaret. I'll remind you of it in a few weeks when you're yelling at me for not pouring my soul into my work." Dana crossed one slim ankle over the other and visually inspected her new lizard-skin shoes, a going-away, good-luck present from her father. "Dad said I should ignore you when you tear into that kind of tantrum."

"Funny. He gave me much the same advice about you." Margaret smiled and stripped the glasses from her nose. "Easy for him to say. He's in Philadelphia. Too far away to hear the repercussions of any tantrums—what a silly word—you or I might have."

Dana had a sudden longing for Philadelphia and the home of her father, where she'd spent most of her life. But in all truth, Philadelphia was no more home to her now than was Branson, Missouri. "Don't worry, Margaret. I'm too old for tantrums."

"Not me." Margaret pushed back in her chair and got to her feet. She wasn't very tall, but her presence was imposing just the same. Margaret Ausbrook wore authority like a well-positioned beauty mark. "A display of temper can be quite effective on occasion. I do hope your father hasn't raised you with so much conscience that you can't indulge in a little foot-stomping now and then."

Dana shrugged noncommittally. She wasn't about to admit how little success her father and grandparents had had in trying to subdue her naturally high spirits. She was, after all, her mother's daughter. "Is it time to face the lynch mob?" she asked, rising reluctantly at Margaret's approach. "Should I powder my nose? Comb my hair?"

"Slit your wrists?" Margaret paused at the door, hand on the knob. "Honestly, Dana, this is just a little press announcement. Not the melodrama you seem intent upon making it. Save your theatrics for the television cameras."

"Television?" Dana's stomach slid to her toes. "I thought you said it would be just the newspaper."

Margaret opened the door and motioned Dana forward. "Don't be a goose. We're announcing the additions of a new caramel cream and a new vice president all on the same day. Don't you think the public has a right to know?"

There were certain members of the public—one, in particular—whom Dana hoped would never even find out she was in town. She didn't care who knew about the caramel cream. "I can't imagine the public is that interested."

Pursing her lips, Margaret began closing the door, propelling Dana through the exit. "Believe it or not, Dana, this is the real world and selling candy to the masses is what you're here to do. Start thinking like a businesswoman. That's what I'm paying you for."

A valid point, Dana conceded as she preceded her mother down the stairs. She was now a salaried employee, a title she'd never before been able to claim. She'd been a full-time student up until now. She had the loan payments to prove it. If only she'd decided to enter law school immediately after getting her bachelor's degree, she might already have this year behind her. But she'd pursued a graduate degree in psychology before deciding law was her true interest. So now, with three diplomas, it was time to go to work. The confectionery wasn't her highest career objective, but she'd give it her best effort while she was here. Her own plans for the future would wait while she took one last shot at settling her past.

At the base of the stairs, two doors faced off. One led to the front of the building where a candy store and reception area were located; the other led into the factory where machines and employees worked in tandem to produce the Ausbrook confections. Dana knew the announcement was to be made inside the plant, but she waited for Margaret to reach the foot of the stairway and open the appropriate door. She felt like a fraud, even though Margaret knew Dana wouldn't stay longer than a year. Today's announcement would come as no surprise . . . except to the one man who'd heard her declare complete and utter independence from her mother's plans. But the chance of Rick Stafford being in the crowd was nil. She didn't think he'd come within a mile of the confectionery. He probably wouldn't come within ten miles if he knew she was here.

"Buck up," Margaret commanded. "It's only a year of your life, not the end of the world. Now remember, I'll make the announcements and introduce you. Then you take a piece of candy from the box, eat it—and do try to look happy about it, Dana—then pass the box around to our guests. More boxes will follow the first and we'll keep handing out caramel creams until—"

"—everyone is sick," Dana finished with a grimace.

Margaret patted Dana's cheek. "You have a lot to learn." She pulled open the heavy metal door and the sounds and smells of the factory, which had been subdued in the upstairs office, poured full strength over Dana.

A lump of anxiety collected in the back of her throat. This would never work. The smell of chocolate gave her a headache. Caramel stuck to her teeth. She couldn't look at a gumdrop without calculating the miles she'd have to jog to work off the extra calories. Worst of all, Margaret was her boss. Was keeping a promise really worth this?

There were a number of people standing in a roped-off area beside one of the conveyor belts. With a brisk pace and a pleased expression, Margaret made her way there, her arm linked with Dana's in a gesture of mother-daughter camaraderie.

Dana wasn't impressed, but apparently the crowd liked it. A couple of cameras flashed. There was a spattering of applause and then Margaret raised her voice to be heard above the hum of machinery. "Thank you for coming," she called. "I've waited for this day for twenty-eight years, ever since my daughter, Dana, was born." With this, she nudged Dana forward, presenting her formally, Dana supposed, to the people. "It gives me great pleasure to announce—"

Margaret's voice didn't break. It stopped cold. There was a rustle of movement in the back and Dana caught a glimpse of someone waving. She couldn't see his face clearly, but she could make out his white shirtfront and the paisley suspenders curving up over his round belly. From the look on Margaret's face, it seemed obvious that she recognized the man, and was not at all pleased to do so. Her clasp on Dana's elbow tightened, but her publicity-conscious smile didn't falter.

"—two new additions to the Ausbrook House of Candies." Margaret resumed the sentence as if the pause had been strictly for effect. It hadn't been. Dana knew it and she assumed the man in the back knew it, too, but no one else seemed to have noticed. Margaret continued with her spiel, giving the history of the Ausbrook Confectionery and working into a pitch for the new caramel cream.

Dana kept her expression lightly serious, as if she were listening to her mother's every word, but she actually let her attention wander to the little man in the back. He wasn't really little. He just wasn't as tall as the man who'd stepped through the doorway behind him...

Was that Rick? Rick Stafford? Her heart bumped into her throat and then rebounded against her ribcage. It couldn't be Rick. He would never... Dana fought the impulse to stand on tiptoe for a better view. She didn't want the video camera to catch her craning her neck to get a glimpse of a good-looking man in the crowd. She made herself glance away, focus her attention again on Margaret, but she couldn't make it stick. Her eyes kept wandering back to the man who looked like Rick.

Could it be? Her memory provided a stored image for comparison. Dana remembered Rick as a young man with lively green eyes and hair the color of corn silk. Her recollections were of a youthful body with muscular shoulders and arms tanned by long hours in the sun and a crooked smile that had done funny things to her stomach. Of course, she'd been a kid then, and any attention from a handsome young male had resulted in a funny feeling in her stomach. That did nothing to explain the churning sensation she experienced now. If the man was Rick, he had matured in all the right ways, she decided, as she tried again to get a better look at him. Boyish angles had sharpened, his features were well-defined and infinitely more attractive. His hair was a darker blond than she remembered, but that wasn't so unusual. Her own hair color had changed some in the past few years, deepening her once bright strawberry-blond to a more subdued autumn shade.

Her personality had deepened some, too, since she'd last seen Rick. Ten years ago, she'd been almost as flamboyant as her hair color.

Rick hadn't much liked her reckless approach to life and liberty then, she recalled, and wondered if he might like her better now. Not that it mattered. Margaret would have an unholy fit if she knew Rick was here.

The thought struck Dana that perhaps Rick and not the man in paisley suspenders had been responsible for Margaret's momentary loss of composure. But no. Margaret had been looking at the shorter man. In fact, Dana realized, her mother had hardly looked at anyone else since, and her eyes sparked with something akin to anticipation.

"...so as the first box of caramel creams comes off the line, our new vice president, Dana Ausbrook, will take a piece of candy and after she's taste-tested it, you may all sample this exquisite new confection." Margaret placed her hand at the small of Dana's back and urged her up to the conveyor.

Dana stepped forward, wishing she were anywhere in the world but here. The responsibility of the career she'd vowed she would not have loomed before her, symbolized by a small square of chocolate-covered candy. And of all things, Rick—it had to be him, Murphy's Law decreed it—was here to see her eat her words...literally.

Dana reached for the pastel-shaded box making its way along the conveyor belt. She wasn't sure what first distracted her—the restless tittering in the crowd or the glimpse of a flying carpet. Actually it was too small to be a carpet, Dana realized within the next few microseconds. It was just a scrap of black and white checked fabric, sailing end over end toward her. She started to duck, but the missile skimmed over her head and landed neatly on the candy box. In a game of horseshoes, it would have been a full-points ringer, but Dana wasn't sure what a beret around a box was worth.

There was a moment of suspended animation as the audience watched the action and then turned to see who had thrown the hat. Above the fluctuating quiet, a grumbly voice, full of barn-stomping mischief, called out, "Hi, Honey! I'm home!"

Dana guessed that the voice and the hat belonged to the man with the paisley suspenders, but she didn't think his heckling was aimed at her. She turned to see how Margaret was handling the disruption and caught her mother in the act of grabbing the candy box, tossing aside the troublesome beret and hurling the box—candy and all—at the heckler. Dana couldn't believe her eyes as the caramel creams scattered in airborne frenzy and rained down upon the hapless spectators.

The machines kept humming. The crowd's collective gaze shifted from the man in the back to Margaret in the front and then one by one turned to Dana. How she had suddenly become the person in charge, she didn't know, but it was obvious from her mother's furious expression that something had to be done. And quickly. "Ladies and gentlemen," she began with a reassuring smile.

"How dare you, Hezekiah Brown!" Margaret's voice and pointing finger rudely interrupted, encompassing the finer elements of good melodrama.

"Margaret—" Dana whispered the warning hoarsely, somehow maintaining that "everything's under control" smile for the watching crowd. "Ladies and gentlemen, please—"

"Ha!" Hezekiah Brown, Dana was sorry to see, began to move closer. "How dare you, Maggie Jane Burton!"

"If you take one more step, I'll call the police!" Margaret bristled like a Banty rooster. "You get off my property or I'll throw more than a box of candy at you."

The crowd shifted nervously. Dana grabbed her mother's elbow and squeezed meaningfully. "Please, don't be alarmed," she said to the group, while she searched for an idea. Any idea. "This is the promotion for our new candy...the 'Honey, I'm Home' caramel cream."

It was weak, Dana knew, but she didn't have much to work with and Hezekiah Brown was only a few steps away. She forced herself to laugh and hoped someone out there would buy her explanation. "We at Ausbrook Confections don't encourage you to 'throw' our chocolates, but we do hope you'll take a box home to share with your honey." The mood seemed to ease a little, but Dana could see she wasn't home free yet. "If you'd like to pick up a complementary box, you may do so in the candy shop right now."

No one rushed to the door. Probably because Hezekiah Brown had made his way through the crowd and was almost nose to nose with Margaret Ausbrook. The tension was so palpable that Dana was afraid one or the other would start a fistfight. Against her better judgment, she positioned herself between them. "Margaret. Hezekiah," she said as loudly, firmly, and cheerily as she could. "Take a bow. You've both turned in an amazing performance."

"I'm going to have you arrested for trespassing, Ki," Margaret announced over Dana's shoulder.

Her opponent grinned. "I want my hat, Maggie Jane."

"Over my dead body," Margaret replied.

Dana thought that sounded like the best idea yet, but she opted for retrieving the beret instead. Rising, she came nose to button with a familiar chest. Rick. Great, she thought, bringing her gaze up to collide with his. The perfect addition to this friendly little gathering. "Hello, Rick," she said dryly. "How nice to see you again."

"Dana, I want you to sue this man." Margaret, still oblivious to her responsibilities and the curious onlookers, pushed a stiff finger under a paisley suspender, pulled it and released it with an elastic pop. "You can't get away with this, Ki. Dana's a lawyer. We're going to sue."

Rick's eyebrows rose and his green eyes looked questioningly into hers. Dana looked back helplessly. She'd sometimes wondered what it would be like to see Rick Stafford again. Foolishly she'd imagined herself as cool, calm and in control. But here he was and she wasn't even breathing normally, a difficulty not entirely attributable to Margaret's tantrum.

"Well," Hezekiah drawled, almost popping his own suspenders with the barreling of his chest. "Rick's a lawyer, too. We'll just sue you back."

This time Dana's brows rose in surprise. Rick? A lawyer?

He shrugged, correctly interpreting her thoughts. "Small world, isn't it?" he said.

"Too small." Margaret clipped the words with importance and Dana half expected her to tell Hezekiah Brown that the town of Branson wasn't big enough for both of them. "Now, unless you want Sheriff Owens to escort you to the city jail, I suggest you take your 'lawyer' and get off my property, Ki."

"I ain't leavin' without my hat."

Dana seized the opportunity and offered him the beret. "I think it would be best if you left," she said.

Margaret's fingers grasped her wrist meaningfully. "Hand him that stupid hat and I'll cut you out of my will," she warned. "He threw it at me and I'm going to keep it . . . as evidence."

"Getting sentimental in your old age, Maggie?"

Definitely time to step in, Dana decided, but Rick beat her to it.

"Let's go, Ki," he said, setting his Stetson atop his head and maneuvering himself between the warring factions at the same time. "We don't want to wear out our welcome on our first visit."

"First and last!" Margaret glared as eagerly at Rick as she had at Hezekiah. "Neither one of you is welcome here."

Rick smiled, slowly and with more charm than Dana thought necessary. Apparently, the rougher edges of his personality had undergone some refinement in the last ten years. "Now, Miz Margaret. Let's not be hasty. My client didn't mean any harm. He just wanted to say hello to an old friend."

"He wanted to spy on his competition!" Margaret's anger was building again.

"Competition! Hell, you think this—" Hezekiah gestured broadly to encompass the whole factory "—is competition for me?"

Margaret sputtered. Dana stepped into the fray, before her mother gave real grounds for a slander suit. "Let's keep this civil, Margaret. I'm sure Mr. Brown will leave quietly." She shot an entreating glance at Rick and added, "with his attorney."

"Right." Rick's hand gripped Hezekiah's shoulder with a firmness Dana could see. "We'll be sayin' good-bye, now."

"I'm not goin' anywhere without my hat."

"It'll be a cold day in—"

At that moment, a dozen or more boxes of caramel creams arrived at the end of the conveyor, toppled over the metal restraint and dumped onto the floor. Several of the boxes split, spilling chocolates across the floor. Margaret stopped arguing long enough to notice the ignominious heap of candies at her feet. Then she came as close as she could to being "nose-to-nose" with her opponent. "I'll show you competition, Hezekiah Brown. I'll use the Recipe!"

Hezekiah paled, then his round cheeks burned a furious red. "You touch that recipe, Maggie Jane, and I won't be responsible for what happens. All hell will bust loose. I'm warnin' you—"

"Don't you threaten me! Why I'll—"

Dana had no choice. She wedged her body decisively between her mother and Hezekiah Brown. "I'll handle this," she said. "Mr. Stafford, if you would be so kind as to escort this gentleman off the premises, I will meet with you later to discuss how best to settle this...disagreement."

Rick nodded, his clamp on Ki an affirmative action in itself. "This afternoon? My office is downtown. Ask anyone for directions." He urged his companion toward the exit. "Welcome home, Dana," he called over the heads of everyone in the crowd. "It was nice to see you again, too."

"All right, Dana, you can move out from in front of me. I don't need a bodyguard." With Hezekiah's departure, Margaret regained a modicum of composure. "And I don't want you to discuss my business with that Stafford boy."

Dana moved from her constraining position and noticed the lump of gooey caramel embedded on the heel of her new lizard-skin shoes. "As your attorney, Margaret, I advise you to shut up."

A camera flashed in her face and Dana frowned into the laughing eyes of a local reporter. "How about a quote, Miss Ausbrook? Something about how it feels to be on the sweet side of the candy business?"

Dana fixed him with a cool stare. "Sticky," she said. "At the moment, it feels very sticky." And bunching the troublesome beret in her fist, she turned on her heel and walked away, head high, her shoe making a "gggglluuump-ssttuuuchkk" sound against the concrete floor with every step.

Chapter Two

Rick Stafford had an office.

Not just any office, but a small, old-fashioned, antique-filled law office.

Dana hated him for that. She hated every piece of oak furniture, every leather-bound law book, every brass-trimmed accessory in the room. It wasn't fair that his diplomas hung, framed and impressive, on the cream-colored walls, while her sheepskins lay rolled and buried in a packing box marked Textbooks and College Records. This was the kind of office she'd planned for herself. And it belonged to Rick.

"May I help you?" The dark-haired secretary asked efficiently.

Dana assumed her professional voice. "Rick Stafford, please."

"He won't be in until Monday."

A whole weekend away, Dana thought. She rubbed her thumb across the band of the beret. Had Rick forgotten?

"May I be of assistance?" the secretary offered in that protective way secretaries have.

"I don't think so."

The brunette eyed her with a hint of suspicion. "Did you have an appointment, Ms.—?"

"Not exactly." Dana paused in front of the chair, then walked to the bookcase instead. Since Rick wasn't here to observe her keen interest in his professional life, she might as well satisfy her curiosity. "It was more along the lines of a date," she said, thinking that would raise her status in the secretary's eyes.

The silence that followed was quite cool. The secretary was clearly unimpressed. "Apparently he forgot, miss. Would you care to leave a message?"

So much for impersonating an old friend of the boss. With a sure but forgiving envy, Dana took one last look at the row of law books before turning her attention to the dark-haired woman. "Would it be possible to wait for him?"

The secretary smiled, in control once more. "He won't be in until Monday. I'd be happy to take a message, though."

Dana took a seat, just to show she was not intimidated. "I'll wait." Placing the beret in her lap, she picked up a magazine and began to leaf through the pages, waiting for the woman to go on about the business of running the office.

When the dull tapping of the computer keys became a steady rhythm, Dana glanced up from the magazine in her lap and took another look at Rick's office. When had he decided to become an attorney? she wondered. Ten years ago his loftiest ambition had been to lead the life of a hermit somewhere in the Rocky Mountains. Of course, her own ambitions had been nothing to brag about. She'd wanted to stay far away from Margaret and the candy factory. Period.

So much for youthful aspirations, Dana thought. Rick had probably never made it to the Rockies and she— Well, here she was in Branson, about as close as it was possible to get to Margaret and the confectionery. Just another of life's little ironies. Like seeing Rick this morning, in the last place she would ever have expected to see him, and in a set of circumstances that—

Dana closed off the memory of the morning's fiasco. She'd been over it already, several times, without reaching a satisfactory explanation. Margaret certainly hadn't offered one. Even after everything else had returned to normal, Margaret had continued to pace the floor, smoking literally and figuratively. All because of a short, balding man named Hezekiah Brown.

Dana's lips curved with sudden humor. Hezekiah Brown, for Pete's sake. A man who wore paisley suspenders and an English beret. What in heaven had happened between that man and Margaret to produce such an emotional earthquake? Margaret never, never, lost her composure. Dana suspected it wasn't the norm for old Hezekiah, either. She hoped Rick had some answers, because she hadn't been able to come up with any on her own.

The typing stopped and Dana glanced to her left to find the secretary watching her. She smiled and resumed a cursory inspection of the magazine. If Rick didn't show up soon, she'd have to make some excuse to Della Street over there behind the desk. Not a happy thought. She flipped a magazine page in frustration. Rick had caused her no end of frustration before. Did she honestly believe ten years would have changed him? Dana flipped another page. Then another. She might as well make up a pressing reason to leave right now and quit—

A door in the back opened and closed. Hurried footsteps sounded in the hall. "Barbara? Any calls? I'm expecting—" Rick paused in the doorway, catching sight of Dana and losing track of his breathing all in the same moment. He hadn't thought she'd actually come.

"Mr. Stafford." Barbara stood, surprise written across her face. "I didn't think you were going to be in today. This woman has been waiting to see you, but I told her—"

Rick nodded, although he was only vaguely aware of his secretary and her explanation. Dana commanded his attention, his thoughts. She was so pretty. He'd noticed that this morning, of course. He'd taken careful note of the changes in her face and form while recognizing the pert nose and sprinkling of freckles he remembered so well. Still, he felt oddly surprised by the woman she had become. "Hello, Dana. Glad you could make it."

Her lips curved, but didn't quite make a smile. Was she nervous? He was, which was ridiculous. Dana Ausbrook was pretty. So what? There were dozens of pretty women in town. She had been his first real love. Big deal. Just because she'd led him in a merry chase once before was no reason to be nervous now. He was older and wiser. He had diplomas to prove it.

"I'm glad you could make it, Rick. I was beginning to think you'd forgotten me."

Her voice had a husky warmth and Rick responded to it. "How could I do that? You once told me you were unforgettable, Dana."

She did smile, then. "Are you sure I only told you once?"

At the moment he wasn't sure of anything, except that he ought not to be standing there, grinning like a total fool. "You might have mentioned it more often. You talked so much, it was hard to keep track of everything you said.''

"You should have kept a diary, Rick." She stood and smoothed her skirt, matching her lighthearted remarks with a lighthearted expression. If he found out her knees were shaking like gelatin cubes, she'd never forgive herself. "Believe it or not, there are people who would pay good money for the things I used to say."

"You're into blackmail, huh?"

She lifted her shoulder in a smooth denial and seized the opportunity to take a deep breath. "Don't be silly. You know my high moral standards."

"Those I do remember." His smile ebbed into a wry curve. "The first time I met you, Dana, right after you stole my truck, I said to myself, 'Now, there's a girl with high moral standards.'"

Dana's cheeks reddened at the memory. Nothing like an embarrassing incident from the past to renew an old friendship. "How good of you to remember, Rick," she replied with sweet sarcasm. "You really shouldn't have."

He didn't appear at all chastened and just kept looking at her and smiling as if he might recall another nostalgic moment of their defunct relationship. "No trouble at all," he said and then seemed to realize Barbara's interest. "Let's go into my office, Dana, shall we?" He turned to his secretary. "Any messages?"

Barbara riffled through some papers on her desk and handed him four message slips. "Nothing pressing," she answered.

Rick nodded as he scanned the notes. Dana watched with a wistful curiosity and the sure knowledge that, after all this time, he was still the sexiest man she'd ever met. It wasn't fair. Why hadn't he grown a potbelly and a receding hairline? He was thirty-two years old, for heaven's sake. He was supposed to look . . . well, tamer. Not so ruggedly attractive. He wasn't exactly handsome, but he had a latent sensuality, an aura of devil-may-care charm. A potent combination. He should have gotten married, she decided. That would have clipped off some of the raw appeal of his bachelor confidence.

"Dana? Do you want to come in now?"

She hid her thoughts, she hoped, behind a smooth facade of professionalism as she walked to the doorway where he stood. He didn't back out of the way, just motioned her to precede him into the hallway and waited as she edged between the door facing and his body. It wasn't the closest squeeze of her life, but she made a special effort to hold her breath and thereby avoid touching him. A silly precaution, she assured herself, but there was no point in taking any chances.

"Nice setup, Rick." She walked purposefully down the hallway to the first door and opened it with confidence. It was a broom closet. She closed it quickly. "Everything's just where it should be."

"I'm glad you like it." He placed his hand on her shoulder and pointed to the second doorway. "My office is behind that door."

She hid her chagrin in flippancy. "How clever of you."

"Not really." He pushed open the door. "I knew it was here all along."

Rick hadn't lost his sense of humor, she thought as she walked into his office. His desk was strewn with paper and manila files. The Rolodex looked ragged and overworked. Two chairs in front of the desk were wood and black leather. The chair behind the desk was a deep, rich red. Dana loved it on sight. "Would you consider selling the chair?" she asked.

He motioned her to take a seat. "I might consider an offer."

"Ten dollars?"

"Tempting, but no."

Dana settled into one of the two matching chairs. "A year's worth of caramel creams? You wouldn't have to shop for Christmas presents."

Rick perched on the edge of the desk, arms crossed, eyes shining emerald with mischief. He was closer than she would have liked, but she ignored the irritating tingle of awareness racing through her veins. "Why not just steal it?"

"Will you ever let me live that down? I didn't steal your stupid truck." She hesitated. "Besides, I don't think I could get that chair out of here by myself."

He laughed and she remembered why she'd first liked him. "It's heavy," he said, "but I'm sure you'd manage somehow." He didn't know why he continued to tease her. The truck incident had been a misunderstanding. It was tactless of him to tease her about it. But she had such an expressive face and he enjoyed watching her, which is what had gotten him into trouble the first time. "Well, Dana, what brings you to Branson?"

"Business," she said, deciding he could make whatever answer he wanted out of that. "I'm working with Margaret at the confectionery."

"As a vice president." Rick shook his head. "I heard Margaret say that this morning, but I thought I must have misunderstood. Didn't you tell me you'd die a thousand deaths, jump into the deepest river, and stick bamboo shoots under all of your fingernails before you went to work in this Podunk town?"

"I'm sure I never mentioned anything about bamboo shoots." She stroked the wooden armrest with studied nonchalance. "I might have said something about not wanting to work here. But I was very young. I didn't know what I wanted then."

"You sure fooled me."

She was uncomfortable with the conversation or with his penetrating gaze. She couldn't decide which. It could, she supposed, have something to do with the scant two inches that separated her knee from his leg. Shifting slightly, she met his eyes with cool aplomb. "So, Rick, you never married?"

Rick could almost see her chagrin as the question hit the air. He loved it. "No. No, I haven't." He paused for maximum effect. "You're divorced, I understand."

Dana nodded, even as she squashed the oddest impulse to offer an apology. "Darren and I weren't suited," she explained.

Rick kept smiling, although he had a sudden urge to wring her neck. "That kind of mistake happens sometimes."

It was a leading statement, but Dana pretended not to notice. "I was surprised to learn you were a lawyer, Rick."

His only answer was a slanting of the lips. She labeled it smug, although she felt churlish in doing so. "I always thought you wanted to lead the life of a hermit. You used to talk about living in the Rocky Mountains."

"I decided I liked the Ozarks better."

"So you did get to the Rockies? I wondered if you—" Her heart skipped a beat and she swallowed the rest of the sentence. She didn't want him to know she'd ever given him a second thought. "You've done well for yourself."

"Have I?"

It was a loaded question, calling for a value judgment on an old argument.

Define success, Dana.

Unlimited wealth and complete independence, she'd replied.

And that was how the original quarrel had begun.

"Of course," she said now. "Don't you think so?"

Rick pursed his lips before allowing them to curve ever so little. "Yes, I'm doing very well for myself. All by myself."

Dana glanced away. The air was stirring with memories. A funny, sad sensation curled in her stomach as a dozen or more "what ifs?" ran through her mind. What if she and Rick had eloped as they'd planned? What if she'd stayed in Branson that summer instead of running back to Philadelphia and Darren? There were no answers, of course. Only the consequences of the choices she'd made.

She brought her gaze back to him, casually, as if she'd only been looking around, getting acquainted with his office. "We should talk about our respective clients," she said, knowing Margaret lent sobriety to any conversation. "Margaret is determined to sue."

"For what? Defamation of caramels?"

A laugh caught her unaware. "I was thinking about citing grounds for alienation of confections."

He whistled in mock dismay. "If you're going to play hardball, this case could get badly gummed up."

They laughed together, the subtle tension eased, and Rick moved...finally...behind the desk. "Well, my client is threatening to sue for custody of a recipe. And that's about as much sense as I could get out of him. What did your mother say about the morning's face-off?"

Dana lifted her shoulder in a dainty shrug. "My high moral standards won't allow me to repeat it. Let's just say that an apology is out of the question."

"Ki wouldn't accept it anyway."

"I meant that Margaret wouldn't settle if he apologized from now until the turn of the century."

"She sounds as stubborn as he is."

"No one is more stubborn than my mother."

"I don't know. I always thought you had that market cornered, Dana."

"We're not talking about me." She watched Rick rock back in the big red chair. It suited him. Just as the jeans and sports shirt suited his unrefined masculinity. Just as the office suited his home-town-boy-makes-good image. "We're talking about my mother and your— Who is Hezekiah Brown, anyway?"

"In relation to Margaret? Or me?"

"Let's start with you. That'll be easier."

Rick smiled to himself. Was any kind of relationship easy to explain? "Ki is...was...my neighbor when I was a kid. After Dad died, Ki helped us keep the farm running. He taught my brother and me how to manage the place and I know he slipped Mom money from time to time, although he denies it. He nursed me through my first and only hangover without ever once telling me what a fool I'd been and he—" Rick stopped himself from mentioning how Ki had helped him survive his first and only broken heart.

"When Ki turned fifty, he decided to sell his land and do some of the traveling he'd promised himself he'd do. He wanted to visit his war buddy, Henry Philipps, and when he did, they started a business, London Country Candies. You've probably heard of it. Anyway, before he left Branson, he asked me to take over his farm and then eventually he arranged the financing so I could buy it. He talked incessantly about getting a college education and convinced me it was a necessity. He swears he didn't help me get the scholarship I was offered from the University of Arkansas, but I've always thought he pulled a string somewhere." Rick shook his head. "In short, Hezekiah Brown is a good friend."

Dana puzzled over the description for a minute. "Why didn't I ever meet him?" she wondered aloud. "I thought I knew everything about you, Rick." A blush stole across her cheeks. "I mean, I thought I'd met all of the important people in your life."

Rick liked the blush. Maybe the years had taught Dana some sensitivity. "Ki left for Europe in May, just before you arrived in town that summer. I'm surprised your mother never mentioned him. Their feud is somewhat of a legend around here."

Dana looked skeptical. "Margaret? Involved in some kind of hillbilly feud? No, no. She's too levelheaded to—" The clear memory of Margaret's livid expression and the caramels scattering across the factory floor cut Dana short. "After this morning, there does seem to be some room for doubt about that, doesn't there?"

"Clear thinking was not the order of the day. However, you did a remarkable job in trying to restore sanity. You jumped on that 'Honey, I'm home' line like a duck after a june bug. You could be in advertising, Dana."

"I think I am." She allowed herself a small grimace. "Margaret tells me I have to start thinking like a businesswoman. Sell, sell, sell."

He whistled softly. "Quite an adjustment for a 'buy, buy, buy' consumer. You used to tell me your mission in

life was to shop until your plastic credit cards disinte-
grated."

"For someone who didn't keep a diary, you seem to
recall a number of things I used to say."

"Seeing you again so unexpectedly must have brought
it all to mind." He looked so relaxed, so noncommittal.
Dana didn't know whether he was enjoying the memories or nursing a grudge. "There's no telling what I might
remember about you, Dana. If I tried."

The tension curled in her stomach again. Tighter, this
time. A gentle tremor sashayed down her spine as she met
his eyes and shared a moment cognizant of what they'd
once been to each other. Not lovers. But almost. Almost.

"Let's keep this as businesslike as possible, Rick. I see
no purpose in verbally sparring over something that
happened years ago."

Rick could see a number of purposes, not the least of
which was the physical attraction still at work between
them. Dana was aware of it, too, or she wouldn't have
bothered to make such a defensive statement. "I think we
can safely leave the sparring to Ki and Margaret, don't
you?"

"Which brings us back to their feud."

"And the recipe. Did Margaret say anything about it?"

"Only what she told Ki this morning. I don't even
know what the recipe's for."

"Trouble, apparently." Rick tapped a pencil against
the desktop. "Do you think Margaret means to take legal action?"

Dana shrugged. "I'm hoping she'll stop ranting and
raving long enough to realize how foolish that would be.
Maybe by the time I get home this evening she'll have
calmed down."

"You're living at your mother's house?"

A funny look crossed her face, but was instantly brought under control. "Where else would I go?"

Rick could think of several alternatives, but none of them, he decided, would meet the high standards of Ms. Dana Ausbrook, princess of the realm. "Did you try Allie Kelsom? She sometimes has an apartment to rent."

It sounded like heaven. An apartment of her own. Independence. But it would defeat her purpose in coming to Branson. "Margaret has plenty of room." Dana defended her decision as best she could. "And Charity's there to look after me."

"Oh, yes," Rick said wryly. "Charity, the housekeeper, caretaker, and all-around watchdog. Does she still read tea leaves?"

"And coffee grounds. She's very good at it."

"I'm sure she is. Can she talk any sense into your mother?"

"I doubt it. But she must know about the feud. Whether or not she'll tell me what she knows is another matter." Dana pushed a stray wisp of autumn hair away from her cheek. "Charity treats me like a ten-year-old."

"Find out what you can. Ki's staying with me for a few days. I'll try and get some answers from him. I suppose we ought to be prepared, although I can't believe either one of them will follow through and actually file a lawsuit."

"I hope you're right. You know, as well as I do, that this is nothing but a nuisance suit at best." Dana sighed softly. There was no reason to linger in Rick's comfortable office. In truth, there had been no reason to meet with him in the first place. She wasn't even licensed to practice law in Missouri. So that left only one explanation for her presence in his office.

She'd wanted to see him, up close and personal, and discover if the attraction was still there. Now that she knew, she probably ought to leave.

As Dana stood, the beret tumbled from her lap to the floor. Retrieving it, she laid it on Rick's desk. "I slipped this out when Margaret wasn't looking. It's really not such a valuable piece of evidence. I'll let you know if anything develops," she said. "In the meantime, you might want to keep your eye on that chair."

He grinned as he slowly got to his feet and came around the corner of the desk. "I'll do that, Dana. In fact, now that you're in town, I'll keep an eye on all my possessions."

"Rest easy, Rick," she said lightly. "Your possessions are in no danger from me."

His lips curved in soft irony. If she only knew. "I'll be on guard, just the same. A man can't be too careful, you know."

With a toss of her head, she walked to the door. He followed, breathing the quiet sweetness of her perfume, telling himself over and over that he would not, under any circumstances, get involved again with Dana Ausbrook.

In the doorway she paused and after a moment's hesitation, she extended her hand. Rick looked at it before closing his fingers around hers in a brief handshake. She had small hands, delicate and fair, and he wished he hadn't touched her. But it was too late. A forgotten fire stirred in his memory and try as he might, he could not ignore it. "Come again, Dana. Anytime."

"It's been nice seeing you again, Rick." Reluctantly she withdrew her hand from his. "I wish..." She met his eyes and left the sentence to dangle. Coming here hadn't been such a good idea, she decided. She hadn't expected to feel so nostalgic, which was the only word she could think of to describe the restlessness inside her. "If you ever have a craving for caramel, give me a call. Candy is my business, you know." With a flip of her hand, she said goodbye and walked down the hallway toward the exit.

She breezed past the broom closet and the curious regard of Secretary Barbara and made her way out of the office. Outside, Dana drew a deep breath of Ozark air and exhaust fumes. She'd faced Rick and survived. She'd even handled the situation with poise and confidence and he had no way of knowing the flimsy state of her nerves. Why, he'd actually been friendly.

So, it was over. On her list of things she least wanted to do, facing Rick had been number one. She mentally marked through it. It was done. She didn't have to think about it anymore.

Except that she didn't understand why her heart was still thudding in her chest like a bongo drum. She didn't know why her hand still felt warm from a simple handshake. She had come to Branson to fulfill an obligation, a promise she'd made to herself years before. The last thing she needed at the moment was an involvement with a man. Any man. Least of all, Rick.

In his office, Rick gave the red chair a slow spin. After all this time, who would have thought he'd be such a pushover for the one woman who'd rejected him? Dana was the last woman in the world he ought to be attracted to. Ki had been right. He should have set his heart on some sweet, homegrown girl long ago.

It was too late for that now. Dana was back, although he had no illusions that she'd stay. She was a city girl, who'd never liked the homespun, artsy-craftsy atmosphere of the Ozarks. On top of that, she'd never gotten along with her mother and she hated the candy business. No matter what she said.

He'd give her a month at most.

The chair stopped and Rick rubbed his palm across the smooth leather. But he might have enough time to work out some old feelings before she left. Maybe then he could forget about Dana Ausbrook. Maybe then he'd stop wondering what would have happened if she hadn't run away.

Chapter Three

Seated at the breakfast bar, Dana nibbled on a croissant and watched Charity sweep the kitchen floor. The broom angled in short, sharp strokes from one side of the wide bar to the cabinets on the other end. Charity never missed a beat as she filled Dana in on the Branson-area news.

"You ought to remember Rayburn Seay, Dana. He used to call you Woodpecker and Red Robin Hood. You got in a lot of trouble once for putting Tabasco in his iced tea." Charity began to pester a minuscule dust ball in the corner.

"It was worth it," Dana said and decided the moment was right to introduce the topic she wanted to discuss. "By the way, Charity, do you know someone named Hezekiah Brown?"

The dust ball scampered across the floor after one swift whack of the broom. Charity straightened, surprise settling in the laugh lines around her eyes. "Where in God's good creation did you hear about him?"

"I guess you do know him." Dana camouflaged her curiosity by taking another bite of croissant. "Is he an old friend of mother's?"

"Hardly a friend."

"I can't recall ever hearing Margaret mention him before today."

Charity sniffed. "His name has been taboo around here for longer than I care to say. I'm surprised your mother would let it pass her lips."

"Why? What happened between Margaret and Hezekiah Brown?"

Charity shook her graying head. "They were crazy-sick in love, I'll tell you that."

Dana tried to imagine Margaret as being "crazy-sick in love" with the short, balding man who'd been at the confectionery that morning. The vision wouldn't take shape. Why, even Leonard Ausbrook had once admitted that Margaret's heart bore more resemblance to a peanut cluster than to a soft, cream center. "That must have been long before she met Dad," Dana remarked, mostly for her own benefit.

"Yep," Charity said. "No one can accuse Leonard of breaking up a match made in heaven. Your mama didn't meet him until later. The feud with Ki was well underway by then."

Feud. There was that word, again. Dana sighed and thoughtfully chewed the last bite of roll. "Does Dad know about this, uh, feud?"

Charity smiled and began wielding the broom again. "If he does, he never let on. Not to me, anyway. But then your daddy don't tell everything he knows, either. He's a very quiet fellow."

A forlorn twinge of conscience made its way through Dana. It had been two days since she'd left Philadelphia on a morning flight and she hadn't as yet phoned her father to report her safe journey. He wouldn't chastise her or even mention that he'd been waiting for her call, but she knew he was and she resolved to make the phone call tonight. Leonard Ausbrook was such a nice man. Quiet, as Charity had said, and on the bookish side, but deeply, sincerely nice. Dana loved him totally, if somewhat impatiently at times, and she wondered quite often why Margaret had married him in the first place. It was a certainty she'd never been "crazy-sick in love" with him.

"Do you think she loved Dad, Charity?" Dana propped her chin on her hands, feeling suddenly like a little girl again, posing impossible questions to the housekeeper because she could never find the courage to ask her mother.

"That's somethin' you'll have to ask *her*, Dana." Charity scraped the dirt particles into a dustpan, her broad forehead furrowed in concentration.

Dana sat in silence for a moment. "I was only two at the time of the divorce, too young to remember any fighting or yelling or anything like that."

"You know your daddy's not a fighting man. I always suspected he was just too nice for Margaret, but what do I know? They had about the friendliest divorce I ever heard tell of."

Dana smiled because she knew it was expected, but personal experience had taught her that from a child's perspective there was no such thing as "friendly divorce." "They're so different," Dana said. "I can't imagine how they even stayed together long enough to have me."

"It doesn't take all that long to conceive a baby."

Being blunt was Charity's way and Dana accepted it, but the words cut deeply into an old scar. All of her life, Dana had secretly nursed the fear that she'd been an unplanned pregnancy, an unwanted child. She'd spent agonizing hours during her youth struggling with the idea that she'd been born by accident rather than design. Even now the thought created an empty, churning sensation in the pit of her stomach. But once and for all, she was going to lay the fear to rest. She was finally going to put the past in perspective and develop a relationship with her mother.

Charity put away the broom and wiped her hands on her flowered apron, as oblivious to Dana's somber thoughts as she was to most subtleties. "I'd better get dinner started. Your mama'll be home here in a minute." Charity walked to the refrigerator, pulled open the door and stood staring at the contents. "What do you want for supper?"

"Salad."

"We don't have the stuff for salad." Charity buried her head in the refrigerator and came out with the beginnings of dinner. "How about coleslaw and ham?"

"That sounds fine." Dana tapped idle fingers on the countertop, wishing Charity would allow her to help do something. "Do you ever see Rick Stafford around town?" she asked and immediately regretted it as a sharp, perceptive gaze cut from Charity's eyes to hers.

"Rick Stafford? You still think about him?"

"No. Yes. Well, sometimes." Dana grabbed for a decisive tone. "I've thought about him once or twice and wondered what happened to him."

"He grew up," Charity offered in a cleverly done, wouldn't-you-like-to-know-more tone of voice. "Turned out to be a fine young man, too."

"Did he?" Dana tried to sound casual. "I'm kind of surprised he never got married."

"Are you, now?" Charity began slicing a carrot.

Dana tried a different tack. "I heard he became a lawyer," she said. "That kind of surprised me."

"I'll just bet it did." Charity laid a cabbage on the cutting board and began rummaging through the utensil drawer. "Especially since you said he'd never amount to anything."

"Margaret said that, not me."

"Well, but you believed her."

There wasn't a good way to deny that, Dana decided. But why was Charity so pro-Rick, all of a sudden? "I don't recall you standing up and shouting about what a fine young man Rick was at the time."

"Wouldn't have made any difference." Charity found what she was looking for and slammed shut the drawer. "You'd already made up your mind and if ever anybody was more stubborn than your mama, Dana, it was you."

"Thanks, Charity. It's nice to know you remember all my good qualities."

"No one loves you more than I do, Dana, but I'm not blind to your faults. You've always been a bullheaded child."

It was on the tip of her tongue to point out that she was no longer a child, but Dana held back the words. Outside, a powerful automobile engine purred and was answered by the hum of the electric garage-door opener. A familiar tension stirred uneasily in her stomach. "Margaret's home," she said. "Just in time to watch the evening news."

"Oh, today was the big press conference, wasn't it?" The sounds of someone entering the house through the garage entrance punctuated the sentence. Charity began to hustle. "Too bad I didn't start the ham to frying before now. We could have eaten while the news is on."

"It's just as well, Charity." Dana's lips slipped into a rueful smile. "I don't think the news will be a particularly appetizing experience tonight."

"Something smells good, Charity." Margaret walked into the combined breakfast nook and kitchen area and settled on a barstool next to Dana's. "I'm unusually hungry this evening, for some reason." Margaret set her purse on the counter and with hardly a wasted motion, reached inside for her cigarettes. "Lord knows, I ought to be sick to my stomach over what happened today."

Charity thumped the skillet on the stove. "Did something go wrong?"

"*Everything* went wrong." Margaret rummaged in her purse and eventually produced a gold lighter. "Didn't it, Dana?"

"The announcement didn't quite go as you planned," Dana conceded.

With habitual ease, Margaret flicked the thumb wheel and when the flame caught, she lit a cigarette. "The announcement was fine, it was that *trespasser* who created the problem."

"Trespasser?" Charity turned her attention from the ham slices to her employer. "Did someone get arrested?"

"No. More's the pity." Margaret blew out a frustrated smoke ring. "It would have done Ki good to spend the night in jail."

"Ki? Hezekiah Brown?" Charity's voice rose with each new pronunciation. "*Ki* was at the confectionery today?" She almost choked on her surprise. "Why didn't you tell me, Dana?"

"I was getting around to it," Dana explained with a conciliatory shrug of her shoulders. "I was going to tell you."

"Hmmph." Margaret reached down and slipped off her low-heeled shoes. "Dana was so busy eyeing that Stafford boy, she never noticed anyone else."

"Rick was there, too?" Charity's expression grew sulky and her cloudy-blue eyes fixed accusingly on Dana. "Now, why didn't you mention that, Missy?"

With a deep breath Dana discarded the idea that she had to accept chastisement from these two women. They had bossed her as a child, but she was a grown-up now and didn't owe them any explanations. "I noticed that you completely lost your cool, Margaret, and created quite a scene, yourself. Do you want to tell Charity about that?"

Margaret reached for the ashtray, unaffected by Dana's accusing tone. "Oh, hell! You know how I detest that man, Charity. When he waved at me from the back of the room, I...well, I saw red. The nerve of him! Coming into my factory as if he had every right in the world to be there." She stared at the engraved lighter in her hand and idly turned it on the counter. "I hope you informed that Stafford boy of my intentions to sue his client, Dana."

"You don't have a case, Margaret. How many times do I have to tell you that? You can't sue a man just because you dislike him."

"I don't dislike Hezekiah Brown, darling. I abhor him!"

It was the Burton temperament at its best, but Dana was unimpressed. "Yes, I think everyone is well aware of that now. And any who aren't soon will be. I'm sure the local media will provide a glowing account of what happened at the Ausbrook Confectionery today."

"What happened?" Charity was bursting with curiosity, but Margaret just drew on her cigarette and exhaled slowly, ignoring all but her own thoughts.

"Unfortunately you're right, Dana. Ki certainly managed to upstage my announcement, didn't he?"

"And with so little assistance from you."

"Don't be smug, Dana. I'm sure the camera caught you eyeing that Stafford boy."

"Will you quit calling him that? His name is Rick and I don't see what he has to do with you throwing candy at the crowd. Besides, I wasn't 'eyeing' him, as you so succinctly put it, during your little press conference. I just thought he looked familiar, that's all."

"Familiar?" Margaret tapped cigarette ashes into the tray. "Of course he looked familiar, Dana. Ten years ago you were ready to elope with him. If I hadn't put my foot down, you probably would have. So don't try to tell me you'd forgotten what he looked like. A woman always remembers her first infatuation."

"Is that why you recognized Hezekiah Brown?"

Margaret's eyes sparked in self-defense and Charity leaned across the counter, fairly bristling with the questions she wasn't getting an opportunity to ask. "That's different," Margaret said. "He's an old enemy."

"He didn't appear to be much older than you," Dana hadn't gotten to be twenty-eight without learning a few ways to circumvent her mother's temper.

Margaret stubbed out the cigarette with unusual care. "That was tacky, Dana."

"Sorry."

A reluctant smile pulled at Margaret's lips. "No, you're not. That's one of the things I like about you. You can sometimes be so effectively insincere."

It was hardly the kind of compliment Dana wanted to hear from her mother, but she smiled at Margaret, anyway. One day, before this year was over, Dana promised herself, she would make Margaret understand how sincere she really was.

"Will one of you stop arguing long enough to tell me what happened, today?" Charity braced her weight against the bar, crossed her arms and waited impatiently for an explanation.

Margaret tapped another cigarette from the pack and lit it. "During my announcement to the press today, Ki showed up in the crowd with that Stafford ... Rick Stafford, in tow. He made a scene, of course—"

"Rick did?" Charity asked.

"No, Hezekiah did. He tossed his hat at me and made a complete ass of himself by yelling something asinine, so I threw a box of caramel creams at him and ended up telling him I planned to manufacture the Recipe."

Charity gasped. "*The Recipe?* What did he say then?"

"He threatened to sue me. So I threatened to sue him back."

"I believe it was the other way around," Dana commented. "You threatened to sue first."

"What difference does it make, Dana? I'm going to sue him for every penny he's got. Then I'm going to sue him again."

"You don't have a case, Margaret."

Drawing from the cigarette, Margaret shrugged complacently. "So you've said. I guess we'll just have to see about that."

"You can't use that recipe." Charity skewed her chubby cheeks into a perplexed frown. "I told you the other day, Margaret, the tea leaves predicted trouble. You'd best let sleeping dogs lie and not even think about making that candy."

"What kind of candy?" Dana asked.

"Chocolate Peppermint Kisses." Margaret's expression was triumphant, her voice firm with victory. "The Recipe will make us famous, Dana."

"Then why haven't you used it before now?"

Charity made a snorting sound, undignified but very expressive. "She can't, that's why. Ki owns half that recipe and there's not a thing to be done about it, either."

What a setup, Dana thought and settled back to enjoy the coming explanation. "And how did Hezekiah Brown, a man you abhor, come to own half of the recipe for a candy that will make you famous, Margaret?"

"It's a long story."

"I'll sleep late tomorrow."

"You have to work tomorrow." Margaret laid the cigarette in the ashtray and began rolling up her tailored shirtsleeves. "There's no such thing as a weekend for a new executive."

"All the more reason to tell me about this fabulous recipe, then. You keep telling me to think like a businesswoman and since I'm the new vice president of the company, I need to know how peppermint candy will make us famous."

"She's right." Charity pointed out. "It's about time you told her, anyway."

Margaret scowled at the housekeeper, picked up the cigarette again and then ground it dead in the ashtray. "Very well, Dana. I'll tell you the story. Once upon a time when I was a very young, very foolish girl, I thought I was in love with Hezekiah Brown and agreed to marry him." She lifted a hand, palm up, fingers outstretched. "It was a mistake, of course, and luckily I found out before—" Margaret's voice faded with the memory and her brown eyes took on a reminiscent shadow. The ensuing silence lasted a moment, maybe less, then Margaret pulled back her shoulders, lifted her chin and resumed the monologue. "At any rate, just before the wedding, I broke the engagement. I was somewhat mad and, well, one thing led to another and I tore the Recipe in half.''

"What happened? Why did you break the engagement?" Dana wasn't about to let Margaret stop with that bare-bones account.

"That, my darling daughter, is none of your business.''

Dana pursed her lips, her curiosity high, but destined to go unsatisfied, at least for the moment. "So what happened to the Recipe?"

"I took half and Ki took half. And that's the story."

Charity eagerly stepped in to fill out the details. "That's not even a fourth of the story, Margaret, and you know it.'' She turned an expectant gaze to Dana, to be sure she was paying proper attention. "Granny Varnell gave the two of them that recipe 'cause she knew they wanted to start a candy business. Do you recall meeting Granny Varnell, Dana? She always thought you were the prettiest little girl, with your bright red hair and freckles. You probably never saw her more than a time or two, though.'' Charity mulled that over for a second, then dismissed it as unimportant. "Well, Granny is about the best cook in the Ozarks and those peppermint chocolates of hers . . . well, that's about as near to heaven as some folks around here are ever gonna get. Hmm, mmm, mmm! You talk about something that makes a body's mouth water. Anyway, she gave the Recipe to Maggie and Hezekiah as a wedding present and—''

"Please, Charity," Margaret interrupted. "I haven't been Maggie for years and no matter what name you call me, don't link it with *his*.''

One corner of Charity's full mouth lifted in a semi-smirk. "You're mighty picky for someone who couldn't even tell her own daughter the whole story.''

"I told her all she needed to know. You're just embellishing a rather dull saga with useless details."

"Dana has a right to know."

Dana decided it was time to intervene before a fight broke out. "I think I've gotten the picture," she said calmly. "You jilted your fiancé on the eve of the wedding, ripped the Recipe in two, threw half of it in Hezekiah's handsome face, and walked off with the other half clutched in your furious fist. Is that a fair account of what happened?"

Uncharacteristically, Margaret released a soft sigh. "It isn't quite the way I'd have put it, but yes, that's close enough."

"He was a handsome man, too," Charity added. "I never did understand why you—"

"The story hour is over." Margaret swiveled around on the barstool and stretched to reach the television remote. "It's time for the news."

Dana subsided with more grace than Charity, who went back to preparing supper with a pronounced pout. As a commercial came into focus on the screen, Dana tuned out the accompanying jingle and watched Margaret as she watched the television screen. Was it possible, Dana wondered, that the indomitable Margaret Burton Ausbrook had an Achilles' heel?

For most of her childhood, Dana had perceived her mother as a whirlwind of drive and activity. Someone around whom the earth revolved out of sheer force of momentum. Dana resented the energy her mother's ambition demanded and, over the years, their personalities had clashed more often than not. Perhaps because they were so much alike. Perhaps because Dana had ambitions of her own. Still, she wished they might have shared long mother-daughter talks about makeup and boys and life in general, and feelings and so many other things. But there'd never been time for discussions.

Dana remembered only impressions. A moment here, when Margaret had smiled the approval Dana always sought. A moment there, when she'd known her mother wanted to say something, but hadn't. And the moments in between, like now, when Dana could only look at Margaret and wonder what made her tick.

"Here it comes," Margaret announced solemnly. "Let's hope they pronounce your name correctly, Dana."

For her part, Dana hoped the whole tape was a garbled mess in which no one's name was clear. No such luck. From the moment the news anchor introduced the segment as "The Caramel Cream Connection," Dana knew they were in trouble. The tape showed an edited, but no more flattering, version of the day's happening from beginning to ignominious end.

"Would you look at that," Charity remarked when the camera zoomed in for a close-up view of the black-and-white checked beret lying on top of the pastel candy box. "I can't imagine Hezekiah wearing a wimpy hat like that."

"Well, he certainly got a good shot of you," Charity said when the telephoto lens narrowed in on Margaret just as she tossed two and a half dozen caramel creams into the crowd. "Good thing you didn't hit anyone."

"He looks better than ever," Charity stated when Hezekiah Brown appeared on the screen in full and glorious color. "I've always thought he was the sexiest man ever to walk out of these hills. Short, mind you, but sexy as—"

"For heaven's sake, Charity," Margaret interrupted. "We can do without the commentary."

Dana ignored them both and leaned forward, knowing that at any moment . . . There he was. Rick came into the picture and her heart beat faster. She wanted to touch a button and freeze his image on the screen so she could examine and study every feature of his face, all the ways he'd changed, all the ways he had stayed the same. But then the camera switched back to Margaret and Ki and the tape ended with a brief comment by the newscaster that "feuding is alive and well in the Ozarks."

Margaret reached for a cigarette, lit it and casually switched off the television. "Not bad coverage," she said.

Dana arched a skeptical eyebrow. "Is that all this is to you? Publicity?"

"No, but I'm not about to overlook the positive aspects of the situation, either. Business is business, Dana, and the bottom line is money. The more publicity you get, the higher your sales figures. Period. I'm going to sue Ki Brown because he deserves to be sued, but if the Ausbrook Confectionery gets a little free publicity out of the deal, I'm not going to throw my hand against my forehead like some nineteen-thirties screen actress and moan, 'Please, let me have some privacy!' " She gave a good imitation, then capped it off with a throaty laugh. "Didn't you learn anything about marketing in all those years you went to school, Dana?"

"I did take a class in business ethics."

"Good for you, dear." Margaret reached across the counter and snitched a carrot slice. "Just remember whose side you're on when that Rick Stafford starts trying to sweet-talk you into copping a plea."

Dana sighed and slipped from the barstool. "You don't cop a plea in a civil suit, Margaret. How long before dinner's ready, Charity?"

"Fifteen minutes or so. Don't wander off, now. I'll be calling you in just a bit." Charity moved the cutting board out of Margaret's reach and leaned across the counter. "What do you suppose Ki's come home for, Maggie? Last I heard, he was having a grand life, chasing women and selling his London Country Candies all over Europe."

"Do you know what he had the nerve to say to me today, Charity?" Margaret ran her fingers through her short auburn curls. "He said I was no competition for him. No competition! Can you believe . . . ?"

Dana didn't linger to hear more. She'd heard Margaret rant and rave enough for one day, and the possibility of actually gleaning any useful information was outweighed by the beginnings of a dull headache at Dana's temples. She considered going to her room and lying down, but Charity wouldn't take it kindly if she didn't show up for supper, so Dana dismissed the idea of a nap and decided to phone her father instead.

No one answered in the stodgy, old Philadelphia house and Dana put down the phone receiver with mixed feelings. It would have been nice to hear Leonard's quite, dignified voice. On the other hand, he'd have asked how the press announcement went and Dana didn't think she could bear to go over it again. Actually, what she wanted to do was to phone Rick, tell him about the broken engagement and the torn recipe and listen to his deep baritone laugh. Rick, at least, would be able to see the humor in this situation.

She stroked the smooth plastic surface of the telephone, then withdrew her hand and nestled it in the pocket of her brown safari shorts. Business, she reminded herself. She meant to keep the relationship with Rick strictly business.

Restless, Dana wandered through the house, reacquainting herself with the patterns and shapes of its design. The house was as modernistic as Margaret and the trends of twenty years ago had been able to make it. Margaret had even put out a sign during construction which read, I Know It's Different. I Like It This Way. Dana, personally, had always felt that the house looked as forlorn as a bottle of expensive wine surrounded by countless jugs of moonshine. However, she never said so. Why voice one more difference of opinion between herself and her mother?

She saved the study for last and unerringly made her way to the window seat. This room, out of all those in the house, provided a sense of security, a place where she belonged. The study felt settled. Its soft, tan walls were covered with memorabilia . . . a news clipping and photograph of a young Margaret with a winning recipe; a dollar bill, framed with age and gilt; an ad for Ausbrook Candies from a local newspaper; a picture of the groundbreaking ceremonies for the Confectionery. Dana gazed affectionately at the cluttered wall, finding in the collection of memories a sense of her own history. She was a part of this.

There she was beside her mother in the groundbreaking photo, her hand next to Margaret's on the shovel. And in other pictures, she stood with her mother, proud to have been included in whatever proceedings were taking place. She had visited her mother for one weekend every other month until she was thirteen, but it was the special occasions she remembered best. The times Margaret arranged for her to come and take part in some grand happening at the confectionery. More often than not, it had been a lot of travel time for a few hours of ceremony, but she'd loved it. She'd been just a child then, filled with her own importance at being Margaret's daughter and so very eager to please her dynamic mother. It had been easy to like the confectionery before she recognized it as her rival for her mother's attentions.

Dana sat on the cushion and hugged her knees. She looked out the window, but trees and late-afternoon sunlight cast the outside world in bright shadows, so she turned back to the warm memories in the study. At age thirteen she'd stopped visiting her mother except for a two-week stint in the summer. The candy business became distasteful to her and she avoided going anywhere near the confectionery. It had been her way of rebelling, of protesting the idea that the confectionery mattered more to her mother than she did. But she had outgrown her youthful insurgency and now all she wanted was to mend just a few of the fences she'd so readily broken or never built in her relationship with Margaret.

Rick had warned her at the time, but back then she'd been so self-righteously sure she knew what she was doing. She'd been so sure about so many things. It was only in retrospect, as she'd grown to understand herself and her world, that she'd been able to accept the responsibility for her choices.

Dana let her thoughts ebb back to the present, but Rick came with them. He was a lawyer now. With his own office. He'd become a respected man in the community. She admired him for that and wondered what would have happened if she'd eloped with him. Would he have gone on to college and become an attorney, then? Would she? Chances were, their lives would have taken entirely different paths. Funny, she'd never realized Rick had career ambitions. She'd misjudged him and the thought chafed her conscience.

She sat for a while longer on the window seat, but then she gave up the fight and reached for the phone on Margaret's desk. She didn't know Rick's number, but it didn't take long to find it out and soon the phone was ringing.

"Hello?"

For no reason her heart began to thud against her ribs. "Hello? Rick? It's Dana."

A momentary silence carried across the wire, then his voice came again, softer, warmer than before. "Hello," he said. "I'm glad you called."

Suddenly, so was she. "I thought I'd let you know what I found out about Margaret and Hezekiah and the mysterious Recipe."

"Oh, you got Charity to talk, huh?"

"Finally. It took a lot of persuasion."

"I'll bet she said they were both as crazy as two squirrels in a pecan tree."

"Not exactly." Dana smiled at his nonsense. "'Crazy-sick in love' was the way she described their relationship."

"Love is certainly not a word I'd use in connection with your mother and Ki."

"Oh, she didn't mean they're in love now," Dana clarified. "Forty years ago my mother was engaged to marry Hezekiah Brown. Can you believe that?"

"Well, yes. I've heard rumors of the Burton-Brown feud ever since I can remember and the consensus of opinion has always been that Margaret jilted him at the altar. No one seems to know why. Did she tell you why she broke the engagement?"

"I was told it was none of my business." Dana leaned back against the window sill, remembering how she used to sit like this for hours, cradling the phone to her ear, listening for every breath Rick drew, waiting for the distant tones of his voice to reach her. She found the memory comforting, and her restlessness faded. "I wish you'd told me about the feud a long time ago, Rick. I didn't know until today that Margaret had such a colorful past. And to think that all this time I believed her highest passion was for assorted chocolates."

"Oh, I think she feels passionately about caramel creams. They travel well, you know."

Dana released a low groan. "Very funny. Has Hezekiah said anything about what happened?"

"No, but he smiled broadly all the way through the evening news, if that tells you anything."

"Did you see it?"

"Every detail. You looked great, by the way. Even Ki said so."

"I'm deeply appreciative." Dana twisted the phone cord around her fingers. "Sorry, but no one here said anything about you. Charity thought Hezekiah looked as sexy as ever, but she couldn't believe he'd actually wear a beret."

"And Margaret?" Rick asked.

"Margaret didn't have much to say...which is a blessing, believe me." Some remnant of loyalty caught Dana by surprise and kept her from mentioning Margaret's views on publicity and marketing and lawsuits. "She did tell me about the Recipe, though."

"Of her own free will? Or did you have to resort to blackmail?"

Dana smiled. "It was sort of a joint effort. Between what Margaret would admit and what Charity added, I think I have the whole story."

"So there really is a recipe?"

"Yes, for a Chocolate Peppermint Kiss."

"Hmm. My favorite."

Dana ignored his interruption. "The Recipe was a wedding present from Granny Varnell. When Margaret broke the engagement to Hezekiah, she tore the Recipe in half and that's how it ended up being at the center of the feud."

"At least we know there's something of substance responsible for that display today."

"I don't know how substantial a Peppermint Kiss can be, but Margaret said the Recipe would make us famous."

"Us?" Rick's tone conveyed amusement and surprise. "Does this mean she's already brainwashed you into thinking like a businesswoman?"

Dana shrugged off the teasing. "You know how I've always planned to be famous."

An odd silence stretched over the wire, broken only by a bittersweet memory which neither of them really wanted to recall. "I suppose I'll have to ask Ki about the Recipe. At least, I can ask about his half of it. What did Margaret do with hers?"

Dana straightened on the window seat. "You know, I didn't even think to ask. She must have it somewhere. I mean, she speaks as if it's as valuable as the Dead Sea Scrolls."

"Maybe it is. Granny Varnell is a mighty fine cook."

"If Granny's still around, why doesn't someone just ask her for a copy of the candy recipe?"

Rick's laugh rippled deep and generous through the telephone receiver. "That would be too simple, Dana. I don't know what Margaret and Ki have in mind, but it's a cinch they're going to put us in the middle of it, if they can. Personally, I'd hate to see that happen."

So would she. But Dana didn't say so. "I've told Margaret fifty times already that she doesn't have a case. To no effect, mind you, but I have given her my best legal opinion."

"It's hard for me to realize you're a lawyer, Dana. I never thought—" He broke off the sentence and a lighter nuance returned to his voice. "What made you decide to get a law degree?"

"A happy circumstance. I was taking graduate courses in psychology and did a paper on the legal rights of the mentally ill. It required some research in the law library and by the time the paper was written, I was hooked. I entered law school the next semester. And, three years later, here I am."

"The vice president of your mother's company."

The phone cord twisted tight across her fingers and Dana jerked her hand free. "That was a low blow, Rick."

He said nothing for a minute, then deftly turned the subject. "Well, I'm sure the Ausbrook Confectionery needs a good lawyer, who can double as a vice president."

Tension pulsed through the wires. "I intend to work very hard at this job."

"I never suggested that you wouldn't."

There were suddenly a dozen explanations in Dana's mind, all waiting to spill across her lips and convince Rick that she hadn't taken the job as an easy out, that she meant to give the confectionery and her mother her best effort. But he wouldn't understand. He probably wouldn't even believe her. She swallowed hard. "How long is Hezekiah going to be in Branson?"

"This is his home." Rick accepted the return to an impersonal topic without hesitation. "I expect him to stay from now on."

"I thought he had a business in Great Britain. London Country Candies, isn't that it?"

"Yes. He built it from scratch with the assistance of an Englishman he met during World War II. Ki and Henry started out making a plain caramel and did so well, they've expanded into a dozen countries and have tripled the size of the original operation. London Country is now an exclusive line of confections. Ki's done rather well for himself considering that he started so late."

"With you as his supporter, I'm not surprised. Was he your inspiration or were you his?"

"If I were guessing, I'd say Margaret did more to inspire Ki than anything or anyone else. There's nothing like a broken love affair to open up the mind to new possibilities. You know, Dana, the old 'I'll show you' kind of incentive."

The conversation was somehow oddly personal. "Motivation comes from unexpected sources, at times, I suppose."

"Yes, it does."

The restlessness returned. "Rick, I've got to go. Charity's calling me to supper, so I guess . . ."

"Thanks for calling. I'll let you know if Ki breaks his silence on the Recipe."

"Yes, do that," she said. "And—" There was, she realized, nothing else to say. "Goodbye, Rick."

"Goodbye, Dana."

Damn, she thought, as she replaced the telephone on the desk and uncurled from the window seat. Why was her pulse racing? Why couldn't her heart beat normally instead of pounding like a tympany drum? What was it with her and Rick, anyway? Ten years changed people, for heaven's sake. She definitely was different from the self-centered teenager she'd been when she'd met Rick.

And it wasn't as if she wanted to pick up the relationship where they'd left off. She was more of a "city girl" now than she'd been then and he was certainly still entrenched in the "country-boy" life-style. So why did she feel like a love-struck teenager when all she wanted was to be friends. There was nothing wrong with wanting his friendship.

Charity called again from the kitchen and Dana left the study, reassuring herself that nothing was going to happen in a year. Less than a year now. Only three hundred sixty-three days. What could possibly go wrong?

Chapter Four

Carefully, quietly, Dana closed her office door. She eased around the desk and dropped into her chair. She kicked off her shoes, hitched her skirt above her knees and propped her stockinged feet on the desktop. With a sigh of utter exhaustion, she popped the tab on a cola can and tipped it to her lips for a long, cold swig of soda.

When someone knocked at the door, she ignored it and closed her eyes, telling herself she was entitled to a break, especially since she hadn't even taken time for lunch. Dana didn't know how her mother did it. Margaret seldom took a lunch hour, never interrupted her work for a coffee break and stayed late almost every night. For the past week and a half, Dana had kept pace, but she was beginning to lag behind. Granted, she was still learning the ins and outs of the business, but she was a lot younger than Margaret and she'd thought that would give her an edge. She hadn't expected to surpass her mother's energy level, but it shouldn't have been so hard to stay even. Yesterday when Dana had remarked, over a dry sandwich eaten long after any normal supper hour, that she was not having fun, Margaret had laughed and said *she* was having a wonderful time. Then she'd presented another stack of paperwork for Dana's perusal and approval. The work just kept coming. Unfortunately, so did a seemingly endless string of interruptions.

The knock came again, more insistent. Dana flipped her skirt down to cover her knees and with a faintly resentful sigh, she put her feet on the floor. "Come in."

"Dana?" It was Will Burton, a distant cousin, younger than Dana by five years, and supervisor at the confectionery.

Dana tried to work up a pleasant expression. "Yes, Will?"

"Could I see you for a minute?"

It was on the tip of her tongue to inform him that she'd resigned or died or something, but instead she invited him in with her best businesslike smile and waved him to a chair. Tired or not, she was still the vice president of the company. "What can I do for you?" she said.

"Well..." Will's speech was slow and deliberate, often repetitive, and Dana found it hard to keep from completing sentences for him. He seemed intelligent enough and was distressingly polite, but as far as Dana could tell, he got up in the morning for the simple pleasure of coming to work. He loved making candy and it was apparent from his plump little body that he enjoyed the fruits of his labors in more ways than one.

"Yes?" Dana prompted.

"I must talk to you," he said. "It's a...uh, a most delicate matter."

"Is this a personal problem, Will? Or is it business?"

He cleared his throat. "Both. Sort of. It concerns Margaret. Your mother."

Dana had been afraid of that. "Okay," she said, hoping he'd take the initiative from there. Will just looked at her, his glance darting toward the door at frequent intervals. Dana leaned forward to encourage her cousin. "Are you spying on me?'' she said with a smile. "Did Margaret send you in here to find out if I'm goofing off on company time?''

His round face grew rounder with horror at the thought. "No. I wouldn't do that. What made you say...?''

"I was joking, Will." Dana shifted back into the chair, wishing that Will had a sense of humor. "I wasn't really accusing you of being a spy.''

He paled. At least, she thought he did. With Will it was hard to tell. "So, what's on your mind, Will?''

He shuffled uneasily in his seat. "Well, it's... I just thought you ought to know. She's acting... well, strange.''

"Who? Margaret?''

He nodded, glad she'd caught on so quickly. "Yes. Margaret. Your mother.''

"What's she done?''

"She's not well.''

"She's not?''

Will pursed his lips. His pudgy fingers tapped the arm of the chair. "I don't know what's wrong.''

"Well, what do you *think* is wrong?''

"Well, the other day she yelled at Rachael. For no reason at all.''

Will obviously found this grounds for indictment, but Dana had received a few of Margaret's yells herself and wasn't overly concerned. "Margaret is a little testy these days," she agreed.

"But there was no call for this." Will's cheeks bloomed with agitation. "Rachael was in tears.''

Dana nodded her understanding and tried to recall all that she knew about Rachael. Rachael Stokes was Charity's granddaughter and she'd occasionally visited Charity when Dana was at the house. Over the years, they probably hadn't met more than a half a dozen times, though, and all Dana could remember about Rachael was her long, brown braids and the habit she'd had of sticking out her tongue in the most obnoxious way. "Does Rachael work here, now?" Dana asked Will. "Funny, Charity didn't mention it to me."

"Rachael doesn't see her grandmother much." Will straightened in the chair and Dana noted the change in posture with interest. "She works in the test kitchen."

"I hope she's better with recipes than her grandmother is." Dana smiled. Charity was an adequate cook, who made simple meals and hated anything more complicated than frying, boiling, or chopping. "I haven't seen Rachael in a long time. It's hard to believe she's old enough to be working here."

"She turned eighteen last May," Will announced. "She's exactly five years and fourteen days younger than me." He paused. "Than I am."

Dana mulled over that information. "I'll bet she turned out to be a very pretty young lady."

"Oh, she's beautiful. Really beautiful." Reverence echoed in the words and tucked in shyly at the corners of his mouth.

Bingo, Dana thought. In Will's mind, he and Rachael were a couple. Whether or not they actually were, Dana didn't know, but it certainly helped to explain the problem Will was having with Margaret. "Why do you think Margaret yelled at her?"

"A mistake." Will was suddenly eager to confide. "She's making a lot of mistakes."

Dana knew to whom he referred, but she asked anyway. "Margaret?"

"Yes. Margaret. Your mother."

If he said that one more time, Dana thought she might just have to yell at him, herself. "Have you noticed anything else?"

"Well..." Will glanced toward the door, glanced back. "The other day when I took some orders in for her to sign, she refused. Wouldn't even tell me why. 'No!' she said. 'No!'" Will repeated it, as if he still couldn't believe Margaret had spoken to him like that. "She's never done that before. She always signs the things I take her. She trusts me, you know. I have a lot of responsibilities here. And I do a good job, too. What am I supposed to do when she won't sign the orders? I can't do my job, if she won't do hers."

"Hmm." Dana stalled for time and a moment's silence.

Will calmed down somewhat. "She's been acting this way ever since the press conference. And you know what that means."

It sounded ominous, whatever it meant. "The incident with Hezekiah Brown was unfortunate, Will, but it's been blown out of proportion. I don't think anything like that will happen again. You really shouldn't worry about it."

His face puckered in a pained expression. "I do worry, Dana. This confectionery is important to me. I want to see it grow and make progress. I don't want something terrible to happen because your mother makes some bad business decisions. And in her state of mind..." He let the prediction trail away, leaving Dana to fill in her own horrifying images.

She schooled the impatience out of her voice. "Everything is fine, Will. The next time you have something needing Margaret's signature, bring it to me. I'll take care of it."

Will looked suddenly offended, as if she'd kicked him for no reason at all. "What makes you think you can get her to sign, if I can't?" he asked.

A good point, Dana conceded, but she wasn't about to admit it to him. "I'll sign them, Will. I'm the vice president. I can do things like that."

"Well..." he said. "Well...you can't sign everything."

She almost snapped at him then, but she controlled the impulse. "I'll take care of it. Just stay out of Margaret's way for a while and everything will be okay."

He didn't like that idea. It was apparent in the stubborn set of his mouth. "I have a lot invested in this business, Dana. I ought to be included in the decision making."

Dana lifted her chin. "Oh? What do you mean, you have a lot invested in the business?"

Will flushed, but didn't lower his gaze. "Just what I said. I've been working here for seven years now. When I turned sixteen I started working after school and weekends. I even took evening classes at the junior college so I could keep my job at the confectionery. I know a lot about this place, Dana. A lot more than some people think I do. And I ought to be allowed to make a few decisions."

"What kinds of decisions?" Dana asked. She was more uncomfortable with his tone of voice than with what he said. It sounded almost like a threat. "What is it you want to be consulted about?"

He seemed to back off his statement a bit. "Well...the chocolate peppermints, for one thing. If we're going to be selling them, I have a right to—"

"How do you know about the peppermints?"

"Oh, everyone around here knows about the Recipe, Dana. And Margaret told Ki she was going to use it on television. It's common knowledge."

"Have you actually seen the Recipe?"

Will shifted in the chair, crossed his legs and then, obviously uncomfortable, put them back the way they were. "I don't know if there is anything to see, but I ought to be included in any decision Margaret makes about it."

Dana found that the most presumptuous thing he'd said. Margaret didn't consult anyone when it came to making decisions and Dana wasn't going to be the one to suggest she start. "I think you're worrying about nothing, Will," Dana said soothingly, hoping to ease her cousin out of her office. "Margaret loves the Ausbrook Confectionery more than anything. She may be a little irritable lately, but don't take it personally. I'm sure she didn't mean to offend you or Rachael. Just do your job the best you can . . . as you always do . . . and try not to worry."

"Well . . ." He stood and brushed at permanently set wrinkles in his slacks. "I thought you ought to know that I'm concerned."

Dana stood, too, mentally pushing him toward the door. "I appreciate that, Will."

"Well . . ."

"Well . . ." Dana nodded and made a move away from the chair. "Thanks for stopping by."

Finally Will walked to the door. "You'll tell her what I said?" he asked.

Dana didn't know what that meant. Did he want her to tell or was it supposed to be their secret? "You can trust me, Will."

"I hope so."

He left and with a shake of her head, Dana closed the door again and returned to her chair. She scribbled a note about Will's problem in getting the purchase orders signed so she'd remember to ask Margaret about it later. She had a fair idea that Will had left off some minor detail in preparing the orders and that was why Margaret wouldn't sign them, but she wanted to follow through on Will's complaint. That was, after all, a part of her job. And she'd take care of the problem just as soon as she'd had a break. Lord knew, she needed a break. Thirty minutes of escape. An hour, at best. She deserved a little bit of time to call her own, didn't she?

Propping her feet on the desk again, she leaned back in her chair and picked up the latest stack of production reports. It was a compromise, but Dana promised herself she'd take a real lunch break later, as soon as she'd lowered the paperwork by an inch or so and providing, of course, that there were no other interruptions.

RICK'S FOOT PRESSED DOWN on the accelerator as the truck made the turn in front of the Ausbrook Confectionery. Usually he drove past and allowed himself a moment to wonder about Dana and how her v.p. training was progressing. But today he wasn't going to drive past. Today, he had a legitimate reason to stop and see her. At least, he'd told himself it would be legitimate to stop and ask her if she'd found out anything else about the Recipe. If Margaret still intended to sue Ki, Rick thought he had a right to know.

Besides, he wanted to see Dana. He'd thought about her far too often during the past several days. He'd promised himself he would bide his time before approaching her and he had. Ten days offered proof that he had willpower and was in control of the situation, didn't

it? The fact remained, though, that he was intrigued by
her presence in Branson. He wanted to know if Dana had
changed, or if she still behaved as if she'd been born a
princess and was therefore entitled to have her way, regardless of who got hurt. Had she matured enough to
understand the consequences of her own actions?

Five minutes later he walked into the Candy Shop and
waved a friendly hello to Millie Beatty, who worked behind the counter selling sweets. "Is Dana upstairs?" Rick
asked, hardly waiting for her nod before making his way
to the door marked Employees Only. He took the stairs
two at a time and smiled to himself as he thought about
the thunderstruck look on Millie's face. He supposed his
presence in the confectionery would be a surprise to anyone. Why, he hadn't been inside since the other day with
Ki. And before that…well, it had been a very long time.
And now here he was, acting as if he had every right to
be there. He just hoped Margaret didn't catch him wandering the corridors. Facing her was not a prospect he
relished.

At the top of the stairs, three doors opened off a short
hall. The one to his right probably still belonged to Margaret. He'd received his walking papers out of Dana's life
in that office and the memory still burned hot in his
mind. With more bravado than courage, he stepped past
the open doorway and moved down the hall with defi-
nite steps. The second door was open, but the third was
closed and Rick's mouth tilted into a rueful smile. He
knocked quietly and got a throaty groan in reply. Glancing over his shoulder to be sure Margaret wasn't charg-
ing down the hall toward him, he reached for the knob
and opened the door.

Dana sat behind the desk, her stockinged feet propped
on the corner, her skirt riding high on a shapely thigh. As

he stepped into her office, she shifted position, lowering her feet to the floor and adjusting the hem of her skirt in one swift movement. She looked up from the papers she held in her hand and her eyes widened at the sight of him, then narrowed with pleasure. "Hello, Rick. You're late."

His heart skipped a beat, but came swiftly under control. "I am?"

"I phoned for a rescuer days ago. What took you so long?"

"Traffic is bad. You know how it is."

Dana shook her head and placed the papers on the desk. "White knights aren't what they used to be."

"I came the instant I heard you were chained to that desk."

Her lips curved. "Did you bring the key?"

"No, but I made your bail. I'm springing you out of this joint. Grab your hat and let's go."

Her shoulders straightened in quick attention. "You mean it? You'll actually take me somewhere? Away from here?" Her hand swept the room in a questioning gesture.

"Sure. I came by to ask if you've found out anything more on the Recipe, but we can go for a ride if you want."

She drooped slightly. "This is business? I hoped...thought you might have come to take me to lunch or something like that."

"It's long past lunch time, Dana. Haven't you eaten?"

"Oh, yes, sure. Hours ago." At breakfast, actually. But she didn't say that. "Well, sit down and let's talk, Rick."

He sensed her disappointment. "Perhaps we ought to go for a drive. I'd hate to have your mother walk in while I'm here. Why don't I just kidnap you?"

"Great idea." A full smile captured her mouth and she was on her feet and by his side in a matter of minutes. "You, sir, have just earned yourself unlimited samples of the Ausbrook candies."

"That doesn't sound like the sell-sell-sell philosophy to me. Margaret won't be pleased."

Dana looked him square in the eye with patent disgust. "Well, don't be fool enough to tell her, Rick. I'm certainly not going to."

He laughed and wondered how, after all that had happened between them, Dana could make him feel so comfortable. "I take it you're not going to ask her permission to leave work, either?"

"I've never been stupid, Rick. I'm not about to pick up the habit now." She grabbed her purse, slung the strap across her shoulder and smiled at him with such delight he had to catch his breath. Dana at her most charming was potent stuff.

"I guess you don't have to worry about losing your job, do you?" he remarked offhandedly and regretted it when a sudden wariness altered her pleasure.

"Did you come to kidnap me or to criticize?" She pursed her lips and thrust her hands into the deep pockets of her skirt. "Don't answer," she cut in before he could say anything. "Because I don't care why you came, Rick. I'm just glad you did. In fact, you have no idea how glad I am to see you."

With her words, a thrill sketched its way down his back. He ought not to fall for this, he knew, but... Well, why else had he stopped by? "I had a feeling you'd be restless by now."

"Restless?" A throaty spill of amusement eased past her lips and Dana enjoyed it. She released any lingering guilt over leaving the office with a silent promise that she'd work twice as hard when she got back. Three times as hard, if necessary. "I'm desperate. I haven't seen the sun in four days. And at night when I sleep—I haven't told another person this—I've started dreaming about vats of chocolate."

"Ah, sweet dreams."

She made a face at him and moved into the hallway. "Any more remarks like that and you can forget about the free samples. Understood?"

"Perfectly." He watched the saucy tilt of her head, admired the silky sway of her cinnamon-gold hair and knew the impulse to catch her in his arms and kiss her until she begged him to stop. "I'll be careful," he promised. "You know what a fool I am for fudge."

Dana tossed a frown over her shoulder. "I don't know why I like you, Rick. Your taste leaves a lot to be desired."

"Depends on who you ask. There are a number of people who think I have excellent taste."

"They're probably all sugar addicts, like you." She walked away, then paused, waiting for him to catch up. "On the other hand, I quite admired your office, so perhaps you do have your sober moments."

Rick grinned and reached for the doorknob of her office door, preparatory to closing it behind him.

"Leave it open," Dana said. "Then maybe no one will notice I'm gone." With an upward flip of her hand she blithely skipped down the stairs.

Rick followed, aware of a conflicting pleasure in her easy rejection of responsibility. He supposed he'd hoped that it would take a bit more effort to pry her away from her job, but then he hadn't really expected her to put up any resistance. After all, the Dana he had known before had avoided work at any cost. Had he really envisioned an attitude change?

Shrugging aside the questions, Rick trailed Dana's steps through the doorway and into the candy shop, where Millie eyed them with obvious curiosity. "You leaving, Miss Dana?" she asked.

"Yes." Dana continued toward the exit without breaking stride. "If anyone asks for me, tell them I'll be back in . . ." The end of the sentence got lost between the air-conditioned shop and the rush of July heat outside.

Rick waved goodbye to a slack-jawed Millie and followed Dana out the door, feeling more like an adolescent than a grown man waffling on the issue of whether or not to get involved again with Dana Ausbrook, Princess Extraordinaire. In a matter of ten minutes, more or less, he'd managed to discover how powerful an old attraction could be. He'd also learned how vulnerable he was to that same attraction. His only defense lay in the knowledge that Dana was not the forever kind. Understanding that was the key to keeping his heart out of danger. Accepting it was the secret to enjoying what little time he had with her.

"My truck is over here." He caught her arm and turned her in the right direction.

Dana shaded her eyes against the sun and squinted at the blue-and-beige pickup, sitting all shiny clean and new in the parking lot. "Oh, good! A truck," she said. "Do you want me to drive?"

Rick unlocked the passenger door and invited her to take a seat. "I'll drive, Dana. I haven't forgotten what happened the last time you got behind the wheel of my truck."

"That was different." She put one foot on the running board and boosted herself onto the cloth-covered seat. "I didn't have a driver's license then."

"I'll bet you don't have one now, either. At least, not a valid Missouri license."

He was right, but Dana shut the door, deciding not to tell him that she hadn't had a minute to call her own, much less time to change over her Pennsylvania license. He probably wouldn't believe she'd really been working...and working hard at that. In fact, he probably didn't believe she actually intended to get the license. So why try to explain?

"Where are you taking me?" she asked instead as he got into the truck. Then, with hardly a pause for breath, she lifted a hand to ward off any information he might have been about to give. "No, don't tell me. If Margaret tracks me down, I want to be able to tell her you kidnapped me and I had no idea where I was."

Rick shook his head and reached for the shoulder restraint. "Buckle up. If Margaret does track you down, at least you'll be wearing your seat belt."

Dana laughed. "You don't really think that will impress her, do you? A woman who smokes like a freight train?"

Rick put the truck in gear and backed out of the parking space. "I know people who smoke *and* use seat belts."

"Not Margaret. She wouldn't wear a seat belt on a million-dollar bet."

"I see the two of you remain on the best of terms." Swinging the pickup onto the highway, Rick headed for the hills. "I suppose some things will never change."

Dana knew he'd said the words facetiously. God knew she'd voiced the same thought herself, many times. But things would change. That's the reason she was here. Margaret probably wouldn't stop smoking cigarettes or start wearing her seat belt, but, one way or another, her relationship with her daughter was going to change. Dana intended to see to that. Not that Rick would understand. He had a large and loving family. How could he possibly know how it felt to want so badly to be loved and wanted and appreciated? He'd always known the security of those emotions. Dana never had. At least not from Margaret, her mother.

The thought brought Will Burton to mind and Dana continued to look out the pickup window as she studied the problem he'd presented. It amounted to nothing, she decided. If all he was worried about was Margaret's judgment on business matters, then he had a lot to learn about business. Even in the short time Dana had worked at the confectionery, she'd come to appreciate her mother's ability to direct, manage, and oversee the company. Just because her judgment was none too sound when it came to Hezekiah Brown was no reason to believe Margaret was making bad decisions about the confectionery. It simply meant she was as susceptible to a man's line as any other woman. For instance, Dana herself was at this very moment seated in a northbound truck with a man she had no business being with. Of course, Rick hadn't given her a line. Dana had supplied that for him.

"You're very quiet. Aren't kidnap victims supposed to yell out the window or something?"

"I'm composing a 'help' note in my mind. I'll write it with lipstick and leave it at the first rest stop we come to."

"What if we don't make any rest stops?"

"You'll just have to keep me, then."

Rick's right eyebrow arched in tawny skepticism. "I'm not sure I can afford to keep you, Dana. As I recall, you're quite expensive."

"I am. I admit it." She smiled at him with wry confession. "But I'm not as expensive as I used to be. During the past few years, I've learned I can't always have what I want."

"A lesson we all have to learn, sooner or later. Somehow, though, I didn't think you'd ever get it, Dana."

From his tone, Dana knew he hadn't forgotten the past or forgiven her for being a part of it. "People change, Rick. You're certainly a prime example of that."

His answer was to pull off the pavement onto a dry, dirt road. The truck bounced like a jackrabbit as Rick drove a wooded half mile to a clearing overlooking a superior view of the green hills and valleys of the Ozarks. Dana remembered it well. She and Rick had spent many long, lovely hours here, sheltered from prying eyes, alone with their dreams and their love. They'd talked some, but had spent most of their time exploring the physical vistas of young love, teasing each other, kissing until their lips were warm and swollen with the touch, stepping close to fulfillment, but backing away from that final commitment. And now that Rick had brought her here again, Dana wished she didn't recall those other times quite so vividly.

She pretended the memories didn't affect her, that she wasn't imagining what it would be like to exchange kisses with him now. She turned to him with a wide smile. "Good job, Stafford. Margaret won't ever find me here."

"This is probably the first spot she'd look. Everyone who was ever eighteen years old in Branson knows about this place. Your mother's probably been here a few times, herself."

Dana laughed at that. "With Hezekiah Brown, no doubt. Somehow, I just can't imagine Margaret with him. They're so very different."

"Are they?" Rick turned toward her, his arm stretching across the top of the bench seat. "Do you think they're as different as we are?"

"Oh, they couldn't be. No one could be as different as we are." The words tripped from her tongue like a pair of mismatched dancers, missing the light touch she intended and falling flat. She salvaged a smile and tried again. "But we do have one thing in common. Our law degrees. Different schools, of course. Different states. Still that's something, don't you think?"

His eyes darkened to a cloudy emerald, but whether it was annoyance or something more akin to desire, Dana couldn't decipher. Whatever the emotion, she felt it and recognized its power. They were no longer teenagers, groping in the dark for love and approval. They faced each other in those few moments of silence as a man and a woman who had unresolved feelings and a past they hadn't been able to forget.

The air felt dry and static and Rick held the silence while Dana grappled for words that wouldn't come. When the quiet stretched to the breaking point, Dana retrieved a thought from deep in her mind and, without consideration of its appropriateness, voiced it. "I'm sorry, Rick. Really. I shouldn't have left the way I did that summer, without a word to you. I regret not telling you my decision, but, well, it just seemed best at the time."

He reached out to brush the back of his hand against her hair, gently, yet the gesture was wistful. Dana's heartbeat pulsed in her ears. Why was she apologizing? Rick didn't want to hear her excuses. What's more, she didn't owe him an explanation. If he'd really been "crazy-sick" in love with her, he'd have hot-footed it to Philadelphia and convinced her she didn't love Darren and couldn't marry him. But Rick hadn't done that. Satisfied that she'd shifted his share of the blame back where it was supposed to be, she kept her eyes fixed on his. When the silence again grew uncomfortably long, she frowned. "It wouldn't hurt you to say you were sorry, too, you know."

"I'd be lying, Dana, if I said it. If you hadn't left when you did, the way you did, I wouldn't be the person I am right now. And I'm pleased with the man I've become. I'm not sure I could honestly say that if we'd eloped as we planned."

His admission rankled, but she smiled agreeably. "Oh, I get it. This is one of those 'I went on to bigger and better things and I owe it all to you' dramas. Is that it?"

"Not exactly." He lifted his hand to stroke her hair again, but she discouraged the gesture with a look. "I don't owe it all to you. Any more than you owe your achievements to me. I'm just saying that sometimes what seems terrible at the time, turns out to be a blessing in disguise."

"A blessing?" She wasn't liking this, not at all. "I'm glad you remember it that way, Rick. I was afraid I might have broken your heart."

"Oh, you did, Dana. But I got over it and learned a valuable lesson in the process."

"What? That you don't always get what you want?"

"I realized I could survive not having you. And from there, it was only a small step to understanding what I could have if I was willing to make the necessary sacrifices."

Dana could have kicked him in the shins for being so patronizing. He didn't have to act like losing her was the best thing that ever happened to him. "So," she said, after several long minutes slid into several more. "Here we are. Back where we started and still a million miles apart."

Rick held her gaze with the sheer force of his own longing and this time, when his hand lifted to her hair, he wasn't satisfied with a touch. He cupped the back of her head in his palm and pulled her forward to meet him in the middle of the bench seat, to bring her into an embrace that had been building for years.

Dana's pulse barely had time to flutter a warning before she was a captive in his arms, her heart held hostage by memories and a newly awakened need. As his mouth came down to cover hers, she lifted her lips in acceptance.

Chapter Five

In all of her life, Dana had enjoyed few pleasures so much that she dreamed of repeating them. The thrill of amusement-park roller coasters had diminished in direct proportion to her age and consecutively higher levels of daring. Funnel cakes, those batter-fried swirls of sweetness, sold at tourist traps around the country, had won first prize with her taste-buds. She'd loved the treat at first bite and had begged, wheedled, bribed, or bought one at every opportunity since. The problem, though, was that she couldn't quite recapture the first delicious sensation. Roller coaster rides and funnel cakes never measured up to the pleasure she recalled and so she'd come to the reluctant conclusion that memory endowed first-time experiences with a charm which could not be duplicated. She'd lived by that assumption, too. Until this very moment, when Rick kissed her and shot her theory to pieces.

She didn't remember when her arms had found their way around him or just when her fingers had begun a restless massage of his back. Her lips were parted beneath his and as the tip of his tongue began to tease her, she responded with a slow, playful pursuit. His mouth moved against hers in a series of sensual nudges, designed to strip her willpower and undermine her resistance. Dana had never been long on resistance, though. Not when it came to Rick and Rick's kisses. Still, it was somewhat humbling to discover that ten years of experiences and dozens of well-thought-out excuses melted like milk chocolate in the heated renewal of this old attraction.

As her pleasure deepened, she admitted that in this case, reality was better than her memories. As another tender minute passed, she decided reality was better even than anything she'd been able to imagine. And she was very good at imagining.

His lips eased away from hers and Rick brushed one last, pleasing touch across her parted lips before retreating. His arms fell away from her in a gradual, grudging motion, lingering here and there on her skin as if bestowing a gift. The slightest tilt tucked in at the corners of his mouth, not a smile exactly, but an expression of satisfaction that Dana suspected she mirrored.

"Perhaps we have more in common than a law degree, Dana."

She knew there was no point in denial. "If you expect an argument, you're going to be disappointed."

"I only wanted to prove that we're not as different as you'd like to believe."

"It isn't that—" Her voice went uneven and rough, as she realized what she had to say. Honesty didn't come easily, but she was determined to be straightforward. She had no intention of staying in Branson and she knew Rick had no intention of leaving, so there was no point in pretending a relationship between them would work. This time when she left, she wasn't going to look back with regret. "I'm only staying here for a year, Rick. I want you to know that before—well, before anything starts.''

"Before anything starts." He rolled the words on his tongue as if he found the idea new and interesting. "Just what did you have in mind, Dana?"

"You know what I meant," she said, knowing he was as aware as she was of the pitfalls in renewing their friendship. There were obvious dangers involved. Kissing, to name just one.

Rick moved, shifting behind the steering wheel again. "I know what you meant, Dana. What I don't understand is why you're here in the first place. Why can't you tell Margaret you aren't interested in working for her or with her? What's going to be different in a year's time?"

She couldn't tell him. Dana had cherished her secret promise too long to open it up for critique. What happened between her and her mother didn't involve anyone else and she didn't feel comfortable discussing it with Rick. "I promised her I'd work for a year at the confectionery as soon as I graduated. It's not such a long time."

That depended, Rick thought, on who was counting and who had the most to lose. "I see. And what happens when the year's over?"

"I've been promised a junior position with Barney, Mayfield, and Simonsen." She wondered why her voice was suddenly so soft. She cleared her throat. "They're a large law firm in Philadelphia."

"I'm impressed, Dana."

"Oh, do you know the firm?"

Rick stopped short of explaining that one of his classmates had applied for a position there during their last semester of law school and, just for the heck of it, simply because he'd known Dana lived in Philadelphia, Rick had applied, too. And been accepted. And turned it down. "I've heard of it," he said. "Very prestigious."

Dana nodded her agreement, then felt compelled to add, "My father had nothing to do with my getting the job, either."

Rick's brows arched in surprise. "It never occurred to me to think he did. And just for the record, Dana, I'm happy for you. It sounds like a wonderful opportunity."

"Yes, it is." She paused, then amended. "In a year."

"In a year."

The silence returned, but more politely, as if the kiss they'd shared had made it welcome. "So," Rick said finally, "You're committed to working at the confectionery for the foreseeable future. Does that mean you'll be developing the peppermint-kiss recipe?"

"I'm still not convinced there really is a recipe. Margaret's not talking, except to renew her threats to sue Hezekiah. I've looked everywhere I can think to look for it, but so far haven't turned up a clue. It doesn't make sense to me that she'd tear a recipe in half and then wait to fight about it forty years later."

"Margaret and Ki have been fighting right along. You just didn't know it. Ki, himself, admits the two of them are worse than the Hatfields and McCoys. But they're not as famous because the Hatfields and McCoys had big families and the Brown-Burton feud involves only two people."

"It appears they're getting ready to remedy that. If they do file a lawsuit, you and I will be square in the middle of their feud. 'I just have that feelin,' as Charity would say."

Rick firmed his jaw with thought. "Charity hasn't offered any more information?"

"No. In fact, any time I bring up the subject, she takes off on a sentimental journey about how Ki and Margaret were 'crazy-sick in love' and should never have broken up." Dana made a rueful face. "Charity isn't overly sensitive to my feelings on the matter. I don't suppose Ki has said anything more specific about the Recipe, has he?"

"Only what I've already told you. He's been pretty busy the past week or so. He's looking for a place to buy."

"He's going to live here?" she asked, shifting in the seat and smoothing her skirt over her legs. "What about his business?"

"I haven't asked. If Ki thinks I need to know, he'll tell me. In the meantime, he hasn't offered any information on what he plans to do about Margaret or the Recipe."

Dana frowned. "Maybe we're talking to the wrong people, Rick. What if we went directly to Granny Varnell and asked her about the Recipe? That might nip this feud business in the bud."

Rick thought it was a little late for that. About forty years too late, but why toss a cloud on the possibility? "I don't suppose it would hurt to visit Granny and find out what she knows about the Recipe."

"Visit?" Dana asked. "Can't we just telephone?"

A low chuckle hummed past Rick's lips. "She doesn't have a telephone, Dana. Besides, she loves to have people drop by. You wouldn't want to deprive her of the pleasure of your company, would you?"

Put like that, Dana could hardly refuse. "How do I get there?"

"The directions are a bit tricky. She lives a good distance from town." He paused. "Maybe I should take you."

Relief poured over her. She'd never been too comfortable talking with the residents of this hillbilly place on her own. "That would be great. When can we go?"

"What about now? You don't really want to go back to work, do you?"

What a question, Dana thought. Going back to the confectionery was not on her most-want-to-do list. But she'd been away from the office long enough. Responsibilities were already calling her back. "I have to get back, Rick. I shouldn't have left in the first place. There's a mountain of stuff that needs to be done. Today." She allowed herself the tiniest sigh. "Let's make it Sunday, all right? I'll just tell Margaret I have to have some time off."

"You've had the last hour off," he pointed out.

"There's no need to be smug." Dana cooled his cheerfulness with a look. "I didn't take a lunch break today. Besides, I haven't said anything to you about why you're not working this afternoon."

"I don't work for Margaret, so I can pretty much set my own hours."

"Lucky you." Dana resisted the urge to explain that it really wasn't Margaret who'd set her work hours. She was expecting far more of herself than her mother was. But Rick wouldn't believe that and she didn't have time to make him understand. "So, on Sunday we'll go to see Granny Varnell, right? Morning or afternoon?"

"Afternoon. Around three o'clock."

"Fine. If nothing else, the visit ought to put the threat of a lawsuit to rest."

"Do you really think so?" Rick settled back in the seat, looking comfortable and relaxed with time on his hands.

Dana glanced at her watch. "Of course. Once we know if there is a recipe, we can get a whole copy of it. Then Margaret and Ki can race to the nearest patent office and let the proper government officials decide who has the right to claim ownership."

"I don't think it's going to be quite that easy, Dana, but we'll see what Granny has to say." His arm stretched along the back of the seat again and Dana thought perhaps it was time to exit this too-intimate setting.

"I hereby declare this kidnapping over, Rick. You can return me to the salt mines, now. Some of us have to work for a living, you know."

He gave a husky laugh, but his arm moved away from her and he lazily reached for the ignition. "If I'd really kidnapped you, you couldn't order me around like that."

"Maybe not," she said. "But consider this, Rick. There is a half pound of fudge calling your name, even as we speak. It's yours, simply for getting me back to that office without getting caught."

His lips curved with modesty. "A hero never considers the reward. But in this case, I'll make an exception. There's a tow sack in the back of the pickup. I could bundle you up in it and sneak you right past Margaret."

Dana shuddered at the thought. "Show a little more imagination, Rick. Burlap has never been my style."

"No, I guess not." He turned the wheel and backed the truck out of the clearing. "How about slipping in the back door?"

She answered with a pained smile.

He nodded. "Right. Back doors aren't your style, either. Well, then, you'll just have to go in the front and act like you own the place." The corners of his mouth slanted upward. "Now don't try to tell me that's not your style."

Dana felt a pang of regret that she had played along with Rick's teasing, letting him believe she had no patience and little respect for the disciplines of hard work. Maybe it had been true of her a long time ago, but it wasn't true now. She wasn't the self-centered child she'd been ten years before. She'd changed. But how did she say that to him? "Just drive, would you?" she said, holding back a sigh. "I'll work out a plan for myself."

"Good idea." He executed a neat U-turn and had them back on the dirt road, heading for the highway in a matter of a minute or less. "Not that I want to appear mercenary, you understand, but if we don't get in scot-free, do I still get the reward?"

"I'm sure Margaret will be happy to reward you for my safe return. You can tell her you found me on the highway, trying to thumb a ride out of town. Who knows, Rick? She might even throw in a dozen caramel creams as a bonus."

The tip of his tongue made a sashay across his lips. "Do you think you might need to be kidnapped again anytime soon?"

"I hope the fudge gives you cavities," she told him crossly.

THE PHONE ON HER DESK rang at five minutes to five and Dana shot it a meaningful glare. She'd worked steadily and hard since returning from her brief escape earlier in the afternoon. Margaret had been no where to be seen when Dana slipped past her office door a little more than an hour ago and, with a mixture of guilt and relief, Dana hadn't looked up from her work since. She'd even disciplined her thoughts to stay clear of Rick and the too-sweet memory of his kiss. She'd needed to get away from the office for a few minutes. He'd provided a respite. It was nothing more and nothing less. The less she dwelt on it, the better.

The phone stopped after that one ring and Dana rubbed her forehead. Only Margaret would be so impatient, she thought, and sure enough, in a moment, Dana heard her mother's footsteps coming down the hall. Resignedly she put down her pencil and waited for the ax to fall.

"Where have you been?" Margaret walked into the room, unannounced and trailing an agitated smoke signal behind her. "I just tried to call you. You didn't answer."

Dana subdued an impulse to rise to her mother's state of turmoil. "It only rang once," she said in self-defense. "I didn't have a chance to pick it up."

"Never mind." Margaret paced to the chair across from Dana's desk. "I need to see you in my office. Right now." She brought her cigarette to her lips, then glanced angrily around the room. "Why isn't there an ashtray in here?" With that, she spun on her diminutive heels and exited with the same zeal with which she'd entered. "Come on, Dana," she called over her shoulder. "We're meeting *now*!"

What a way to end the day. Dana took her time in getting up from her desk. She shuffled a few papers, stacked them with some pride in the Out box and tapped her finger philosophically on the stack still needing her attention. Tomorrow, she promised. She straightened the gores of her skirt, ran a soothing hand through the hair at her temple and, thus prepared for battle, she started down the hall to Margaret's office.

Will crested the top of the stairs just as Dana reached the doorway and she questioned him with a lift of her brows. He shrugged, hugged his clipboard to his chest and mouthed a warning. "I told you so."

Dana dipped her chin in a nod, as if she understood his meaning completely, and entered the office ahead of him. Margaret paced the floor, pausing every few seconds to look out the window at the factory below. She made no comment and Dana took a seat and slipped off her shoes, deciding she might as well make herself comfortable. Will stood at one corner of the desk, nervously flipping the metal clip on the clipboard. The sound was harsh and unpleasant, but Dana tolerated it because she knew as long as Will was present, *she* wasn't going to get chewed out. And from the rigid set of Margaret's shoulders, it was clear that *someone* was in trouble. Plenty.

"Will you stop that racket?" Margaret snapped when the metal clipped the board for the thirteenth time. "Sit down, Will. You make me nervous."

Will sat, plucking at his pants legs as he did so. Now that, Dana thought, made her nervous. She wished she had a breath mint to offer him, although she didn't have any real hope it would keep him still.

"You wanted to see us?" Will asked, his voice tense and irritating.

Dana winced. Didn't the man have a grain of sense? In this mood, Margaret would probably jump down his throat for breaking her train of thought. But Margaret didn't turn on Will, she stayed silently by the window, her cigarette burning to ashes in her hand. Just as it seemed certain the ashes would fall to the floor, Margaret moved to her desk and stubbed the cigarette into the ashtray. She crossed her arms at her chest and directed a tight, angry glare at the far wall. Even with the irate body language, Margaret was an attractive woman, petite and delicate looking, with auburn hair, frosted in silver. She dressed nicely, emphasizing her femininity. Yet she was undoubtedly the strongest, most independent and the smartest lady Dana had ever met.

A subtle blend of love and pride invaded Dana's consciousness. The feeling surprised her, yet she welcomed it. Most of the time, she kept strict control of her emotions when she was around her mother. She'd been hurt too many times. But occasionally, at the oddest moments, the full force of her admiration made itself known. She was proud to have Margaret as her mother.

"There has been an offer to buy Ausbrook Confectionery." Margaret's glare left the wall and centered squarely between Dana and Will. "An anonymous offer."

Will snapped his clipboard in response. Dana sat a little straighter. "Did you accept?" she asked.

Margaret abandoned her pose and flung a hand outward in a wild gesture. "Nine years of college and that's the first question that springs to your mind? No, Dana, I did not accept. I built this company from scratch and no one is going to walk in and take it away. Especially not Hezekiah Brown!"

"I thought the offer was anonymous," Dana said.

"He's behind it. He wants to put me out of business, and if he can't buy me out, he'll try to do it some other way. I know that man. He stops at nothing." Margaret walked behind the desk, pulled out a drawer, glanced inside and slammed it shut. She began searching through the clutter on her desk until her hand landed on the almost-empty pack of cigarettes.

Dana mulled over the possibilities of the disclosure as she waited for Margaret to light the cigarette and calm down. She glanced at Will, who looked as pallid and wan as it was possible for a person of his size and coloring to look. Poor guy, she thought. The confectionery was "his life." The idea that it could, at some point, be sold probably shocked him to the center of his soul. Dana felt a little sorry for him.

"We have ten days to consider the offer." Margaret resumed her position at the front of the desk, but she seemed more in control, less emotional. "That will give us time to plan our strategy and put him off guard." She paused to puff smoke toward the ceiling. "Ki will be expecting a resounding refusal within minutes. I want him to be lulled into a false sense of security, then we'll nail him."

"Ki Brown?" Will's voice quavered, sounding like a boy on the edge of adolescence. "You think he made the offer?"

"I know he did. Haven't you been listening to me?"

Will looked chastened and nervously began to flip the metal piece of the clipboard again. Margaret reached over and snatched it out of his hands. "Give me that! How many times do I have to tell you, Will, that this clipboard does not look very professional. Order yourself something that looks halfway decent. Something in leather." She dropped the clipboard onto the desk and scuffed the palms of her hands together. "Now, Will, you need to keep your ears open in case rumors about a sale begin to circulate among the employees. We'll need to keep close tabs on morale. I'm sure you'll know how to handle that. Dana, you prepare the necessary legal papers."

Dana jerked her attention from Will's forlorn face to Margaret. "You mean a letter refusing the offer?"

"No, of course not. I can do that myself. I want you to draw up a petition to file in court."

"A lawsuit?" Dana wished her mother wasn't so single-minded. "Margaret, you can't sue Ki Brown just because you think he made an anonymous offer to buy your company. Even if he'd made the offer to your face, you have no grounds for a lawsuit."

Margaret drew on her cigarette, slowly, as if she were making perfect sense and Dana was the one being unreasonable. "I'll think of something. You just draw up the papers."

"Could I—" Will broke into the conversation, but the words seemed to keep getting stuck in his mouth. "Could I ask? What . . . what was the price?"

For his trouble, he received a withering frown. "You want to know the money figure?" Margaret asked.

Dana decided Will needed some support. "I'd like to know, also, Margaret. Was it insultingly low?"

Margaret named a figure that was far from low. Dana, in fact, thought it was flatteringly high, but she didn't say so, of course. "Ki is too good a businessman to name a price I'm honor bound to refuse," Margaret continued. "I confess, though, that I'm surprised he came across with this amount."

"It, uh . . ." Will started, stopped, began again. "It sounds very generous. Maybe we ought to . . . consider—"

Margaret cut off his suggestion with a swift, no-nonsense clarification. "Just so we understand each other, I will burn this place to the ground before I sell it to Hezekiah Brown. Do I make myself clear?"

Will nodded, his jaw slack with worry or annoyance . . . it was hard to tell which. "Yes, ma'am. I only thought . . ." He let the words trail away and turned to Dana, obviously looking for support. "Don't you think it's a good offer?"

Surprised, Dana glanced at her mother before answering. "Frankly, it sounds too good." She held up a hand to ward off another attack from Margaret. "Even though we're not interested in selling, I think it bears further investigation." Margaret stiffened, but took out her frustration on the ashtray, tapping the cigarette sharply against the rim. "There's always the possibility," Dana continued, "that Hezekiah Brown didn't make the offer."

"He made it," Margaret snapped. "I guarantee it."

"You don't think he made it, Dana?" Will's words cut across Margaret's and Dana chose to answer him. He looked so uncomfortable and, without the clipboard to occupy his hands, he'd begun plucking at the creases in his trousers. She couldn't figure out why he was so nervous. Margaret was certainly in a tear, but she wasn't mad at Will.

"I don't know," Dana said. "But it can't hurt to think about the possibility for a few days. Maybe something will come to light."

"I'll tell you what's going to happen." Margaret walked behind her desk and drummed her fingers on the paper-strewn top. "I'm going to move full-scale ahead with the Peppermint Kisses. I'll show Ki I won't take this lying down."

Dana felt her patience give way. "For someone who built this candy factory from scratch, you are not behaving very professionally, Margaret."

"I own this place. I can behave any way I please. Besides, there's nothing professional about this situation, Dana. This is strictly personal."

"I can help with the new project." Will leaned forward in his chair, clasping his fingers into a pudgy knot. "You want me to do that, Margaret? I could arrange for someone in the test kitchen to begin working on it right away.''

Dana bent over to slip her feet into her shoes and studied her distant relative from a new angle. Will's cheeks had gone from flustered white to eager pink. His eyes sparked with an energy Dana didn't think he could possibly possess. Did he think that developing the Peppermint Kiss recipe would save the confectionery and solve Margaret's problems? Or was it the idea that he could spend more time with Rachael in the test kitchen that brought about the change in his demeanor? Dana didn't really care. Margaret was intent upon wreaking havoc one way or another, whether or not Will caught onto that fact. All Dana could do was try to cast some logic on the situation or else keep her opinions to herself. Maybe she could alternate strategies.

Shoes on, Dana straightened and rose to her feet. "Are we through?" she asked. "It's past five and I still have work to do."

Margaret pursed her lips. "Yes," she said finally. "I just wanted the two of you to know what's going on. We'll meet again next week to talk about this again."

It was a flat dismissal, but Will lingered even as Dana walked to the door. "But you didn't answer me. What about the Recipe?"

"I'll tell you what to do, Will, as soon as I decide. Good night, now, and be sure to check that new shipment of boxes before you leave. The last one had a flaw in the design and had to be returned for correction." Margaret pulled back her chair and sat regally, once again becoming Queen of the Ausbrook Confectionery. "By the way, Dana, you need to settle your account with Millie before Friday. If you like, we can deduct the price of the fudge and caramels you gave away today from your next paycheck.''

Caught, Dana sighed as loudly as she could. "Do I get a discount?"

"Ten percent." With a last, lingering smile, Margaret turned her attention to the work on her desk.

"After you've worked here two years, you get twenty percent," Will said as he walked past Dana and out the door.

"What a benefit," Dana muttered and moved to follow Will. She stopped at the doorway. "Margaret? Will talked to me today about some orders. He said you wouldn't sign them."

Margaret didn't glance up. "He'd left off the supply codes. I don't know where his head is these days. He's generally meticulous about the orders. I just handed them back and told him he had a problem. Obviously he hasn't figured out what he did."

Dana shrugged. "I thought I should mention it to you."

"That's fine." Margaret showed no concern, and Dana wasn't even sure she was listening.

"Margaret?"

"Yes, dear?"

"I am not having fun."

"Don't worry about it." Margaret continued to concentrate on her work while she reached blindly for a cigarette. "I'll be sure to tell you when the real fun begins."

"Thanks." Dana frowned, started down the hall, came back. "You want to go somewhere for dinner?"

Margaret looked up and for the first time, her determined mouth softened with affection. "I suppose you'd expect me to treat?"

"Well, you did just threaten to dock my salary."

"How about a chili cheese dog at the Hot Dog Heaven?"

It sounded awful, but Dana decided it might be worth the sacrifice. "That'd be great. I'm starved. I didn't have time for lunch."

"In that case, why don't we knock off work—" Margaret glanced at her watch "—in an hour. Sound good?"

Not exactly what Dana had in mind, but close enough. "Sure. I'll be in my office with my mouth watering."

"Good deal."

Dana wandered down the hall to her cubicle, her stomach growling a protest all the way. She hoped Rick was enjoying the candy. It seemed pretty clear that she'd have to find some other means of bribing him from now on.

Picking up the lunchtime cola can she'd left on her desk, she took a sip of the now lukewarm and disgusting soda and wondered pensively how Rick would feel about chili cheese dogs at the Hot Dog Heaven.

Chapter Six

It was closer to seven-thirty that evening before Dana finally pried Margaret away from the confectionery. To Margaret's dismay and Dana's relief, the Hot Dog Heaven was closed for remodeling, so they ate at one of the many "country kitchens" on Branson's main boulevard. Margaret grumbled about the food, but Dana shed the complaints with determined cheerfulness and did her best to direct the conversation away from shoptalk. The subject of candy making cropped up, of course, as did the infamous Recipe. However, Dana felt that overall the time spent with her mother was pleasant. If it wasn't quite the camaraderie she wished to share with Margaret, at least it wasn't the tense, frustrating distracted moments of the past, either. Relationships progressed slowly, Dana reminded herself, and was grateful for what she could get.

By Sunday afternoon Margaret's mood had shifted several times and Dana was as edgy as a mouse caught between the cheese and the cat. She tried to phone Rick and arrange to meet him away from the house, but there was no answer, so she waited, wondering if she ought to warn Margaret of his impending arrival or take her chances on a quick getaway. She opted for the latter and stood at the front-room window, keeping a discreet watch.

"Are you going someplace?" Margaret stopped on her way past the doorway.

"Who? Me?" Dana could feel the guilt slide across her face. Why did she always feel like such a child in her mother's presence? "Oh, I'm just kind of thinking about it," she said as nonchalantly as she could. "Why? Do I look transient or something?"

Margaret stepped just inside the broad archway. "You look like Cinderella waiting for the pumpkin to turn into a golden carriage. Is that a new dress?"

Glancing down, Dana tried to look as if she couldn't recall what she was wearing. The dress was new, a splashy red and white, cut for sunny, summer days in the sun. It left bare a semimodest expanse of silky tan shoulders and made a wide flare just below the hips. She'd chosen it with care and wished now she'd had enough foresight to put on a robe over it. At least, until she got away from her mother's curious eyes. "Oh, this?" She plucked at the fabric and shrugged a blithe dismissal. "I just haven't had a chance to wear it before now. It's a bit too bare for the office."

Margaret's gaze ran over Dana once more...sort of like a calculator totaling the sum of several figures. "I like it. You look very nice. I'll bet that Stafford boy would love to see you now."

If she'd appeared guilty before, Dana knew it was nothing compared to the way she looked now. Still, she stalled. "Rick? Do you really think so?"

"I'm sure of it," Margaret said dryly. "Why not give him a call and invite him over?"

Dana caught a sudden splinter of annoyance before it pierced her mood. "Maybe I'll just do that. I could ask him to bring along someone to entertain you…Hezekiah Brown, for instance. Now, wouldn't that be cozy?''

"Good idea, Dana. I'm sure it would make for a most interesting afternoon. Let's do it.''

Dana sighed, wishing Margaret knew when to back off, and wishing she would outgrow this embarrassing compulsion to confess to her mother. "Rick's on his way to pick me up now.''

"I know. He phoned while you were in the shower.''

"Oh. You talked to him?''

"Don't worry. I was polite.''

Dana pretended to believe that. "Did he, uh, say where he was taking me?''

"For a drive.''

Relieved, Dana smiled more easily. The last thing she wanted to do was to try to explain just why she and Rick were going to visit Granny Varnell. "Yes,'' she said. "We're going for a drive.''

"I hope you know what you're doing. You know, Dana, you can take the boy out of the country, but you can't take—''

"Honestly, Margaret, you were born and raised here, too. And Rick spent more time away at college than you did. That makes you more of a…a hillbilly than he is.''

"That's hardly a glowing recommendation.'' Margaret's expression turned impervious. "You can do better than Rick Stafford, Dana.''

"Better?'' Dana's voice rose as the irritation found a niche inside her. "What does that mean? I don't categorize people the way you do, Margaret. Rick is my friend. Period.''

"People don't plan to elope with a friend, Dana.''

"For heaven's sake, that was years ago. I thought I loved Rick and wanted to marry him, but you told me I could do 'better,' so I married Darren Hesterly instead. He had background and family credits out the kazoo, but I found out a little late that I didn't love him. After living with him for a while, I didn't even like him very much. And I never cared for his family. You're the one who—'' Dana almost bit her tongue in trying to stop the rush of words. Why did she let herself get caught in these pointless confrontations? The past was past, the mistakes made. Power struggles at this stage were meaningless. ''I'm sorry, Margaret. That was unfair. It was my choice to marry Darren and I don't want you to think I blame you for the failure of my marriage. I take complete responsibility for my actions.'' Dana paused, took a deep breath. ''Then *and* now.''

For a moment, Margaret looked as if she were going to challenge the words, but something intangible and softly wistful touched the corners of her mouth, lingered briefly and was dismissed with a shrug. ''Good for you,'' she said. ''Keep that stubborn chin in the air.''

Dana had never heard that tone in Margaret's voice before. It was almost sad, but why would Margaret . . . ? A truck pulled up outside and Dana swung toward the window in time to see Rick get out and start toward the door. The brim of his hat dipped low on his forehead, shading his rough-cut features. He wore a short-sleeved shirt, cool yellow against the deep tan on his arms, and jeans of soft blue denim. His boots were textured brown, polished with the sheen of good leather. Dana recognized a familiar stir of awareness in her stomach. Rick was, she admitted, a very attractive man. Her heart pumped out an eager greeting, and relief, or maybe simple happiness, washed through her.

The doorbell rang and she realized, too late, she'd forgotten about Margaret. By the time Dana reached the entryway, Margaret was already opening the door and there was nothing to do but stand back and hope the confrontation would be bloodless.

"Well, Rick." Margaret swung wide the decorative front door. "How nice to see you. Come in."

Rick touched two fingers to the brim of his hat, then removed the Stetson from his head as he stepped inside. "Evening, Miz Margaret. How're you doing?"

"I'm doing well, Rick. How about you?"

"Fine." He shot Dana a quizzical glance. "No complaints."

Dana raised her brows to show that she hadn't the faintest idea what her mother was up to, but Margaret was all smiles and that alone was enough to make anybody nervous.

"That's good," Margaret said. "How's your mother? I haven't seen her in a month of Sundays. Did all your brothers and sisters finally get grown up?"

Rick hooked a thumb in his pocket. A subtle amusement edged into his eyes and tugged at the corners of his mouth. "Mother is healthy and happy," Rick said. "She still loves to quilt and has more orders than she can handle. I have one brother still living at home, but the rest of us drop by to visit every few days so there's always someone in and out."

Margaret nodded a pleasant acknowledgment. "I can't imagine how your mother managed to raise all seven of you kids by herself. I could never have done it."

That was certainly true. She hadn't even managed to raise one, Dana thought, and then she was ashamed of herself for her disloyalty. Margaret was cut from different cloth than Rick's mother. She had different accomplishments. Motherhood wasn't for every woman.

"My mother had a lot of help." Rick tapped the Stetson against his leg. "We had good neighbors."

"Yes." Margaret nodded. "How is Hezekiah? I understand he's staying with you."

"Yes, ma'am, he is. Just until he finds a place of his own."

Margaret ruffled up like a wet hen. "You mean he's going to *live* here?"

"This is his home." Rick's voice didn't alter, but Dana knew he was on the alert. With good cause.

"He can't do that." Margaret gave each word a rubber-band snap. "What about his business? He can't just walk away from it."

"He can't?" Rick asked in a surprised drawl. "I always thought Ki could do just about whatever he wanted."

Margaret's frown tightened. "Hasn't he told you what he intends to do?"

"No, ma'am."

"Oh, he's bound to have said something." Margaret pressed a knuckle to her chin as she considered the possibilities.

Dana stepped into the temporary lull to rescue Rick from certain disaster. "Shouldn't we be on our way, Rick? I'd like to have time to browse through some of the craft shops along our way." For her trouble, Dana received nearly identical stares from both Rick and her mother.

"Browse?"

"Browse?" Rick's voice echoed Margaret's in disbelief. "You want to *browse* through some *craft* shops?"

Dana kept her expression innocent. "Yes, I do. Is there something wrong with that?"

"No, no." Rick said, recovering first. "But you're right. We ought to leave. If you're ready."

"I'm ready." Dana jumped right in with an eager nod. "We have to go, Margaret." She moved toward Rick. "I'll see you later, all right?"

With a shake of her head, Margaret waved them out the door. "You're about as subtle as hot pepper sauce, Dana. Go on. Go on."

"Goodbye," Rick said.

Dana mumbled a goodbye and hurried out to the pickup. Once inside, she waved to her mother and breathed a sigh of relief when Rick started the truck and drove away from the house. At the end of the driveway, he stopped and offered a quizzical smile. "Were you in a hurry to leave?"

"I guess I was pretty obvious, wasn't I?"

"It was the mention of browsing at the crafts shops, I think, that gave you away." Rick dropped the Stetson on the seat between them and finger-combed his thick, wheat-colored hair.

Watching him, she felt suddenly calm and sure of herself. "I might have picked up a taste for crafts during the past few years."

His eyebrows arched in skeptical amusement. "And I might have been enjoying the chat with your mother, too. Don't pretend you weren't dying to get away from there, Dana. Remember, I was the one who listened to all the complaining you used to do about Margaret and how she tried to run your life and how you were going to make your own decisions and how she made you crazy and what you were going to do to reciprocate."

It was true. She'd whined to him at every opportunity about how Margaret mistreated her. She'd even wondered if part of her attraction to Rick hadn't stemmed from her need to have someone to listen to her. But that was then, it had nothing to do with now. "I was only trying to protect you, Rick. Margaret was getting ready to tear into you because she can't get her hands on your friend, Hezekiah."

Rick grinned. "You came to my rescue. Now, I appreciate that, Dana. I really do."

"Smart aleck. Next time you can fend for yourself."

"I can do that, you know. I've been fighting my own battles for as long as I can remember. Your mother doesn't scare me."

"Yes, well, I'm not scared of her, either. I just know when Hezekiah Brown's name comes up in the conversation, it's time to take cover. I've been shell-shocked several times during the past few days."

"Does he get mentioned that often?"

Dana opened her mouth to tell Rick about the anonymous offer to buy the confectionery, but changed her mind. Much as she'd like to know his opinion, she couldn't do so without breaching her unspoken oath of loyalty to Margaret and the company. "His name comes up often enough to keep me off balance," she said instead. "I've never seen Margaret act like this. She's completely unreasonable about the man. She's still threatening to sue, but I'm dragging my feet about drawing up any papers. I can't believe she's serious."

"Ki's not a whole lot better," Rick admitted. "Except that he doesn't talk much about suing Margaret over the Recipe. He just says that if Margaret means to try to produce the chocolate peppermints, she'd better be prepared for war." Rick let his glance stray from the road and focus on Dana. A mistake, he realized almost immediately. She was too distracting, sitting there, so close to him, yet so far away. The sundress she wore revealed shoulders he knew would be smooth and satiny to his touch. Her hair curved across her skin in strands of copper so soft and silky he ached to feel it slide through his fingers. He wanted to kiss her. The need made a lump in his throat, stirred a smoldering fire deep inside him. And Rick forced his eyes back to the highway.

Dana shifted slightly on the seat. "You don't really think this could end up in court, do you?"

"At this stage of the game, it's anyone's guess. No one has to have a good reason to file suit."

Her lips pursed in a considering line and Rick resisted the impulse to reach over and take her hand. After a minute or two, Dana offered him a rueful smile. "I hope Granny Varnell can shed some light on the Recipe and why it makes two normally sane, sensible people act like children."

Rick didn't think the Recipe was the real issue, but he decided to let Dana reach that conclusion on her own. At the moment, he was more interested in her reaction to Granny Varnell. Unless he missed his guess, the upcoming visit was going to provide a wealth of useful information. Not all of it about Margaret, Hezekiah and their Recipe, either. No, Rick wanted to see what Granny thought of Dana and, more to the point, what Dana thought of Granny.

THE VARNELL CABIN was just that, a cabin, built more years ago than anyone could or would admit to remembering. Over time, the house had been occupied by six generations of Varnells, but now only Granny was left. She was old and ageless, a woman worn by time, but blessed with the joy of living. As Rick drove up to the cabin, she came around the side, a sunbonnet on her head, a basket on her arm.

Dana thought it looked like a scene right out of the eighteen hundreds—a cabin, sitting on a cleared patch of ground with trees growing to the sky on all sides. A rocking chair graced the square porch and a wedding-ring pattern quilt hung across the rail. A wild rose bush climbed the side of a stone well and amazingly, offered several full blooms to the hot August sunshine. The whole effect was quaint and charming. Dana half expected the cabin to have dirt floors and hand-hewn logs for furniture.

What she didn't expect was the surge of sudden, unreserved liking she felt when Granny Varnell smiled and gripped her hand after Rick made the introductions. "Dana Ausbrook," Granny said with clarity. "Now, haven't you turned out to be a pretty little thing. 'Course, you always were a fetching child. Got your mama's look about you."

"Thank you." Dana didn't know what else to say.

Granny chuckled as she pulled the basket close to her body and ambled up the wide steps. "Come. Sit a spell. I don't get much company these days."

"Why, Granny Varnell, there's a constant stream of callers coming and going at your house." Rick followed the elderly woman up the stairs, unobtrusively offering his arm for her support. "Where would the local folks be without your potions and advice?"

"Potions?" Dana asked, her interest well caught. "Are you a—" Witch and pharmacist were the only words that came to mind, so Dana switched her question. "Do you make medicines?"

"I know a bit about herbs and such." Granny settled into the rocker, set aside the weathered basket and removed her sunbonnet. Picking up a cardboard fan, she began to fan herself. "How's your family, Rick? I heard that Sallie Jo's agonna get married next spring. Is it that boy from Springfield?''

As Rick chatted with Granny, Dana glanced around for a place to sit. There weren't many choices. Granny had the rocker, Rick perched half on, half off the porch rail, so Dana chose the top step and positioned herself as best she could in the shade. Squinting against the sun, she studied the area surrounding the cabin. The lawn with its patchwork design of scrawny grass and bare ground would never win any horticulture prizes, but at the edge of the house, Dana could see signs of a well-tended garden spot. Granny Varnell had to be eighty years old or more, Dana thought. Surely she couldn't take care of a vegetable garden by herself.

"Your gardener must be a magician, Granny Varnell." Dana leaned back against the wood post and gave her eyes a moment to adjust to the shaded porch. "How did he get those plants to grow in August?''

"Gardener?" Granny laughed, a deep, rolling sound of pleasure. "I'm the only gardener around this place. I used to raise everything I ate, but anymore, I just plant a few tomatoes and a row or two of potatoes.''

"And onions and corn and squash and okra," Rick said with affection. "Don't let her fool you, Dana. There's more in that garden than a few measly plants.''

"I'm afraid I don't know much about gardening.'' Dana absently rearranged the material of her dress as she shifted on the wooden step. "I'm not even very good with house plants.''

"Dana's a city girl." Rick crossed his arms at his chest and offered a no-offense smile.

"I know." Granny slowed the rocker to a soft creak. "You lived with your papa back east in...now where was it?''

"Philadelphia," Dana supplied. "Pennsylvania."

"Yes. I remember your papa. A gentleman. I don't think he knew what to make of this mountain country."

"No." Dana began to trace a knothole in the porch floor. "In fact, I don't know how he and Margaret got together in the first place."

"Pairin' up is a mystery. Seems sometimes the ones that oughta don't and the ones that ought not to, do." The floorboards squeaked in meditative harmony beneath the gentle sway of the rocker.

"Hezekiah Brown and Margaret Burton, for instance?" Rick glanced at Dana.

She felt his hesitation in mentioning the names, but despite a twinge of discomfort, she wanted to know what Granny Varnell knew about the "crazy-sick-in-love" Margaret. "Yes," Dana said, lending her own question in support of Rick's. "Did you think they were an odd pair?"

"Can't say, exactly. I remember how stubborn they both were." Granny stopped fanning for a minute. "Stubborn as two mules stuck rump to rump in a one-horse stall. Neither one'll make a move less'n the other one moves first."

Rick laughed aloud and Dana had to smile. Margaret, she knew, would not like the analogy, but it seemed appropriate to Dana. "They're still that way, Granny," she said. "Only now they're fighting over the Recipe you gave them as a wedding present."

A slow grin crinkled Granny's cheeks. "Is that so? A recipe, you say?"

"From what Dana and I have been able to find out," Rick explained, "you gave them a recipe as a gift. But they had a fight on the night before the wedding. Margaret tore the Recipe in half and the two of them have been fussing about it ever since.''

''Well, land's sake. Is that a fact?'' The fan in Granny's hand began to flutter back and forth, back and forth, her expression wreathed in a smile. ''Now I'm mighty happy to hear that. I never thought anythin' I ever gave for a gift would still be treasured forty years later. A recipe. Now that's somethin'.''

Dana leaned forward eagerly. ''Do you remember the Recipe, Granny Varnell? We . . . Rick and I . . . were hoping you would. We thought it might settle the feud if you could give us a copy of it.''

At that, Granny stopped rocking altogether and turned a bright gaze on Dana. ''Why, honey, I've never used a written recipe in my life. If I gave one to your mama and her fiancé, I probably just wrote down what I remembered. What was the recipe for, anyway?''

''Chocolate peppermint candy,'' Dana said. ''Margaret calls it a Peppermint Kiss and Charity says it's as close to tasting heaven as some folks will ever get.''

Granny's amusement rumbled in gravelly notes from her throat. ''Is that what Charity says? Well, I was once a pretty fair cook. Leastwise, I never got any complaints. But heaven? I won't say I ever made anything so tasty as that.''

Rick flicked his Stetson across his pant leg. ''Well, you made up something that's caused quite a feud between Margaret and Hezekiah. They both want to make the peppermint candy and sell it around the world. You could be famous, Granny.''

''Famous? Now why would I want to be famous?''

''Well, for one thing, everybody would know your name,'' Rick said with a grin. ''It would be on billboards across the country.''

"Thank you very kindly, Rick, but I don't care to have my name on some board. Besides, everybody I know knows who I am. So I must be famous already."

Dana ran a hand beneath the weight of her hair. The afternoon heat was beginning to get to her. "There's money involved, too, Granny. If the candy should be manufactured and sold, you could be entitled to some of the profits."

Granny set the rocker in motion with a push of one frail-looking foot. "I got no need for profits, Dana. I've got a home and a garden and a harvest of friends and neighbors. Besides, I gave that recipe for a gift. I wouldn't take it back, even if I could."

It was a moot point anyway, but Dana didn't say so. "Can you remember anything at all about the candy? The ingredients? How it was made?"

"My memory isn't so good as it used to be." Granny tucked a strand of gray-white hair into the bun at the back of her head and looked mostly unconcerned. "But I'll study on it a spell, if you think it's that important."

"It might be," Rick said. "At this point, we're still hoping the mules can be led out of the barn without kicking each other in the head."

Granny Varnell laughed and got to her feet. "Want to see my garden?" she said to Dana. "I'll give you some sage to take home with you. And a jar of my pickles. You'll like 'em, won't she, Rick?"

Rick hovered close to Granny as she started down the steps with one hand extended in invitation to Dana. "Her pickles are out of this world, Dana. As close to heaven as—"

Dana laughed and accepted Granny's hand. "I get the picture," she said. "Is there anything you can't do, Granny?"

"Well, I'm not much good with the menfolk. Haven't had a beau in fifteen years."

"That's hard to believe." Dana matched her step to the older woman's as they left the porch stairs and walked toward the garden spot at the side of the house. "You're an attractive woman, Granny Varnell."

"That's because I eat my greens. Lots of spinach and poke salad and turnip greens make a gal healthy and sassy." Granny winked and wrapped her hand around Rick's forearm. "Look there." She pointed to a row of squatty, dark green plants. "In a little more'n a month, those turnip greens'll be mighty fine eatin'. You ever tasted turnip greens?"

Dana shook her head, feeling as if she ought to apologize for the omission. "Not voluntarily. Charity might have slipped some in on occasion. She used to cook up some awful things when I'd be visiting Margaret. During one visit, I subsisted on peanut butter and crackers. Charity isn't exactly a great cook."

"She's a good woman," Granny said. "And when she reads the tea leaves, it's a good idea to pay attention. She knows what she's talking about."

"She predicted trouble for Margaret over the Recipe," Dana said.

"That prediction turned out to be true enough." Rick hooked his thumbs in his jeans' hip pockets and rocked on his heels. "Who would have thought there'd be such a stir about a recipe?"

"Hmm. I wonder what I put in that recipe." Granny took her hand from Rick's arm to shade her eyes against the sun. "Forgot my bonnet, didn't I? You children want something to drink? I got some lemonade in the house."

"A drink of water would be nice." Dana licked dry lips at the thought. She hadn't realized how thirsty she was.

"If it's water you want, come on over here." Granny turned and led the way to the stone well. Reaching over the rim, she grabbed the rope and yanked until a metal tube made a splashing exit out of the well. Rick held the cylinder as water spilled into the shallow pail sitting on the well's lip. When Granny offered the dipper, Dana took a long, deep drink of cold springwater and thought she'd never tasted anything so refreshing. Oh, she'd had well water before, years ago, but it hadn't tasted this good. Dana drank her fill, then offered the dipper to Rick, who followed suit.

Granny watched them, hands on her skinny hips, a smile full on her lips. "Good, ain't it? I got water piped in the house, but I always come out to the well for my drinkin' water. Water from a faucet just don't taste the same. Come on in the house. There's something I want to show you."

The cabin had enough modern conveniences to ease Dana's mind about the older woman's comfort, but there was nothing superfluous within its walls. Rag rugs covered the floor and, when Dana commented on their bright, homey look, Granny explained how they were made. She insisted that Dana choose one to take home and wouldn't take no for an answer. "I've been braidin' rugs all winter and have more'n I'll ever use. You take it, now, and enjoy it."

Rick observed the exchange from a couple of steps behind the women, his attention focused on Dana, trying to read her thoughts by the expressions dancing across her face. He thought for a moment that she meant to refuse the rug and was glad when she accepted the gift with a gracious smile. This wasn't her idea of charming, he knew from past experience. Dana preferred luxury to the quaint hospitality of this old cabin and she undoubtedly found Granny's simple tastes too lower-class and down to earth.

For a fleeting moment, Rick wished Dana could see the beauty he saw in Granny Varnell and her way of life. But Dana, for all her smiles and apparent interest, would never understand the philosophy of the mountain people. He knew that, knew that she'd leave at the end of the year, if not sooner. So why did his heart yearn for her? And why was he spending time and energy on a relationship that would only bring him unhappiness in the end? Therapy, he told himself, and then wondered if the cure wasn't worse than the ailment.

"Did you say something, Rick?" Granny paused at the entrance to the root cellar, bracing her foot on the rusted tin door.

"Let me get that for you." He moved forward and pulled open the door, then stood back to allow the women to precede him down the steps and into the damp room below.

Dana brushed by him and her hand sneaked its way into his for a brief squeeze of fingers that caused a warm spiral of pleasure which Rick couldn't have controlled if he'd tried. "I'm glad you came with me," she whispered and then disappeared into the darkness of the cellar where Granny was already showing off the quart jars of vegetables and fruits she'd canned for the coming winter. Rick waited at the entrance, his spirits unaccountably lighter, his hand tingling with the memory of Dana's touch.

From the cellar, Granny took them back to the porch and entertained them with the stories of her childhood and some long, tall tales of the area. Dana laughed until she cried when Granny recounted the miseries of Ezra Midnight and his moonshine still. Rick laughed because

Dana laughed and Granny...well, Rick assumed Granny just liked to hear the sound of her own amusement.

It was dusk when Rick suggested it was time to leave. Dana gathered the jar of pickles, the fresh herbs and the braided rug in her arms and thanked Granny one last time for the gifts, especially the handmade rug. Granny patted Dana's hand and said it wasn't much. Just something for chilly nights, when the floorboards got stiff with a winter cold. Dana answered with a soft smile and bent forward to place a kiss on the old woman's wrinkled cheek. "May I come to visit you again?" she asked.

"Anytime. Anytime at all."

The goodbyes lingered on for the next five minutes, but finally Dana and Rick got into the truck and drove away, leaving Granny Varnell waving and calling after them. "Come again. Come again."

As he drove, Rick glanced at Dana from time to time, wishing he could read her thoughts one minute, and glad he couldn't the next. Silence cushioned the interior of the truck for several miles until he felt he had to say something to break the intimacy before it broke him. "I don't believe Granny knows much more about the Recipe than we do. I thought she'd at least remember giving it to Margaret and Ki as a wedding gift."

Dana's hand moved lightly over the braided rag rug. "I guess memory is kind of tricky at her age."

"She has a wonderful memory for stories, though, doesn't she?"

Dana nodded, but continued staring pensively out the window, and Rick tried for her attention once more. "I'm beginning to think we may get into a genuine lawsuit over this recipe."

"Mmm-hmm." Her tone revealed no concern, no real sign she'd even heard his question. Rick focused on the road and allowed Dana to dwell on her own thoughts for a while.

About halfway home, she released a long sigh. "It's so quiet here," she said softly, as if her voice might break the stillness in half. "I don't think I ever noticed that before."

"Quiet?" Rick glanced at her and smiled at the dreamy look in her eyes. "It seems noisy to me compared to what I remember from when I was a child, especially the summers when tourists are everywhere and the line of traffic into town goes on for miles. Branson used to be just pleasantly crowded in the summers, but every year the crowds got bigger and the season lasted a bit longer. And now, since the city annexed that long section of the highway containing all the hotels and tourist attractions, there's even more traffic in the downtown area than there used to be. No, quiet isn't the way I'd describe Branson anymore."

"Maybe it's a mood more than an absence of sound. The whole Ozarks area has capitalized on tradition and a way of life that no longer exists. Except it does exist here—beneath the surface—in people like Granny Varnell." Dana paused and stared out the window for several long minutes. "She's the first person I've met who seems completely at peace with herself and her world. That must be a fine feeling to know."

Surprised, Rick slowed the truck and allowed his attention to stray from the road. Dana appeared lost in thought, her face softly shadowed by the night, her hair softly gleaming in the moonlight. Peace wasn't something he'd ever thought much about and yet, he knew it as an integral part of himself, as a part of his life and of his heritage. "Are you at war with your world, Dana?" he asked gently.

She didn't answer for quite some time and Rick began to think she wouldn't, or couldn't. But then she gave a little shrug and a tiny smile tracked the outline of her mouth. "At home, at Dad's house, it was always very still. I sometimes imagined the whole city of Philadelphia would shatter into fragments if I raised my voice a single decibel. I didn't realize then that the city was noisy and it was only our house that stayed so still. It wasn't quiet, like here. It was an intimidating stillness, with ticking clocks and footsteps in the hall or out in the street. And people spoke in hushed tones with the proper diction and dignity. Then, when I'd come to visit Margaret, there was noise and movement everywhere. Raised voices, excitement, energy from all directions, something happening all the time."

For a moment the silence returned, then Dana's expression softened with wistful memory. "I used to tell myself I had the best of both worlds. A quiet, studious father and an energetic, career-minded mother. One home for quiet times, one home for noisy fun. But I was never quiet enough for one place and never noisy enough for the other. I never really fit. Not like Granny Varnell fits her cabin and her garden patch. Not like you fit your rustic office, your small-town lawyer image."

Her unexpected admission caught Rick off guard. He didn't know what he should say. "I'm sure you'll fit into the Philadelphia law firm like a hand in a made-to-order glove," he offered.

Her smile took on a sad tilt. "I'm afraid peace isn't a place, Rick, but a state of mind. I just don't know where to find it."

Again he was at a loss. He'd had no idea Dana felt that way about her childhood. He'd seen only her rebellious side, the temperamental princess upset because her mother, the queen, wouldn't grant complete independence. He hadn't realized Dana might be insecure and vulnerable about her place in life. And he hadn't realized how lucky he was to have known the security of a loving, caring, boisterous family. They hadn't had much, but it had been enough. And Dana, who'd had so much, felt she didn't belong.

On impulse, Rick offered the only comfort he could think of. "My family's getting together next Saturday to celebrate Mother's birthday. Would you like to come?"

"Yes." She sounded almost eager. "If you're sure you want me to be there. I mean, your family won't think—won't mind, will they?"

"They have no hard feelings for you, if that's what you're afraid of. I'm sure they think you have incredibly poor judgment not to have married me when you had the chance, but if I'm not mad, how can they carry a grudge?"

Dana tossed him a meaningful frown. "Gee, Rick, you make it sound so positive. Should I apologize to your family the moment we arrive or wait until after the birthday cake is served?"

"Your choice." His throat filled with laughter. "Maybe you could just wear a sign around your neck. Something suitably remorseful."

"How about, 'Forgive me for not taking this conceited lug off your hands. I know it was a disappointment, but can I still have some cake and ice cream?'"

"Never mind the sign. Sackcloth and ashes ought to give them the idea."

"Do you have this sort of fantasy often?" Dana asked. "It could be dangerous, you know."

Oh, he knew, all right. But he saw no reason for her to know it, too. "We're almost at your mother's house. Shall I go in and chat with her a while?"

"Not unless you're willing to wear a sign around your neck. One that says something about how you've been a perfect gentleman this afternoon and haven't laid a hand on her precious daughter. You probably ought to mention, too, that you know nothing about Hezekiah or his plans for the Recipe." Dana reached across and patted his shoulder. "She won't believe a word of it, of course, but if you're fool enough to want to chat with her, you deserve whatever she dishes out."

"It's good to know I have your support." Rick drove up to the house and stopped the truck on the wide circle drive.

Dana turned toward him. "You are going to lay at least one hand on me, aren't you? Maybe a pair of lip—"

He cut off her teasing with a serious kiss. No preparation. No room for hesitation. He just reached over, pulled her into his arms, and claimed her lips for his own. In the back of his mind, he recognized an element of anger, a fragment of resentment that she'd chosen not to marry him and that now she could speak so lightly of the decision. He wanted to punish her for that and yet, he also wanted to console her for the tender loving care she'd missed as a child. But at the first murmur of her response, the anger and resentment vanished, the sympathy disappeared, metamorphosing into simple, undeniable desire.

Damn, why did she have to taste so good, feel so right in his arms, fit so perfectly against his pounding heart? He'd wanted this all day, had thought of how he would kiss her, of how she would respond. But now that she was here, giving back kiss for kiss, making him ache with need for her, he realized it was he who had the most to lose, he who had to maintain control.

Reluctantly Rick pulled away, schooled his expression in outward calm and ran a caressing fingertip across her cheek. "Now this is dangerous." His voice searched for and found a teasing note. "What if your mother sees you?"

"What if she does?"

Rick refused to be drawn back to her lips. "I've got to get home, Dana."

Once she would have read rejection into the words and it would have sent her angrily grasping for the door handle and a way out of the truck. This time she gave a soft, exasperated sigh. "Thanks, Rick. I haven't had such a pleasant afternoon in ages. I'll see you next Saturday, right?"

He almost forgot his resolve. One kiss, he'd promised himself. No more. No chance of losing the war that way. "Saturday," he confirmed. "Count on it."

"I will." She slid from the seat and shut the door. Lifting her hand in a wave, she watched Rick drive off. Then, clutching Granny's gifts to her breast and Rick's kiss to her heart, she opened the front door and walked inside.

Chapter Seven

Dana closed the glass-paned front door behind her, placed her things on the hall table, and looked up in time to see her mother storm past.

"It's gone!" Margaret threw up her hands and walked into the study without giving Dana so much as a glance. Her angry voice carried clearly back to the hall. "I'm not going to stand for this."

Charity ambled into view and her blue eyes narrowed on Dana. "Well, I'm glad you got back."

"Why are you here? You don't usually work on Sundays."

"There's an emergency." Charity pointed a finger at the study and the raucous sounds emanating from the room. "She's lost it."

"Yes, I can see that." Dana fought a grin. It would never do to show a lack of concern. "On a scale of one to ten, what kind of crisis is this?"

"About a hundred and two."

"Charity!" Margaret yelled from the study.

Charity folded her hands at the waist of her dungaree pants and shook her head. "If she keeps this up, we're gonna have to shoot her with a tranquilizer gun."

"Charity!" The call came again, muffled but demanding. "Did you check the kitchen?"

"Yes, I did!" Charity yelled back. "It's not there, either."

Dana lifted her eyebrows in a question and Charity rolled her eyes in answer. "It's the Recipe," Charity said. "She's lost it."

"The Peppermint Kiss recipe?"

"Yes, Dana." Margaret came to stand in the study doorway, a furious frown on her lips. "The Peppermint Kiss recipe has been stolen."

"But you didn't have the whole recipe, Margaret."

"I had *half* of it, Dana, until today. And now my half of the Recipe has been stolen."

Leave it to Margaret to go for the dramatics, Dana thought and reluctantly followed Charity into the lion's den. Some thirty minutes later, the three of them agreed the torn piece of paper on which the Recipe was supposedly written was not where it had been. Dana's initial amusement had faded into a vexed ill humor. Margaret was and remained incensed, as if someone had come in the black of night and carted off the entire confectionery to never-never land. And it didn't take long to substitute the name of Hezekiah Brown for that unknown someone.

"This is absolutely the last straw." Margaret slammed a book on top of her desk, sending paperwork scooting off and across the floor. "I'm not taking any more of this nonsense from him. He can't just walk into my house and take my recipe. And don't tell me I can't sue him for this, Dana. My civil rights have been violated and I'm going to have him arrested."

"Margaret, be reasonable," Dana pleaded. "The Recipe is probably just misplaced. When's the last time you remember seeing it?"

"Yesterday," Margaret snapped. "Or the day before. I don't recall, but I know what you're thinking, Dana, and I did not misplace that recipe. Ki stole it. We can discuss it for days, but he did it."

"All right, all right. Suppose he did." Dana paced to the window seat, clenched her hands and slowly relaxed them in an effort to remain calm. "How did he get in the house?"

"How the hell should I know? But somehow he got his hands on my recipe."

"Half of a recipe," Dana corrected.

Margaret stared her down. "Don't quibble, Dana. This is too important."

Charity shoved a book back onto the top shelf, pulled down another and leafed roughly through the pages. "Ki's never even been in this house, Margaret. He couldn't have gotten in by himself without tripping the alarm and I certainly never let him in."

Margaret swung a thoughtful gaze to Dana, who raised her hands in immediate denial. "I didn't let him in, either," Dana said.

"Someone else must have taken it for him." Margaret reached for her cigarettes, but paused when the pack was in her hand. "Rick. Rick Stafford was here this very afternoon."

Dana twisted on her heel, not sure if she was more frustrated than angry or more angry than frustrated. "Margaret! Would you please stop this ridiculous witch-hunt? Rick did not take your precious *half* of a recipe. Today was the first time he's stepped foot inside this house in years and you were with him every second. Don't start accusing him of stealing."

"There's no need to leap to his defense, Dana." Margaret's brows arched upward. "I didn't accuse him. I merely stated that he was here this afternoon. And we all know his relationship with Ki."

"They might as well be father and son." Charity clarified the matter as she climbed down from the stool on which she'd been standing. "I think Rick'd probably do anything in the world for Hezekiah."

Dana turned her frustration on the housekeeper. "Rick would not steal for anyone."

Charity blithely dusted her hands on her hips. "No, he wouldn't. He's a fine young man and if you ask me—"

The phone on Margaret's desk shrilled an interruption for which Dana was grateful.

"That'll be Ki calling to find out if I've missed the Recipe, yet." Margaret grabbed the telephone receiver as if it were a snake from which she planned to extract every ounce of venom. "Yes?" she said into the mouthpiece. "It's for you, Charity," she said a moment later and handed over the phone, disappointment obvious in her every movement.

Dana continued to search for the Recipe, fighting her frustration and wishing Margaret wasn't so quick to jump to conclusions.

Charity talked for a few moments on the phone before hanging up. "Rachael thought she might have left her sunglasses when she was here the other day," she explained and then glanced around the room. "Where were we? Oh, yeah, we were discussing Dana and Rick and—"

"We were discussing the missing recipe." Margaret blew a long stream of smoke at the ceiling. "And how Ki managed to steal it."

"Why don't you ask him, Margaret?" Dana's voice echoed with irritation. "Just pick up the damned phone and ask him."

Margaret's brown eyes met Dana's challenge. "All right." Margaret stubbed out her cigarette butt with a grinding motion. "All right, I will ask him. But not on the phone. I'm going over there and put the question straight to his ugly face."

"Good for you," Dana said, agitated enough to give her blessing to any action that got Margaret away from her. "Maybe Charity will drop you off on her way home."

"Uh-uh," Charity stated definitely. "I'm not gettin' involved in anything so ill-advised. And I don't have to look at the tea leaves to know this is the stupidest idea you've ever had, Margaret Ausbrook."

"I can drive." Margaret began gathering her car keys and pocketbook. "I'm not scared of Hezekiah Brown. What can he possibly do to me?"

It was what Margaret was going to do to herself that worried Dana, but she was too mad to show concern. "That's the right attitude, Margaret. If he slugs you, you can sue him. It's what you want to do anyway."

Margaret nodded agreeably. "There will be no slugging, Dana. The duel will be verbal and lethal. As my attorney, you probably ought to come with me."

"As your attorney, I advise you to stay the hell away from him."

"That does not sound very professional, Dana."

"So sorry, Margaret. When I come to bail you out of jail, I'll behave more professionally."

Margaret headed for the door. "I'm going to kill him with words. It won't be painless for him, but I won't get put in jail for it, either."

Dana looked at Charity, who was shaking her head from side to side. "You'd better go with her, Dana," Charity said. "Nothin' good's gonna come from this. And somebody with some sense ought to be there."

It was positively the last thing Dana wanted to do. "If she won't listen to me now, why should I go along as a witness to the crime?"

Charity shrugged. "She's your mother and at the moment, she's as crazy as a tomcat in the full of the moon. Somebody's gotta be responsible."

"Oh, come on, Dana," Margaret called from the entryway. "Who'll protect Rick if you're not around?"

Rick. Hezekiah was staying with Rick. If Margaret barged in there and started throwing around accusations... With a shudder of complete and utter exasperation, Dana turned to follow her mother. "Why didn't you shoot her with the tranquilizer dart when we had her cornered in here?" she said to Charity on her way out of the study.

"Just keep her away from the caramel creams," Charity answered. "They're too expensive to be used for ammunition."

No one seemed to consider the emotional expense, Dana thought as she walked outside and firmly pulled the door to behind her. Margaret was already in the car and had the engine running. Dana closed her eyes for a moment as she gathered together her inner resources. It was not easy being Margaret's daughter.

"Dana, hurry up!"

That did it. Dana marched to the car and jerked open the door. "I'm not going anywhere with you unless you put on a seat belt."

Margaret looked stunned, but Dana felt better for having taken a stand on something.

"Get in the car, Dana. I don't know what gets into you sometimes—"

Dana closed the car door and started back for the house. As she reached the door, Margaret called her. "All right. All right. I'll wear the seat belt. Now will you get in the car?"

Dana's lips curved in a smug smile which she didn't even try to conceal as she got into the car and watched Margaret's exaggerated snap of the seat belt.

"Now can we go?" Margaret flipped the shoulder strap irritably before reaching for a cigarette. With the car's lighter in hand, she shot Dana a warning glance. "Just don't say a word about my smoking, okay?"

"Jogging would be better for you."

"I tried that. The smoke just blew back in my face."

Dana tried to hold on to her ill humor. She really did. But somehow a smile worked its way through. "Are you sure I wasn't adopted?"

"I'm positive. I have the stretch marks to prove it." Margaret backed the car out of the drive and replaced the cigarette lighter at the same time. "Besides, you're so much like me sometimes it's scary."

"Dad used to tell me the same thing."

"What? That you were like him?"

"No, it scared him that I was so much like you. We had many long talks about 'appropriate' behavior and the foibles of being too determined. But I always felt that underneath it all, he secretly admired my rebellious streak."

"He's very proud of you, Dana. So am I." Margaret began to fiddle with the shoulder restraint again. "I just wish you hadn't inherited Leonard's sense of responsibility. I hate wearing seat belts."

"Live with it, Margaret. It'll do you good to do something sensible for a change."

"I beg your pardon. I'm a very sensible person."

"Except about your health and those occasions when Hezekiah Brown's name is mentioned."

"Leave my health out of this. There's a long history to my feud with Ki, which I'm not about to tell you. I just can't let him get away with stealing the Recipe."

"How can you be so sure that he did?" Dana swept restless fingers through her hair and prayed that Rick had gone straight home after leaving her. She didn't think she could handle this alone. "Maybe it really is misplaced."

Margaret cracked her window to release the smoke from her cigarette. "For the last time, Dana, the Recipe is not simply misplaced. I've kept it between the covers of that book for years. I certainly didn't move it."

"But to accuse Ki of stealing it—"

"Who else would do it, Dana? Tell me that. Ki has the other half of the Recipe. What good would it do anyone else?"

"Well, if it's not any good without the other half, why did you keep it all these years?"

Margaret's Cadillac was fairly new, but it had developed a few rattles over the miles. In the next few minutes, Dana heard every one of them. She decided it was one of the few times her mother had ever been reduced to silence. But if she'd hoped Margaret might be composing an answer to her question, Dana was disappointed. Margaret didn't say another word until they reached a turnoff on the main highway. "Rick bought this place from Ki, you know. I have to admit he's done wonders with it.''

Dana glanced at her mother in surprise. "I didn't think you and Rick were on visiting terms."

"I've driven past a few times."

"Why?"

Margaret frowned. "Just because, Dana."

She wanted to pursue the subject, reach further into Margaret's motivations, but at that moment, a long, low house of cedar and stone came into view and Dana realized she was seeing Rick's home for the first time. He lived here. He had painted the woodwork, planted flowers and planned his future here. And she could have been a part of it.

"Here we are." Margaret stopped the car and shut off the engine. Anticipation gleamed in her eyes, and for the first time Dana realized that Margaret relished the idea of confronting Hezekiah. There was more to this than a missing recipe, Dana thought. But Margaret got out of the car and marched purposefully to the front door and Dana followed, her own reluctance fading at the thought of seeing Rick.

"Margaret. Dana." Rick said after opening the door to their knock. His gaze went past Margaret directly to Dana and quizzed her in silence, but to his credit, he didn't look shocked. "What a pleasant surprise. Ki and I weren't expecting company, but you're—"

"Where is he?" Margaret asked and, without further amenity, brushed past Rick to enter the house.

"Hello, Rick." Dana stepped forward. "Congratulations. The war has just entered your camp."

Rick glanced after Margaret. "I didn't hear anyone sound the attack."

"Oh, she did that at home." Dana moved into the foyer and waited for Rick to close the door, shutting them momentarily into a private moment. "This has been one very exciting afternoon."

"Yes, it has," he said softly, his eyes finding hers in the gentle shadows of the entryway. "But I didn't think your mother had anything to do with it."

Warmth flooded her body for no apparent reason. Except that Rick stood within inches of her, the memory of being in his arms hovered ever present between them. For the first time, Dana decided coming here hadn't been such a bad idea. "She's lost the Recipe, Rick. And she's convinced that—"

"I took it."

Dana reached for his hand. "No, no. You distracted her so that Ki could get in and steal it from her study."

Rick's eyes sparked with a wry humor. "I did that?"

"Mmm-hmm. All within the five or ten minutes you stood in our hallway chatting with her."

For a full minute there had been a growing commotion in the back of the house and just then a raised voice ripped down the hall. *"The hell I did!"*

"We'd better get in there." Rick pulled Dana behind him as he walked quickly toward the noise. He stopped inside a kitchen of stark black and white and shiny copper; an impressive kitchen whose centerpiece at the moment consisted of one short redhead standing with her hands on her hips and talking as fast as she could talk to one short, balding man with a red face.

"Why would I do something like that?" Ki stood on one side of a wrought-iron-and-glass breakfast table, his fists pressing down on the glass, his blue eyes fixed on Margaret. "I have no business at your house, Maggie."

"My point exactly." Margaret's composure was better than it had been in the study at home, but not much. She certainly didn't seem to be making any better sense. "You have no business snooping around my confectionery or my house."

"Is that so? What about the Recipe, Maggie?"

"Aha! So you admit it."

"I admitted nothing, but you can't claim that I have no interest in whether or not you produce that recipe."

"I do claim it. I'm calling the authorities and I'm having you arrested this time, Ki. You can't do this to me and get away with it."

A flash of amusement glimmered through Hezekiah's obvious annoyance. "Before you call the sheriff, Maggie, you might want to consider just where you are. In this house, you're the trespasser and more apt to be arrested than me."

"Don't threaten me, Ki, I can—"

"Stop it." Dana couldn't stay silent any longer. "You're both acting like children and it's—well, it's ridiculous."

"This is not your problem, Dana." Margaret didn't take her eyes off Ki.

He ignored her glare and turned toward Dana. "I don't believe we've been properly introduced. And to think, Maggie, you were once so proud of your good manners."

"Dana, this is Hezekiah Brown," Margaret said through gritted teeth. "He's a con man and a thief. Please avoid him at all costs."

Dana would have liked to point out that it was at Margaret's insistence that she was meeting Ki like this in the first place. But just because her mother was behaving so badly, Dana made an extra effort to be cordial.

Besides, she rather liked the way Hezekiah smiled. When he came around the table, ignoring Margaret, to acknowledge the introduction with an outstretched hand, Dana noticed how stocky and muscular he was. When his hand closed over hers in a handshake firm with confidence and sincere interest, she understood that he was more than a match for her mother. "It's very nice to meet you," she said. "I've heard a lot about you."

"I'll just bet you have," he said with a dry chuckle. "None of it is true, however." His chest barreled out as he relinquished her hand and turned to face Margaret. "I am not a thief, Maggie, and you'll please apologize for calling me one."

"Not if you begged me. You stole my recipe."

"Your recipe?"

"Don't play dumb. I discovered it was missing this afternoon. Do you have an alibi?"

"He's been here with me all—" Rick's words got cut off quickly and evenly.

"You were with Dana until an hour ago." Maggie tossed the interruption at Rick as if it left a bad taste in her mouth. "Come on, Ki. Where were you this afternoon?"

Ki's lips pulled tight and then took on the appearance of a smile. "You still let that temper get the best of your better judgment, don't you, Maggie? If I had been at your house this afternoon to steal the Recipe, I damn sure wouldn't admit it and I'd also have a real fine alibi. But the simple truth is that I didn't steal it. I don't have any use for your half of that old recipe."

"Words are cheap, Ki." Margaret stated flatly. "You'd do anything to keep me from producing the Peppermint Kisses. Anything."

"Wait a minute." Rick stepped forward, his voice and manner authoritative, his posture commanding. "Would one of you please tell me what this is about? One half of a recipe cannot be that important."

"Depends on who you ask." Ki ran a thumb along the collar of his chambray shirt. "Now, Maggie here will say her half is worth more than my half. I'd say neither one of 'em is worth a buffalo nickel unless either Maggie or I wanted to make the candy. And since she's kicking up such a fuss, I guess that's what she's planning to do." He challenged Maggie with the statement and a stare.

"You started this, Ki," Margaret began, but Dana moved into the discussion and cut her off.

"Isn't that what this fight is all about? Which one of you is going to make the candy?"

"Now that Ki's stolen my part of the Recipe, he probably thinks he'll be the one to do it, but I'll fight it every step of the way."

Ki narrowed his eyes with renewed anger. "When you tore the Recipe in half, Maggie, I told you I'd never use it unless you used it first. I could have, you know. At any time over the past forty years, I could have duplicated the ingredients in your half of the Recipe. But I've kept my word. Why would I go back on it now?"

"The Recipe is gone, Ki." Margaret's voice cooled with the first sign of doubt. "Who else could possibly use it?"

"What?" Rick interrupted. "Did you just say that you don't need the whole recipe to make the candy?"

"It wouldn't be hard to figure out what was missing in the Recipe," Margaret confirmed as if it were a minor point hardly worth mentioning. "Especially since my half of the written recipe has the—" she stopped herself "— I almost gave away the secret ingredient."

"I'm afraid you're mistaken," Ki said. "The special ingredient was listed on my half."

"Do you mean—" Dana turned to her mother "—that you could have produced this candy at any time during the past forty years? Without Ki's half? And he could have done it without having access to yours?"

"Of course, Dana." With a frown, Margaret looked at Rick. "Could I have something to drink, please? My throat feels very rough."

"Good idea." Rick walked to the counter without a moment's hesitation. "I think we all need some refreshment. Dana, how about you? Ki?"

Dana nodded absently as the others specified a choice of beverage. She couldn't concentrate on anything other than Margaret's revelation that the recipe, in and of itself, was not important. If Margaret could have manufactured the candy at any time during the past forty years, what had stopped her from doing so? Obviously there had never been a written agreement, forbidding use of the Recipe. Ki said he'd given his word not to use it, but a verbal promise wouldn't have stopped Margaret. So why had she kept a torn piece of paper containing one-half of a recipe for a candy that would "make her famous"? Was it possible that the Recipe's importance was sentimental? Did it represent emotions that hadn't quite died?

Dana mulled over the possibility as Rick handed her a glass of iced tea. She looked from her mother to Ki and noticed an intangible tension in the glances that passed between them. It was the same sort of sensual energy that flowed whenever she and Rick were together. Maybe it was only the memory of the emotion they'd once shared, the lingering whisper of what might have been. Dana accepted the feeling as a natural consequence of her past relationship with Rick. She wasn't sure she could accept it so easily in connection with her mother.

"So, Maggie," Ki said as all four of them took seats at the table. "How many people, would you say, know about the Recipe?"

Margaret sipped her drink, amazingly serene after the ferocity of her earlier attack. "You know this town, Ki. Half the population knows the history of the Peppermint Kiss recipe. Now, how many knew where I kept my half, I have no idea. Charity was aware of its location, but—"

"Well, if she knew, then so could anyone who's talked to her in the past ten years." Ki cupped his hands around his frosted glass. "Charity never could keep a secret."

"It's a little unfair to blame her, don't you think?" Dana asked.

"No one's blaming her, Dana." Margaret lowered her eyebrows in a maternal frown, then arched them knowingly at Ki. "Dana thinks I simply misplaced the Recipe. She doesn't believe it was stolen."

"Are you sure there's no possibility she's right?" Rick tossed in his two cents' worth and was immediately corrected.

"For the last time..." Margaret's voice went tight and obstinate. "I didn't misplace the thing. There is an explanation and I'm not at all convinced it doesn't have something to do with you, Ki."

Hezekiah lifted his glass and eyed Margaret with cool regard. "You always were too quick to judge me, Maggie."

"Is that so? Well, then, tell me what you're doing back in Branson."

"This is as much my home as it is yours. I always planned to come back here when I retired."

Margaret set her glass on the table with a thump. "Ha! You're no more thinking of retiring than I am. You forget I know you about as well as anybody, Ki."

He laughed. "You forget how very long ago that was, Maggie."

"Time doesn't make one bit of difference. And you know it as well as I do."

Dana shared a confused look with Rick across the table, but she wasn't really confused at all. It was becoming clearer by the moment that Margaret and Ki were engaged in an extremely personal conversation covered thinly by their accusations concerning the missing recipe. The idea made Dana uncomfortable, and yet she felt oddly encouraged by this unexpected perspective on her mother. She'd never considered that Margaret was vulnerable to the same emotions, the same errors in judgment as other people. That realization comforted Dana, somehow translating into a realistic hope that a true mother-daughter relationship was possible.

"Well, to tell the truth," Ki began, "I did have sort of an ulterior motive in coming home now." He dabbed a thumbprint pattern in the sweaty side of his glass. "About a month ago, I heard a nasty rumor that Ausbrook Confectionery had scheduled testing on a chocolate peppermint." He raised a silky gaze to Margaret's face and stifled her protest before it fully formed on her tongue. "Now you can about imagine what I thought when I heard that, can't you, Maggie Jane? It kind of gave me a sick feeling in the pit of my stomach and I decided I had as much right to that recipe as you do. So, I came to Branson to check out the rumor and see if there was any truth to it. O' course, that wasn't the only, or even the main reason I came home, but it was a part."

"You came here to stir up a bunch of trouble, Ki," Margaret snapped. "Don't bother to deny it."

His smile smoothed the lines in his face. "I do like stirring up trouble, I admit it. But this time, you've done it by yourself, Maggie. I hardly had to help at all."

Margaret stood, reaching for her car keys. "I knew you were behind this. And just so we understand each other, Ki, I no more believe you heard a rumor about Ausbrook Confectionery's plans for the Recipe than I believe you were as innocent as you claimed to be forty years ago. I never even *thought* about making the Peppermint Kisses until you showed up and started tossing hats at me. So, do what you feel you must, because you can be sure I'm not going to sit idly by and watch you steal this out from under me." She turned to Dana. "Let's go, Dana. We've had all the truth we're going to get today."

"You wouldn't know truth if it walked up and spit in your eye, Maggie." Ki was on his feet, his cheeks flushing with agitation.

"Ha!" Margaret snapped.

With a roll of her eyes, Dana stood and caught just the edge of Rick's amusement as he got to his feet along with everyone else. He had the right idea, she thought. In this case, laughter probably was not only the best, but the only, medicine available. "Thanks for the iced tea, Rick. What I got to drink of it was great."

"Anytime." Rick lowered his voice slightly to carry through the argument going on at a higher decibel. "But next time, let's try not to double-date. It's too hard to talk."

Dana's lips curved with gratitude that he was able to take her mother's eccentricity and make it seem . . . well, almost ordinary. She appreciated that. She really did.

"I'm leaving," she announced close to Margaret's ear and snatched the car keys from her mother's grasp. "Goodbye, Mr. Brown, Ki. It was very nice to meet you."

Ki stopped arguing. So did Margaret. In the lull, it seemed they were both somewhat embarrassed at creating such a scene. After a moment Margaret turned on her heel and left the room. The outer door opened and slammed a minute later. With a softly apologetic shrug, Dana waved goodbye to Rick and followed Margaret's retreat to the car. The driver's seat was vacant, so Dana got in and started the engine. Margaret inhaled a freshly lit cigarette and stared straight ahead, but she did have on her seat belt; an action which Dana interpreted as both an apology and a warning that the silence was to continue without interruption.

Being quiet was no hardship for Dana. She spent the time wondering what kind of person Margaret might have been had she married Ki instead of breaking off the relationship at such a young age. What kind of mother would she have been then? It wasn't an idea Dana really enjoyed thinking about. After all, it put her own identity on the line; brought up questions regarding her existence. Yet, it needed to be considered. Dana felt disloyal to Leonard for even recognizing the attraction between her mother and Ki, but she knew that as an adult, she had to acknowledge Margaret's past. No matter if it hurt. No matter if the picture that emerged of Margaret Burton Ausbrook was not the portrait Dana had wanted to create.

"He couldn't have heard a rumor." Margaret broke Dana's reverie with a sharp, quick conclusion. "There wasn't a rumor for him to hear."

Dana decided her comments were unnecessary and unwanted, so she just kept driving.

"He knows more than he's telling, Dana. I think we'd better file a restraining order as soon as possible." Margaret nodded to herself and then swung a questioning look to Dana. "Isn't that the proper legal move?"

Dana gripped the steering wheel with firm resignation. "You could do that. A restraining order would simply be an order by the court prohibiting Ki from using the Recipe." Dana paused, but had to add, "Either half."

"Then let's do it. How soon can you get the legal papers ready?"

"It won't take long to prepare a petition." Dana cast a wary glance at her mother. "It might take longer for me to get permission to represent you in the Missouri courts. I'm not licensed to practice law here."

"Why not? You'll be handling legal matters for the company. We should have gotten this taken care of already." Margaret tapped ashes into the ashtray, her every move a study of considered thought. "Who do we have to ask?"

Dana had a sudden vision of Margaret calling the governor and requesting that he stamp Dana's forehead with a red-inked "permission granted." She hastened to disabuse her mother of the idea of helping. "I'll take care of it, Margaret. It shouldn't take too long."

"Then you'll file the papers, correct?"

"Correct." It wasn't the answer she wanted to give, but if that's what Margaret was determined to do, then Dana didn't have much choice. "Then I'll file the papers," she said.

Chapter Eight

During the next week, Dana worried about her decision to represent Margaret in the lawsuit. If she'd been able to feel that the case had merit, that the confectionery stood at risk, perhaps she wouldn't have had to struggle with her conscience. Maybe if someone other than Rick was the opposing counsel, she'd have laughed at her mother's obsession with a recipe and proceeded to handle the legalities, leaving it to a judge to set the record straight as to what constituted a nuisance suit.

The bottom line, however, was that Margaret called the shots and Dana, regardless of any personal interest in the company or the case, was merely an employee. She had little choice but to follow Margaret's instructions and take the necessary steps to petition the court for a restraining order. She wanted to discuss the whole situation with Rick, but the opportunity didn't arise. From eight to five, she danced attendance on the thousand and one details of learning the candy business. From five to eight, she listened to Margaret explain what she planned to do about the Recipe, when she planned to do it, and how surprised Ki would be when she did it. Dana retired to her room a little earlier each night to catch a few moments' respite before the next day began.

By the end of the week, she was well on her way to obtaining special permission to represent the Ausbrook Confectionery in the Missouri courts until she could obtain entrance to the state bar. Official acknowledgment would take several days, but Dana already felt the pull of professional ethics against her desire to talk over everything with Rick. Her only consolation at this point was the faint hope of persuading Margaret not to file the lawsuit.

When Saturday dawned, cloudless and hot, Dana faced the day and the scheduled Stafford family get-together with mixed emotions. Rick picked her up at one o'clock and before he'd driven a quarter mile down the road, Dana had decided to bring up the subject of the Recipe and the lawsuit. One conversation, she reasoned, wouldn't constitute a breach in ethics, especially since nothing as yet had been filed.

But Rick spoke before she could open the discussion. "I'm glad you're going with me today. Mom will be happy to see you."

"I'm looking forward to getting reacquainted with your family, too. As I recall, they were a boisterous lot."

"Hell-raisers is the way Ki puts it, but all my brothers and sisters, except for one, have calmed down considerably since the onset of maturity. Even my mother says it's mighty quiet when we're all together, compared to what it used to be." Rick laughed at his own thoughts. "I guess we're just waiting for the next generation to reach the age for trouble-making. Then we can all enjoy it again without having to sap our own energy."

"The next generation?" Dana asked. "How many little Staffords are there?"

Rick tipped back his hat and considered the question. "Well, let's see, Curtis has two boys, Kenny has a three-year-old girl and another baby on the way, Jenny has a baby girl, so I guess that makes two nephews, two nieces and one undecided.''

"Somehow I thought there'd be more.''

"Five seems like a pretty fair number to me, considering everyone but me is under thirty.''

Dana smiled and offered a little shrug. "What about the others?''

"Sallie Jo's planning a wedding for next spring. Tommy will be a senior in high school this next year. And Annie is still as wild as a November wind and as ornery as Zack Wiggons's Brahma bull. She's always up to mischief of one sort or another.''

"Oh, yes. I remember Annie. If it hadn't been for her, I would never have taken your truck.''

"Aha, after all these years, you finally admit it,'' he accused with a teasing smile. "And don't try to blame my sister, either.''

"I admit nothing and you're beginning to sound like Margaret when she's tossing around questionable accusations.'' Dana paused, her thoughts returning to her original intentions. "I suppose Ki recovered from the battle?''

"Without so much as a minor wound. Except that he didn't like it when I told him he'd behaved almost as childishly as your mother did.''

"It was quite a scene, wasn't it?''

"If I hadn't seen it, I wouldn't have believed Margaret Ausbrook could so completely lose her cool.''

"Wait until you hear her plans for the Recipe.''

Rick turned an uncomfortable, but forthright, gaze to Dana. "Don't tell me, Dana. I suppose you might as well know now that litigation is pending. Yesterday, I filed a petition for a restraining order against Margaret and the confectionery to stop her from using the Peppermint Kiss recipe.''

Dana felt as if he'd just knocked the breath out of her. "Why, Rick? I was going to talk Margaret out of—"

"There's more to this than the ownership of a recipe, Dana, and neither you nor I are going to be able to work out a reasonable, or even a rational, settlement. The fight belongs to Margaret and Ki and if they choose to drag it into court, it's not my place or yours to try to stop them." He paused and when Dana said nothing, he pushed a thumb under the brim of his hat and glanced impatiently out the window. "Look, Dana, you were going to file. I just beat you to it."

"An action in which you obviously take great pride, Rick." Dana crossed her arms to cover the increased rise and fall of her breasts. Surprise and anger, annoyance and a sense of betrayal blended into a silent whirlwind of tension. "You may as well take me home. We shouldn't be spending time together now that we're adversaries in this case."

"Don't be silly. It makes no—"

"It makes a difference, Rick. It damn well makes a difference."

"Right now, Dana, this afternoon, this time of being with you is personal. Entirely and strictly personal. Now, if you choose to allow your mother to come between us again, then, yes, I'd better take you home. However, if you're the woman I think you are, you'll admit that the lawsuit is not your idea and it's not your problem. We can't discuss it because we represent opposing camps, but as I live and breathe, I swear it doesn't change my feelings for you. You have to represent Margaret because she's your mother, I have to represent Ki because he's my friend. But when this is over, I'll still like you. Hell, I like you now. Can't we just enjoy the afternoon and forget there's any reason not to be together?''

Dana hated to admit it, but he'd won the argument the moment he'd said she was allowing Margaret to come between them again. As flat and repugnant as the idea was, there was a ring of truth to the words. A resounding ring. And Dana still harbored enough rebellion against her mother to respond to it. ''Will it overinflate your ego if I agree too quickly?''

''I'd rather you'd admit you did steal my truck.''

Dana frowned. ''Will Annie be there this afternoon?''

''In all her glory.''

''Then she can explain exactly how it happened.''

''Sure she can,'' Rick drawled. ''Annie can set me straight.''

ANNIE STAFFORD LAUGHED until she doubled over. ''I'll never forget the look on your face, Rick,'' she said in between bouts of hilarity. ''You were slicked up like a summer whistle, all set for a hot Saturday-night date. You'd angled for weeks to get a date with Bethany Hillsberry. She was such an airhead, Rick. I had to do something. I'd planned to siphon out the gas, but then Dana and—'' Annie turned to Dana. ''Who was that with you?''

''Lynn Duncan.'' Dana scooted her chair closer to the table. ''She used to live next door to Margaret. When I was in town, we ran around together.''

''I'll bet your mother didn't know what a hellion Lynn was.'' Rick put in. ''She was worse than you, Annie.''

Annie wrinkled her nose at her older brother. ''Anyway, it couldn't have been better timing. I talked Dana and Lynn into driving the truck out to Taneycomo Dam for me and they took off just as you walked out of the movie with Bethany draped across your arm. The look on your face, Rick, when you realized your truck was speeding down the road . . ." Annie dissolved into laughter again. "And then Bethany left you flat when Eddie Hankins drove by in his souped-up Chevy. I loved it."

Dana laughed along with Annie. How could anyone not join in her complete and simple enjoyment? In the past two hours Dana had laughed more than she'd laughed in a year. Some of the reminiscing was wistful rather than funny, but for the most part the Staffords were a jovial, congenial family with an endless string of happy memories.

"You're lucky you've lived as long as you have, Annie." Rick sat astraddle the ladder-back chair, his arms crossed on the top, leaning slightly forward. He was between Dana and his mother and across the table from his laughing sister.

"It's a wonder I didn't turn gray years ago with all the mischief you kids cooked up," Mrs. Stafford said.

"And I missed out on it," Tommy, the youngest, complained. "You should have had me first, Mom."

Curtis, who sat at the far end of the table with his oldest son on his lap, chuckled. "If she'd had you first, Tommy, she'd never have had the rest of us."

"Oh, go on." Annie waved a hand in a grand gesture of impatience. "Rick and I set the standard. If it hadn't been for us, the rest of you wouldn't have known how to go about stirring up a tempest in a teapot."

There were general guffaws all around, but Annie persisted in her argument until everyone was laughing again. Dana loved every minute spent with them, yet she knew a sure envy for the warmth and security each of the Stafford children had known from birth. They might have been poor and they might have gone without the extras of life, but they couldn't doubt the love and acceptance that bound them all into a family unit.

Dana felt welcome, but in the back of her mind there was the nagging thought that she'd rejected her chance to become a part of this family, to actually belong here in this kitchen with them.

"So, Dana," Annie said after the sibling debate had died down. "What have you been doing the past few years? We haven't given you a chance to say much of anything."

"Didn't I hear you got married?" Jenny entered the kitchen in time to hear Annie's question. "To some guy back in Philadelphia?"

A sudden discomfort stuck in the back of Dana's throat. "The marriage didn't work out." She felt Rick's eyes on her, sensed a quiet tension in the room. "We divorced within a year."

"Did you have a big wedding?" Sallie Jo asked, revealing her own intense interest in the ceremony of marriage rather than the details of Dana's experience. "I'm trying to decide what color theme to use for my own wedding next April."

Dana smiled, envious of the innocent blush on Sallie's cheeks and the romantic plans in her head. "I had an elaborate wedding, Sallie Jo. Unfortunately I chose the wrong man to share it with."

Sallie Jo embarked upon a list of wonderful qualities held by her fiancé, but beneath her impervious monologue lay a crisp silence.

"Let's clean up." Annie broke the tension with her suggestion and soon the room was abuzz with laughing voices and the clank of dishes. Dana turned, steeling herself to face Rick's disapproval. His eyes held hers for a moment, but all she could see was her own wistful regret mirrored there. She sighed, knowing she'd made a wrong choice ten years before, but not quite ready to admit that she should have chosen Rick instead.

The rest of the afternoon passed without incident. There was a volleyball game which turned into a free-for-all of sibling rivalry and fun. Later, there was homemade ice cream and cake and more reminiscing. By dusk, there was a gradual leave-taking. No one seemed in a hurry, yet the group dwindled until only Annie and Tommy, Rick and Dana were left to keep Mrs. Stafford company.

It was full dark before Rick asked Dana if she was ready to leave. She wasn't, but she could hardly say she wanted to stay longer. After all, she'd spent almost the entire day here and it was time and past to go home. Home to Margaret, who would be pacing the floor, smoking and creating a dust devil of restless energy in her wake. Dana didn't want to go back. She wanted to pretend she belonged here for just a few more minutes.

But she stood with Rick, thanked his mother for a lovely afternoon, bid an affectionate goodbye to Annie and wished Tommy the best of luck in his senior year. Then she gathered the day's memories and walked outside.

Rick escorted her to the truck, but didn't reach for her hand. Several times during the day, he'd caught himself reaching toward her and had drawn back, reluctant to display even a casual touch in front of his family. He'd invited Dana because it had seemed like the thing to do at the time. Now he wasn't so sure. She'd been so quiet today and when Jenny had asked about her marriage . . . well, Dana had looked stricken, as if she hadn't wanted anyone to know she'd chosen some Pennsylvania preppie over Rick. But, of course, everyone had known. The memory stirred some old embers of resentment and his foot pressed too heavily on the gas pedal.

"You're lucky, Rick, to be a part of that family." Dana spoke softly, the inflection in her voice revealing a wistfulness, a loneliness he'd never heard there before. "Do you always have so much fun together?"

"Usually. Mom never allowed us much room for argument, so we had to substitute something for the fighting we wanted to do. I guess that's how all the teasing got started. I don't know how Annie got away with all she did, though. Most of her stunts make hilarious stories in retrospect, but at the time...well, she's lucky one of us didn't tie her in a tow sack and toss her off a cliff."

Dana laughed at the memory of Annie's expressive face and dramatic gestures. "Your mother certainly seems to take it all in stride."

"Mom is a unique person. She raised us almost single-handedly. I don't know how she managed."

"She did a good job."

"We all think so." Rick slowed the truck, feeling a shift in his emotions, but unable to control the part of him that sensed and responded to Dana's mood. "Did you enjoy the afternoon? It wasn't too much family for you?"

"You know I loved every minute of it. It's so...different from what I'm used to. My family is dishwater dull compared to yours."

"I'd hardly classify Margaret as dull."

"Well, she isn't much fun."

"Ki thinks she's a barrel of laughs." Rick hoped to win a smile, but received only a slight tilt of the lips. "Maybe you take her too seriously, Dana."

"Maybe, but she is my mother and it's a little hard to just shrug off her eccentricities."

"The whole town is eccentric, Dana. Haven't you noticed? Everything is as elaborate and alluring as the bid for tourists' dollars can make it."

"That doesn't make me feel any better."

"Would it help if I confessed that I saw Annie bribe you into taking my pickup that day?"

Dana swung toward him in surprise. "What? You were in the movie. With Bethany."

Rick grinned and shook his head. "No, I was in the lobby and I saw my sister go through her 'please, help me' routine. I had a pretty good idea what she was up to."

"Why didn't you stop her? I would never have driven off in your truck if you'd been there."

Rick slowed for the stoplight. "I figured it was a heck of a way to get introduced to you."

An all-too-familiar tingle ran along Dana's spine. She wasn't sure she believed him, but it made a good line. A darn good line. "There were easier ways, Rick."

"Not when I knew you were Margaret Ausbrook's daughter."

"I thought you weren't afraid of my mother."

"I was then."

"But not now?" Dana teased.

"Not now." Rick made the turn onto Branson's main downtown street. "She's already done her worst as far as I'm concerned. She convinced you I wasn't good enough for you."

The words formed an echoing silence. It was several minutes before Dana answered. "You can hardly lay all the blame at her door, Rick. It was my choice not to go through with the elopement, not Margaret's."

He said nothing for a few minutes, although there were dozens of things he wanted to say, questions he wanted to ask. But what did it matter now? Why did he want to hear Dana admit she'd made a mistake in not marrying him? What possible difference could it make? Rick parked the truck in front of his office and turned to Dana with a ready explanation. "I'm going inside to get a copy of the restraining order for you. Margaret will be receiving a copy Monday, but I thought you might like to look it over before she sees it."

Rick thought he was being more than fair, but Dana offered only a nod in reply so he tried again. "If you think you can talk her into settling the case out of court, I think Ki would be willing to compromise."

"Once Margaret sees that order, Rick, she won't be open to any compromise. However, I'll see what I can do."

He waited a moment. "Do you want a copy of the order or not?"

"Yes, of course." Her tone marked her impatience, her whole frustration with the situation. But Rick didn't know what else to offer her. After all, his first loyalty in this case was to Hezekiah. Dana had never given him cause to feel any loyalty to her. With precise, sharp movements, Rick got out of the truck and unlocked the front door of his office. In a moment he heard the other truck door open and sensed Dana's presence behind him.

Inside, he switched on a light over the secretary's desk and then went back to his office. Dana followed. So did a taut silence. As he shuffled through the papers on his desk, he observed Dana's movements as she wandered from bookshelf to file cabinet, from wall to desk. She paused behind one of the black leather chairs and Rick found himself watching the restless stroke of her hand across the smooth leather.

When he raised his eyes, his gaze collided with hers and he knew a pressing urge to take her into his arms, to kiss her and caress her and show her where she belonged. The muscles in his upper arms tensed, his whole body felt thick, his throat ached with words he simply would not allow himself to say. Dana wanted comfort. She wanted to assuage her loneliness and soothe her sense of isolation in the warmth he could offer. Rick knew her motivations as well as he knew his own. Yet as their eyes held, as awareness spun a seductive web, Rick accepted his own vulnerability and made a last-ditch effort to deny it. "Here it is," he said and handed her a copy of the restraining order.

She took the paper from him and glanced at it as he moved toward the doorway. "Margaret won't be happy about this," she said.

"Then that'll make two of us."

"Three. I'm not at all pleased, myself." Dana walked slowly to where Rick stood waiting. "I wish you'd waited."

"And I wish you hadn't come back."

The remark stung, but Dana kept up her chin. "I guess that makes us even."

"Even?" Rick made a sound similar to a laugh. "No, Dana, we're a long way from being even." He turned off the lights and prepared to leave the office.

"So what you said this afternoon about liking me and wanting to spend time with me was idle talk? Just a way to fill the conversational gap until a chance to 'get even' came along?"

Rick wanted to shake her for misunderstanding. But he didn't. He reached for her. He felt as if he'd been reaching for her all his life...and coming up with empty arms. But now she was moving toward him, melting into a need they'd both tried to hide for too long.

Surprise softened the tension in her lips and Dana didn't think to protest. As his mouth claimed hers, she admitted to herself that she'd wanted this all day, had longed for the security of Rick's touch, the knowledge that he wanted to be with her. She'd been unsure of herself all afternoon, uncomfortable in his family circle, knowing she didn't belong, yet sensing that Rick wanted her there. And she knew he wanted her now. It was apparent in the pressure of his kiss, in the way his body cradled hers. And it felt good to be wanted, to be needed. Dana gave over to the sensations coursing through her body.

His lips covered hers with soft, sipping movements. His chin, newly shaven that morning, gently abraded her skin with a few hours' growth of beard. Her hands came up to stroke his face and exult in the texture of his rough-soft jawline. His arms tightened around her and Dana felt small and feminine against the understated virility of his powerful body. She sank into the warm desire flowering to life inside her. A desire she'd known before. Ten years before. When she and Rick had been too young and scared to fulfill their adolescent yearnings, but mature enough to long for it with the sweet innocence of their love.

As the memories surfaced, Dana welcomed them and pressed closer to Rick's caressing warmth. Was it possible, she wondered, for love to linger long after it should have died? Was she still carrying the torch for Rick? Or was it simply that she wanted to experience the sense of belonging his arms provided?

The possibility was enough to cool her response and Rick pulled back, letting his lips linger briefly at the side of her mouth, before he moved so he could see her face, examine her expression. He didn't know what he was looking for. Or what he hoped to see, but the expression in her eyes convinced him that she had been as disturbed by the kiss as he had. The knowledge wasn't comfortable. He didn't want to be disturbed. He didn't want to feel anything at all. He did not want to fall in love with her again. She'd hurt him once. Hurt him badly. And he wasn't eager to chance his heart again.

"I think I'd better take you home, Dana," he said, none too steadily.

"Yes." She moved past him quickly and Rick fought the impulse to pull her back into his arms. But he stayed behind and locked the door, instead. Better to play it safe, even though safe was not satisfying.

Dana said nothing on the drive home and Rick respected her silence. When they stopped in front of Margaret's house, Dana folded the copy of the restraining order in half and tucked it in her pocket. "Thanks for getting this for me, Rick."

"I thought you ought to be prepared. As you said, Margaret won't be happy."

"It won't be the first time." Dana got out of the truck and closed the door. "Good night, Rick. I enjoyed today." She wanted to say more, but didn't know what else to say. So, with a final pat on the truck's side panel, she waved goodbye and went into the house to be alone with her thoughts and the conflicting desires of her willful heart.

Chapter Nine

"Somethin' on your mind, boy?" Ki leaned back in the lounge chair and propped his feet beside Rick's on the porch railing. "You've been staring at the hills practically all afternoon."

"Waiting for wisdom, Ki." Rick twisted the glass in his hands and watched the watery remains of an iced drink slosh from side to side. "You know, 'My help cometh from the hills.'"

"Yeah, I've heard that. How long are you gonna wait for it to get here?"

"As long as it takes, I reckon." The water in the glass settled and Rick set it in motion again. "How old were you, Ki, before you figured out that women are a lot more trouble than they're worth?"

"I've been saying it for years but, just between you and me, it ain't true." Ki sniffed and squinted pensively at the view. "If the truth be known, I'd say a woman, a good woman, is about the best thing that can happen to a man. And I'm here to tell you that if Maggie Burton wasn't such a mule-headed, stubborn female, I'd have made her a good husband for all these forty years."

Rick looked at his companion in surprise. "I thought you couldn't stand the sight of her. I thought the two of you were feuding."

"We are, but it wasn't my choice to begin it. And I don't mind the sight of her. Maggie's still a fine-looking woman, but lordy, she does make me mad. 'Bout as mad as I ever care to get."

"I don't believe I've ever seen you as angry as you were the other day," Rick said with a chuckle. "Your face was as red as an overripe tomato."

"I don't doubt it. All Maggie has to do is walk into the room and my blood pressure shoots sky-high. She does get my dander up."

"Why do you let her do that, Ki? I'd have thought that forty years would have brought some apathy to at least one of you."

"Yeah, folks'll tell you that age brings perspective, but that don't hold true with Maggie. She still pulls my strings like nobody else has ever been able to do." Ki jerked a handkerchief from his overalls' pocket and ran it twice around his sweaty beer bottle before rubbing it across the top of his bald head. "Look at me. I was doin' okay in Britain, minding my own business, tossin' around the idea of retiring and coming home, feeling pretty good about myself. And what happens? Before I can make a decision, my partner, Henry Philipps, tells me he's heard this rumor about a Peppermint Kiss recipe coming on the market in the States. Now, mind you, rumors are always circulating in the candy industry, just like in every other kind of business. Usually I don't pay much attention. But a rumor about a Peppermint Kiss?

"Now, I'll grant you there's always the possibility someone else just came up with a similar idea for a chocolate peppermint, but it isn't likely they'd call it a Peppermint Kiss, is it? So, I figured Maggie's decided to use the Recipe and wants to get my reaction, find out if I'll kick up a fuss. She starts the rumor about manufacturing the candy and waits to see what I'll do."

"So you came home."

With a gruff laugh, Ki took a swig of beer. "Damn right, I did. She's not going to get by with this. That recipe's half mine."

"Which brings up a good point, Ki. Where did you hide your half of the Recipe?"

"Would you believe I don't rightly remember?"

Rick set his glass on the deck floor. "No, I wouldn't believe that. Now, Margaret might. But I think you know exactly where it is."

"Well," Ki drawled in noncommittal good humor. "Maybe I do and maybe I don't. Either way it doesn't matter, cause Maggie's gonna throw one holy fit when she gets notice of that restraining order." He chuckled with the thought.

"I told Dana about it yesterday," Rick said, his gaze returning to the haze settling over the hills. "I also gave her a copy of the order."

"Oh, so that's why you're sitting out here, thinking about wisdom and women. You shoulda just let her be surprised."

Rick frowned. "I couldn't do that, Ki. I felt like I owed her the courtesy of a warning."

Ki mulled that over with an in-and-out pursing of his lips. "How she'd take it?"

"Like I'd stabbed her in the back. She wouldn't even admit that she was going to file the same paper for Margaret against you."

"You think she will?"

"Of course. You just said Margaret would have a fit when she gets the notice. She'll probably insist on driving Dana to the courthouse to file the countersuit."

"I take it Dana doesn't like being caught up in mine and Maggie's feud."

Rick let his feet hit the floor with a thump. "I'm not crazy about it, either, Ki."

"You didn't have to take on the case, Rick. I wouldn't have pressed you."

"I know that. But I have to do it. You're too much like family to me. I owe you whatever help I can give." He offered Ki a rueful frown. "Besides, the lawsuit keeps me from getting in over my head with Dana. If we weren't on opposite sides in this, there's no telling what kind of heart trouble I'd be in already. This way, at least, I've got to try to be objective."

"You do what you feel you have to do, boy, and don't be worrying about my troubles with Maggie. If Dana's the woman your heart's set on, then for pete's sake, don't let this nuisance of a lawsuit get in your way. I'll certainly understand."

"There are ethics involved, Ki, and I won't compromise my self-respect for Dana or anyone else. But there's more to it than that. Even if I was sure my heart was set on having Dana, I know her heart isn't set on having me. She's never liked Branson, plans on going back to Philadelphia in less than a year, and I don't think there's a thing I can say or do to change her mind. I'd only be setting myself up for another heartache. And you remember how long it took me to get over her the last time."

"I do remember, Rick. I do. You must have written me a hundred letters that autumn. Then you spent almost a month with me in London before I finally talked you into coming home and going to college." Ki lifted his bottle to the waning Sunday sun and examined it from every angle. "There used to be some pretty fair moonshine made here in the Ozarks. I remember visiting ol' Ezra Midnight's still with my daddy and wondering why a man would take all the risks to make illegal whiskey. I finally just asked and do you know what ol' Ezra said?"

Rick shook his head, only half interested in Ki's reminiscence.

"He said he didn't figure it as a risk. If it wasn't for the revenuers, he wouldn't be in business. And if it wasn't for him, the revenuers wouldn't be in business. So, he thought it worked out to be a pretty fair trade."

"So what does that mean?" Rick asked, knowing Ki would tell him whether he asked or not.

Ki puffed out his chest and set down the bottle. "It means life is a trade-off as often as not. Dana left you with a broken heart, but you traded it for a college education. Before she came along, Rick, you weren't what I'd call real motivated. But afterward, well, you became a pretty determined young fellow."

Rick waited, knowing there was more, understanding that Ki was trying to help him in his own inimitable way.

"So, what I'm sayin' here, Rick, is that what happened then traded out all right. Don't hold it against her now. Don't be like me and look back forty years later and wish you'd been a little wiser and a lot less proud."

Rick considered that for a long moment, rubbing his palms together in thoughtful meditation. "Do you regret what happened between you and Margaret?"

"Regret's a strong word. It means different things at different times in a man's life. Do I regret loving Maggie Burton?" Ki pursed his lips. "No, never for a minute. As to the rest . . . well, sometimes I have wished I'd tried harder to win her back. And I wish I hadn't run off with the boys on the day before the weddin'. We had one whopper of a bachelor's party and I didn't see any reason not to have a bit of fun over in Joplin on my last night of freedom. Hell, I was young and had no better sense than to get drunk as a skunk right off the bat. My friends left me in the care of a fancy woman they'd hired to entertain me. I can't recall bein' entertained a'tall, but nevertheless, the rented lady drove me back to Branson and delivered me, lock, stock and beer bottles to Maggie. Well, suffice it to say, Maggie didn't take kindly to my idea of a last wild fling. She broke off the weddin' plans then and there, tore up the Recipe, and told me where to put my hat.'' Ki's voice trailed off. ''My one real regret is that I let her paint us into a corner that neither one of us could get out of without losing face. And if there's anything Maggie can't bear to do, it's lose face.''

Ki wiped a large hand across his jaw, as if erasing the memory. ''On the other hand, I wouldn't be the same person if things hadn't worked out the way they did. I'll tell you for sure, if'n I'd married her back then, I wouldn't of spent the next thirty years peacefully learnin' what I did and didn't like about the world. No, sir. I'd of learned what *she* did and didn't like. And I'd surely never have gone to visit my World War II buddy, Henry, ten years ago and we'd never have started talking about candy, and London Country Candies wouldn't be on the market now.'' Ki nodded, pleased with his rationale. ''Why, hell, if I'd gotten married forty years ago, I'd probably be fatter than a grain-fed hog now and I'd be sitting around on Sunday evenings awaitin' for my grandchildren to drop by and play a game of checkers.''

''You might have kept more of your hair,'' Rick pointed out, tongue in cheek.

Ki's hand went automatically to his bald pate, then he grinned slowly. "Naw, Maggie would have pulled it out and I'd have less than I do now. But bald men are better lovers, you know."

"You're pulling my leg."

"Nope." Ki pushed to his feet. "I'm being straight with you, Rick. And it's more wisdom than you're gonna get from those hills this afternoon, I guarantee it."

Rick stood, too, laughing, glad for Ki's fatherlike friendship. He put his arm around the older man's shoulders. "How about a game of checkers, Gramps?"

"To hell with you, boy. I've got tickets to the Silver Dollar Music Show. Want to go?"

"Sure, why not?"

"Well, if you can't think of a reason, don't expect me to do it for you." Ki picked up his beer bottle and walked inside the house. "Are ya coming or ain't ya?"

Rick waited only another minute, his eyes on the nearby hills, his thoughts on Dana. "I'll be right there," he said.

"IS SOMETHING bothering you, Dana?" Margaret walked into the study at a brisk pace. "You've been staring out that window all afternoon."

Dana turned her head, hugging her knees tighter to her chest as she did so. "I'm just thinking."

"About ways to improve the confectionery, I hope."

"No. About you and Dad, mostly."

Margaret came to stand by the window seat where Dana sat. "Have you talked to Leonard this week?"

Dana confirmed it with a nod. "He's fine. Grandmother and Grandfather are both well. They all say they miss me, but I don't see why. It's not as if I saw them all that often, anyway. I haven't lived in the house with them since I started college. I guess it's because they know I'm too far away to just drop in for a visit.''

"You're a joy to have around, Dana. Of course, they miss you. I know Leonard truly wanted you to move back into the house after you and Darren divorced. I sort of hoped you would, too.''

"I couldn't do that."

"Yes, I know. You take your independence very seriously.'' Margaret touched Dana's hair lightly, affectionately. "I guess you got that from me.''

Dana didn't think independence could be inherited from a parent. Learned, perhaps. In her case, certainly, Margaret's self-sufficiency had had a tremendous influence. "Why did you and Dad divorce?" she asked softly. "Why did you marry him in the first place?''

With a heavy frown, Margaret moved away, placing herself behind the desk, busying her hands with paperwork. "We've been over that a dozen times, Dana. Why do you keep asking?''

"Because you never give me an answer."

Margaret stacked papers on one corner of the desk and began sorting through another stack. "Leonard and I are good friends, Dana. We should never have tried to be anything else. I met him quite by chance when I was at a very lonely point in my life. He was wonderfully intelligent and so calm. I liked that about him. I still do. But in day-to-day living, I couldn't handle his constant composure. If he'd ever once lost his temper, I think we might have made it, but it just wasn't in him. Leonard is the most gentle man I've ever known.''

"But did you love him?" Dana braced her chin on her knees, hoping Margaret wouldn't back off the conversation now.

"How could anyone not love Leonard?" Margaret's lips slipped into a subtle curve. "I still love him, Dana, but I never was in love with him, if that answers your question."

It didn't, but then Dana wasn't sure there was an answer that would satisfy her. "Are you still in love with Hezekiah Brown?"

Margaret glanced up in sharp alert. "What on earth made you ask something like that?"

Dana shrugged. "I guess I want to know."

"I refuse to discuss that with you, Dana. It's too..." The words trailed off as Margaret reached for and lit a cigarette. "It's too ridiculous."

It was probably too close to the truth, Dana thought, but didn't pursue it further. Instead she swung her feet to the floor and eyed her bare toes pensively. "Would you tell me I was being ridiculous if I said I thought I might still be in love with Rick?"

Margaret didn't even look up. "Yes."

Dana nodded and rose. "I'm going to fix some tuna salad for a sandwich. Want one?"

"Is that it?" Margaret blew a smoke ring impatiently. "You ask a question like that and then decide to make a sandwich?"

"I refuse to discuss it with you, Margaret. It's just too ridiculous." With a haughty lift of her chin, Dana walked to the doorway.

"Sometimes I think you're too much like your father, Dana. It worries me."

Dana smiled. "Do you want a sandwich or not?"

"Yes, thank you. A sandwich will be fine." Margaret buried her attention in a catalog and Dana left the study, feeling that in some small way she'd taken a step in the right direction. Now, if she could just decide which direction to take with Rick, she'd feel like she'd accomplished something. She couldn't quite define her feelings for him, but she knew Margaret was wrong. The idea that she might be in love with Rick was far from being ridiculous—so far, in fact, that it scared her.

"DANA? ARE YOU IN HERE?" Will Burton knocked on her door and entered without waiting for an invitation.

Dana gave the file-cabinet drawer a solid push and tried not to look irritated. The last thing she wanted to do on this typical Monday morning was to listen to Will rattle off his usual list of Monday-morning complaints. "Hello, Will," she said. "How are you today?"

"I've been better, Dana." He scooted a chair close to Dana's desk and placed himself in it. "I've been better."

With a nod of pseudounderstanding, Dana sank onto her chair and pulled it up to the desk. She clasped her hands and waited for her cousin to enlighten her. It was amazing, she'd decided, that he thought he'd found a sympathetic listener in her. She wasn't sympathetic, but Margaret had told her to listen to him, so she listened. As yet she hadn't learned much, but she still held out some small degree of hope. After all, Will Burton did know about making candy. Eating it, too, but that was neither here nor there. With a mental jerk, Dana realized he'd asked her a question. "Oh, uh, I'm not sure what to think about that, Will."

He nodded, as if he'd fully expected her to answer that way. "I've thought about it a lot of times, Dana, and last summer when I was on vacation, I visited the Randel Stevens Candy Factory in New Jersey. You should see the way they've modernized their building. I was so impressed. And the machinery. Well, it's state of the art."

When he paused, Dana nodded a reluctant encouragement. She saw no point in mentioning that Randel Stevens was only about ten times the size of Ausbrook Confectionery. Will would only dismiss that as a minor inconvenience.

"I believe we're missing a real opportunity," Will continued. "We have the market. Branson pulls in thousands of tourists every summer and they buy our candy. The individually wrapped hard candies sell fairly well and the taffy is always a good seller. But we're not covering the demands of the whole market. And if we don't do it, someone else is going to. Look at these figures I've compiled." He placed a computer printout in front of her and leaned over to direct her attention. "See? The sale of single specialty chocolates, like our caramel creams and the assorted bonbons, is considerably higher than for the wrapped candies, in proportion to the amount distributed. Now if we began an expansion project within the next few months, we could be meeting this demand by May of the following year. Do you see where I'm headed with this?"

Dana tried to make sense of the numbers in front of her and the plan Will was trying to outline, but he kept waving his finger across the sheet and past her nose until she could hardly concentrate on anything except the random movement of his hand.

"Here, look at this." He put another printout on top of the first. "This is a compilation of the equipment we'd need to get started. I already know where to order it and how long it will take to get it installed. From there it'd be easy street." Will smiled, enthralled with his plans. "Can't you see it?"

Dana couldn't. All she could envision was a headache. "Have you talked this over with Margaret?" she asked.

It was obviously the wrong question. Will picked up his printouts and began rolling them into a tight circumference. "I thought you were interested in seeing the confectionery grow. Not stagnate like some isolated pond."

He acted so outraged Dana wanted to laugh, but she knew she absolutely couldn't, mustn't. "I am interested, Will. It sounds like a fine idea to me, but Margaret will have the final say—"

A low roar came from down the hall. It sounded like a lion with a thorn in its paw. Will whirled toward the door, apparently intent on rescue, but Dana stood her ground. She had a strong suspicion that Margaret had just received her notice of the restraining order. By the time Dana had counted to five, Margaret was in the doorway, brushing past Will as if he didn't outweigh her by a good ninety pounds.

"Dana, look at this." Margaret dropped the court order on the desk and patted her pockets. "Damn it, I forgot my cigarettes. Will, get them for me, please. Can you believe it, Dana? He's done it. Ki has filed a lawsuit against me."

Dana picked up the sheet of legal-size paper and gave it a casual glance. "You've been telling him for weeks that you intended to sue him, Margaret. Did you expect him to sit around and wait for you to do it?"

"I didn't expect you to defend him, Dana. But then, I knew your love life was going to get in my way. I suppose with that Stafford boy being Ki's lawyer—" She glanced over her shoulder. "Will, didn't I ask you to get my cigarettes? They're on my desk. Bring them here, please."

Dana wouldn't have done it, but Will hesitated only a moment before leaving the room, presumably to return with the requested cigarettes. "Sit down, Margaret." Dana took advantage of the moment alone with her mother and indicated the chair opposite the desk. "Listen to me for just one minute. I want you to understand that my relationship with Rick Stafford has no bearing on this lawsuit. I advised you not to take your grievances to court. You ignored me. Obviously Ki ignores Rick's advice, too. So, we're all going to court. But don't make the mistake of thinking I take this as personally as you do. I have no quarrel with Rick and you're not about to get one started."

Margaret sat and gazed up at Dana with clear hostility. Then she sighed, long and audibly. "If you're going to be my legal advisor, Dana, and you want to represent the Ausbrook Confectionery in this matter, you'll abide by my wishes. It's unprofessional for you to be consorting with Hezekiah's attorney while the case is pending."

Dana took up a position perched on the corner of the desk. She wasn't towering over Margaret, but she did gain some small advantage in height. It was time, Dana knew, to take a stand, whether or not she alienated her mother in the process. There were moments, and this was one of them, when self-respect outweighed every other consideration. "If you want me to represent you and the confectionery in this matter, Margaret, you'll give me the long-overdue credit for knowing what I'm doing. I did not attend law school to have you sit here and give me a lecture on professional ethics. There's no call for it and frankly, I find your attitude insulting."

"I'm your mother, Dana. I can't help it if my attitude doesn't meet your approval. I don't trust Hezekiah Brown and I certainly don't trust his attorney."

"But you ought to trust me." Dana's brown eyes clashed with Margaret's and neither looked away.

Will hurried in and handed over the package of cigarettes along with Margaret's gold lighter. "Here you are, Margaret," he said. "Now what's this about a lawsuit?" He looked eager to glean the details as he backed into the chair beside Margaret and faced her with clasped hands and a concerned expression. "Why would anyone want to sue you, Margaret?"

Dana crossed her arms at the middle button of her rose linen jacket and watched the drama unfold.

"It's just one of those things, Will." Margaret, with cigarette in hand, was calmer, but tension and anger still registered in her movements. "Ki is trying to legally outmaneuver me, but he's in for a rude awakening. We'll countersue."

"When?" Will rubbed his hands together.

"The sooner the better." Margaret reached for the legal document and read through it again. Will leaned forward to read over her shoulder and Dana watched the two of them with mixed exasperations. A lot of good it had done to become a lawyer, she thought, when no one in this office seemed to need one.

"This applies to the whole confectionery." Will's voice rose to high tenor. "He can't close down the whole confectionery."

"Don't be silly, Will." Margaret looked around for an ashtray, cupping her hand beneath the burning end of her cigarette. "It doesn't say anything about closing the confectionery." She settled for tapping her ashes onto a coaster instead. "That's right, isn't it, Dana? The court can't close us down, can it?"

"The court certainly could if it found reasonable cause." Disgusted, Dana walked around the desk and opened the bottom drawer. She retrieved an ugly ashtray from the very back and put it in front of Margaret. Then she pointedly emptied the coaster and wiped out the residue with a tissue. "However, this is a very simple restraining order specifying that you, Margaret, and any employee or associate of the Ausbrook Confectionery is prohibited from developing a recipe known as Chocolate Peppermint Kisses until such time as the court can determine the interest of the plaintiff, Hezekiah Brown, in the aforementioned recipe." Dana dusted her hands. "And that is all it says."

Will didn't look convinced. "But what about our work in the experimental kitchen?"

"What about it?" Dana sighed, cautioning herself not to rise to the level of hysteria displayed by her mother and by Will. "Anything already going on in the kitchen is not affected. The order applies only to this particular recipe and we're not working on it now, anyway." She glanced at Margaret. "We're not, are we?"

"No." Margaret crossed her legs and leaned back against the chair, her eyes fixed murderously on the ceiling. "I cannot believe Ki did this."

"I can't believe it, either." Will mimicked Margaret's posture, but he couldn't quite capture her angry expression.

Dana had a sudden wish for Rick to be here to see the spectacle. "I don't know why you're so angry, Margaret. You wanted to face Ki in court and now you're going to. You have a hearing date set and everything."

"I wanted Ki to have to face me in court, Dana, not the other way around."

"You'll each get your say."

"That isn't exactly what I wanted."

Defeated by her mother's illogic, Dana gave up her perch on the desk corner and went to the more comfortable chair behind the desk. "The court has no interest in what you want or don't want, Margaret. A judge is only going to consider the legal aspects of your quarrel with Ki. And that means, pure and simple, that the judge will decide whether both of you, one of you, or neither of you, own that recipe."

"I know how it works, Dana." Margaret breathed out a smoke ring, then stubbed out the cigarette. "Will I get an opportunity to tell the judge all the shenanigans Ki has tried to pull? Like stealing the Recipe and trying to buy the company anonymously?"

"You have no evidence that Ki did either one of those things. In fact, you—"

"This will be in the papers." Will straightened in the chair, his eyes round with a new concern. "The publicity will not be good, Margaret. Sales will go down. Costs will go up."

Margaret quelled his gloom and doom with one glance. "For heaven's sake, Will, this is not a national scandal. Besides, publicity is almost always good for business. Sales will go up. Isn't that right, Dana?"

"You've been in this business a long time, Margaret, and if you say sales will go up, then I'm certain sales will go up." She smiled at Will, simply because she was tired of frowning. "There's nothing to worry about, Will. Margaret has everything under control."

"I have a bad feeling about this." Will sat forward, nervous tension replaced with eagerness. "Maybe we should reconsider selling. That anonymous offer still stands and we could—"

"*What* are you talking about?" Margaret's temper rose to its legendary fame. "I thought you understood my feelings about that, Will. Apparently I must say this one more time. If I ever again hear you mention selling this company as a viable option, you will, at that moment, be unemployed. I consider such talk treasonous and you will govern yourself accordingly."

Will's mouth hung slack with astonishment, but righteous indignation soon pulled it shut with a snap. "I understand," he said. "I was under the impression that I was part of the management of this confectionery. Obviously I was mistaken." He stood and for the first time Dana wanted to applaud his performance. At last, he was standing up for himself. She even thought for a minute he might quit. But he didn't. "I'll take my opinions and plans for the Ausbrook Confectionery out of this room and let you two get on with ruining it over some stupid forty-year-old lovers' quarrel." He gathered the roll of computer printouts and marched to the door, where he turned for a last parting shot. "And Margaret, you need to quit smoking."

Dana could have cheered for young, ineffectual Cousin Will, who at last had managed to say something that needed to be said.

Margaret, obviously, felt no such admiration. "Idiot. He's such a kid."

"We all are, at one time or another." Dana folded her hands and relaxed a little. "And he's right. You do need to quit smoking."

"Don't start with me, Dana."

That pretty much clarified the mood, Dana thought and watched Margaret reach for the package of cigarettes. But she didn't light up. She only held the pack, turning it over and over in her hands. "So, are you prepared to represent me in this case, Dana?" she asked finally.

"I've requested special permission to appear in the Missouri Courts and I have every reason to believe it's now simply a matter of receiving official notification."

Margaret nodded and continued turning the cellophaned package in her hands. "Yes, I know about that. My question, however, is personal. Are you prepared to represent me in this case?"

Dana sat very still, hoping against hope that her mother was not going to turn this into an ultimatum. "I am prepared to represent you to the best of my ability, Margaret."

"Then you'll agree with me that since Rick Stafford has now shown his true colors by siding with Hezekiah, you should have nothing more to do with him."

A furious trembling began in her fingertips and worked its way through her like a tidal wave of incredulous anger. Dana stood, hardly aware that she did so, and braced her hands on the desktop. "I am twenty-eight years old, Margaret. I am perfectly capable of making my own decisions and my own mistakes without any assistance from you or anyone else. From now on, you will either treat me as an adult or you will find someone else to be your whipping boy. I won't stand for this anymore.

"I came here to work at the confectionery because I hoped it would give us a chance to form a real mother-daughter relationship. I thought you might want that, too. My God, Margaret, we've never even spent the sum total of two hours in getting acquainted. It's always you telling me how things ought to be done, how things will be done, how it's best for me if I do things your way. You never once have asked me what I like, what I hope to do, what I dream about. I'd like to ask you those questions. I'd like to know who you are when you're not running this business. I'd like to talk to you sometimes as if you were a friend, not my mentor and not my mother." Dana ran out of words abruptly and wished she could withdraw some she'd already said. But Margaret had pushed her too far this time and there was no going back.

"I'm sorry if I've hurt you," Dana said, because she had to apologize. Childhood training went deep, although it couldn't completely obliterate her dignity. "But you needed to hear that, Margaret."

The cellophane crumpled in Margaret's hand, but her expression remained tight and unrevealing. "I had no idea you felt that way, Dana."

"I know." In a single, smooth movement, Dana picked up her briefcase, slung her shoulder bag on her arm, and walked to the door. She stopped there and made a half turn. "One more thing, while we're clearing the air. My love life is none of your business, but before you go casting any stones at it, you'd better take a good, hard look at your own."

Dana stepped into the hallway and tried to still her trembling with several slow, deep breaths. She half expected her mother to follow her, tossing more futile arguments into the already crowded air. But there was no sound from inside her office. No footsteps. No commanding voice. No protests. Nothing.

There was a certain element of satisfaction in reducing Margaret to speechlessness, Dana supposed. But she felt none of it today. None, whatsoever.

Chapter Ten

Dana spent the next several hours walking through Silver Dollar City, Branson's famous theme park. She needed somewhere to go and she couldn't go home, so she chose a place where she could blend into the scenery and think. Not that she really wanted to think, but the scene with Margaret had upset her, left her feeling alone and agitated, with no outlet for her anger.

She'd finally done it. She'd given her mother a piece of her mind...and now she wanted it back. It had needed to be said, Dana knew that, but what consequences would arise from it? Would anything change? Would Margaret now miraculously understand the type of relationship Dana so desperately wanted to build? Dana walked and thought and replayed the scene a dozen times until she finally left the park to seek out the only person she knew she could talk to.

It took a full hour and a half, including the forty minutes spent inching along in Branson's summer traffic, to find Rick. Dana tried his office first, but he wasn't in. After two wrong turns and one backtrack, Dana found his house and then wondered what she would say if he were there.

"Hi." It was the best she could manage when he opened the door. His shirt hung open, revealing a strip of bronzed body above the waistband of well-worn jeans. Dark blond hair curled across his chest and down the flat planes of his stomach. Dana swallowed a tremulous panic as she raised her gaze to his. "Working at home this afternoon?"

"Thinking about it." He smiled and pulled wide the door. "I see you're not working at all. Don't tell me you've been fired." He said it flippantly, with a thread of casual teasing.

"Life should be so easy." Dana tossed her jacket and purse on the hall table and walked into his living room.

"If you haven't been fired, you must have quit." Rick followed and stood, barefoot, in the open entrance. "And your mother threw a fit."

"*I* threw the fit."

Rick arched his eyebrows. "Do you feel better?"

"No." Dana turned to look out the window. "No, I feel awful. Just awful."

"Do you want to talk about it?"

It was the most soothing question she'd heard in days and Dana felt calmer just knowing Rick cared enough to ask. "I've done this to you a lot, haven't I, Rick? I cried on your shoulder many times during the summer we were together."

"A few times, maybe."

Dana gave a rueful smile. "You know Margaret and I butted heads at least every other day that summer. And now when it happens, I rush to cry on your shoulder again."

"You haven't even touched my shoulder."

"I really told her off, today. She..." Tension drew her fingers into fists. "I don't think I've ever been so angry.

She told me that since you'd shown your true colors by representing Ki, I should have nothing more to do with you and that she'd known all along *my* love life was going to get in her way. I should have quit right there and then. If there was some way to resign as her daughter, I'd do that, too."

Rick shoved his hands into his jeans' pockets and gave a low whistle. "I take it she received her notice of hearing today."

"Yes. And I hate to say this, but she's crazy, Rick. My mother is crazy."

He offered a gentle smile to her distress. "At least it isn't catching, Dana."

"It wouldn't make any difference if it was. Margaret doesn't get close enough to me to pass on a common cold. The only thing I'm ever likely to catch from her is criticism." Dana felt tears wad up in her throat, and she turned away from Rick until she could bring them under control. This was not what she'd intended to do. She'd just wanted to see Rick, be with him for a while. Crying over her mother's lack of maternal instincts was not why she'd come. "Look, Rick, I'm sorry. I didn't mean to drop all this on you. It's not your problem and . . ."

His arms came around her and pulled her back against him, his breath felt warm and sweet as it touched her hair. "You haven't dropped a single tear on my shoulder, Dana. I'm a little disappointed."

"Sure you are. I've interrupted your plans for the evening with my sob story and you're disappointed." She patted his hands where they clasped her waist and released a soft sigh. "Thanks, Rick, but you don't have to put your honesty out on a limb for me."

"What are friends for?" His mouth nuzzled a titillating circle just below her ear and Dana caught her breath.

"And I am disappointed. When you used to cry on my shoulder, I knew exactly how to comfort you."

She melted. Whether it was the tantalizing whisper of his tongue on her skin or the memory of other days and other comforts, Dana couldn't determine. But she knew that she wanted his touch, his kiss, his embrace. Anything and everything he would give her, she wanted.

The pattern of her breathing increased as she began to turn in Rick's arms. His hands moved at her waist, guiding her. His lips trailed across her cheek, tempting her. Dana brought up her hands to cup his face, but got distracted by the expanse of bare male chest and let her fingers splay across his skin. She shivered with the touch and lifted her mouth to his.

He claimed her kiss softly, with a gentle pressure that didn't come close to matching the fierce longing whipping through Dana. She wanted more. An intangible, inarguable demand to be closer, ever closer to him, swept over her, and her heart pounded with the intensity of that need. But although Rick held her tightly, although his lips caressed hers with unspoken hunger, she knew he was holding back. Even the seductive dance of her tongue, teasing, mating with his, did not fan the fire to an engulfing flame. He was warm to her touch, but there was no fever heat to his caress, no burning need in his kiss. She drew back, sought the answer in his eyes, and found only an emerald shadow of desire.

"Now, do you feel better?" His solicitous smile was a lie. Dana sensed it, but didn't know how to challenge it.

"Was that all you intended to do? Make me feel better?"

"Of course. I hate to see you upset."

Dana pulled out of his embrace, grappling to understand the distance Rick had so carefully placed between them. "Rick, I—" In search of a reason, the words stumbled. Silence fell and Rick moved to escape it.

"Would you like something to drink? I have soda or fruit juice, even a wine cooler, if you'd prefer that." He took several judicious steps away from Dana and toward the kitchen. Why had she come here this afternoon? Just when he'd decided his heart was too much at risk with her. It would be all too easy, fatally easy, to fall in love with her again and then where would he be when her year was up? He kept moving toward the kitchen. Once there, he placed two glasses on the counter and glanced up to see Dana hesitating in the doorway. "What will it be?" he asked as smoothly as he could. "Soda or juice?"

She regarded him with eyes of sable darkness and shadowed confusion. One slender shoulder lifted in a shrug. "I'll have whatever you're having."

With a nod, Rick carried the glasses to the refrigerator and filled them with ice, wishing he knew what to say to put their relationship back on a strictly friendly footing. "Ki will be sorry he missed you, Dana. He's gone to Springfield for a couple of days."

"To escape the heat?" She pushed a wispy strand of disheveled copper hair behind her ear and Rick fought a powerful longing to bury his fingers in the thick, lustrous strands.

"It's just as hot in Springfield. There's only a thirty-mile difference."

"No, it's hotter here. Trust me."

Rick snapped the lid on the container of orange juice and handed Dana one of the drinks. "Oh, because Margaret's here, you mean."

"Yes." She accepted the glass and for just a moment, caution flickered in her eyes. "Rick, I . . ." Dana backed up to the door frame as if she needed the support. "I don't want to go back to her house. Could I...stay here? Just for tonight?''

Tension jerked through him in quick alert. Why had he told her Ki was gone? The thought brought him up short. Did he really need protection from Dana? Was his heart that close to the edge?

"Dana." It was all he could think to say.

"I'll sleep on the couch. Really, it won't..."

Apparently his distress registered clearly on his face, because she stopped in midpersuasion and the room pulsed with emotion. "You know and I know, Dana, that if you stayed here, you wouldn't sleep on the couch."

Her finger traced a path along the rim of her glass. "I've thought about that, Rick. I've thought about it a lot since the other night at your office and—"

Don't say it, he thought. *Please, Dana, don't—*

"—I'd like to stay."

Rick felt his heart slide into overdrive, beating like a frenzied drummer in solo performance. If he'd been pressed to choose just one wish, he'd have chosen to spend a night with Dana. Over the past ten years, dreams of her had awakened him more than once, had left him lonely and hungry for a consummation he would never know. And now, here was his unstated wish, offered freely and without restriction and he had to say no. His body throbbed an outraged protest, but he had to say no.

"I can't let you stay, Dana." He took a step toward her, but stopped with the upward tilt of her chin. "I've thought about it a lot, too, and I wish the situation was different. But it's not." She refused to meet his gaze and Rick felt compelled to offer some explanation. Anything except the truth that he was so close to being in love with her, he couldn't think straight. "There are ethics involved here, Dana. Ki trusts me and even though he would never say a word about it, I'd know that in some small way, I'd compromised his friendship. I can't do that.''

"The other day you said the lawsuit didn't make any difference." Her eyes swung to his in challenge. "You told me not to confuse business with personal feelings. It didn't matter, you said."

"Well there's a big difference between spending a few hours with my family and spending the night together."

"Oh, I see. As long as our relationship doesn't get *too* personal, then the question of ethics doesn't enter the picture. Is that what you're trying to say, Rick?"

He was no longer sure, but he knew she was escalating things into a quarrel to cover the rejection she felt. "You know exactly what I'm saying, Dana. You're angry with Margaret, so professional ethics aren't a high priority for you at the moment."

Dana straightened. "Oh, in other words, sleeping with you would be a means of getting back at my mother. Is that it, Rick?"

Anger stiffened his jawline. "Isn't it, Dana? Isn't that why you're here now? Not because you want me, but because you know Margaret disapproves and you want to hurt her any way you can?"

"That's not fair, Rick." Dana came away from the door. "Margaret has nothing to do with the way I feel about you."

"Then why did you come here this afternoon?"

Her lips formed a tight line. "I wanted to talk to you. I needed to be with you. There aren't that many people I can talk to, Rick. Not like I can talk to you. I'm sorry if you thought—" Orange juice sloshed from her glass and splattered on the tiled floor. She looked at it, brought her eyes up to meet his. "I'm sorry."

He wanted only to reach for her, to take her into his arms and soothe the loneliness from her body, to make her know he cared, would always care. He reached for a towel and dropped it over the spill. "I didn't mean to argue with you," he said. "I meant—" Rick didn't know what he'd meant to do. He'd never intended to drag out the old resentment. Or to place her mother squarely between them as he'd often accused Dana of doing. "Look, forget I mentioned Margaret. You're right. She really has no place in this."

Dana bent to wipe the juice from the floor. "Is it because I ran away before, Rick?" She rose slowly, twisting the dish towel in her hands. "I know I should have told you I was going back to Philadelphia, but I was confused at the time. And scared. I didn't know what to do. So I did what Margaret wanted...I left and hoped you'd understand." The towel went limp as her eyes met his. "I've been honest with you this time, Rick. I told you I'd be leaving at the end of the year. This time we both know the consequences. Doesn't that make a difference."

It made one hell of a difference, Rick thought, but he'd be damned if he'd admit it to her. "This has nothing to do with what happened before. There's a strong attraction between us, Dana. I can't deny it. But that's not a strong enough reason to toss aside the convictions and principles I live by." Several strong reasons coursed through him, but Rick blocked them with reason. Making love to Dana would create more problems than it could possibly solve. "Besides, I'm still a traditional soul. I think love and commitment ought to come first."

What could she say to that, Dana wondered. It wasn't as if he'd left her any option except to respect his answer, whether she believed him or not. "All right, Rick."

She set her nearly full glass of juice on the counter. "Thanks for listening to my troubles. I'll see you around."

She barely made it to the doorway, before he stopped her. "You don't have to go, Dana."

"Don't I?" She made the effort to create a wry smile. "If I stay any longer, I may compromise your principles and I wouldn't want to do that."

Rick frowned at her oversimplification of the issues and Dana felt some small degree of satisfaction. "I didn't mean—" He stopped, backed away from whatever he'd started to say. "All right, then. Let's go out somewhere. Will you have dinner with me?"

"Won't that create a conflict of interest? A question of ethics?" She couldn't help rubbing just a little salt in the wound. He deserved it, she thought, for believing she felt no love and no commitment toward him. She did. It wasn't enough, perhaps, to alter her life's plan, but she wasn't without principles herself. "Don't you think that's a big risk?"

He eyed her with a frustration clearly building in intensity. "We'll go to Springfield."

"Ki's there."

"Then we'll go someplace here."

"And take a chance on Margaret seeing us together? Good idea, Rick. That will teach her a lesson."

His patience snapped and Dana felt the backlash. "You make it very hard to be your friend, Dana."

"Maybe friendship isn't what I want."

"Maybe it isn't." He raked his fingers through his hair. "But it's all I'm offering. Life is a pay-as-you-go account, Dana. You can't use people like you use a charge card and expect your small monthly payments to earn any interest. Ten years ago, I offered you everything I had in the world, but that wasn't enough for you. You listened to Margaret and beat a path back to the rich guy in Philly. That was your choice and I accepted it. But don't expect me to invite you back into my life and charge it off to experience when you leave. No, thank you."

"I've tried to apologize for that, Rick. I thought it—"

"No apology is necessary, Dana."

"So what do you want me to say?"

"Yes or no." Rick brought his glass to his lips and drained the juice in one long swallow. "Yes, you'll have dinner with me or no, you won't."

"Don't you think it would be a little hard to eat and glare at each other at the same time?"

He put his glass in the sink and when he turned around, his mouth wore the beginnings of a smile. "We'll take turns. I'll arm wrestle you for the honor of eating first."

"What about professional ethics?"

"Okay, I'll arm wrestle you for those, too."

Dana tried to catch hold of her fading annoyance. "This is serious, Rick."

"Yes. My stomach is taking it very seriously."

"So, do we just forget everything that's been said here?"

Rick hitched his hands in his back pockets. "No, Dana. We won't forget, but we don't have to talk about it. We're on opposing sides of a lawsuit and we owe our respective clients some measure of professionalism, so we won't mention the lawsuit. I have no desire to talk about it, anyway. Do you?"

"No." Dana shook her head, still struggling to get past his words to the real reasons behind them. "What about Margaret?"

"I promise not to mention her, either. If you feel the need to do so, well, I'll certainly listen. As to our other difference of opinion—" Rick held her gaze with quiet determination "—we won't discuss that, either."

"That doesn't leave us much to talk about."

"I think it leaves us a vast territory for exploration, except for the tab. Dinner will be my treat."

Dana couldn't believe she was falling for this. She had all but asked him to make love to her, been flatly rejected and now, not five minutes later, she was agreeing to have dinner with him ... and enjoying the prospect. Which only showed how vulnerable she was. "Don't expect me to argue with you over the bill, considering that I'm going to have to get an apartment."

Surprise edged into the corners of his mouth. "An apartment? Of your own?"

"You don't expect me to invite you to move in, do you?"

He smiled. "No. I was just surprised. I've always thought of you as, well, as a princess who needs someone to cook and clean and make her bed." He paused. "Sorry, I guess that isn't very flattering, is it?"

She sighed, wishing she still had the energy to get mad. "Since I always pictured you as living like a hermit, eating out of cans in a filthy hut with dirt floors and furniture, I suppose I can't be offended." She moved forward, caught the middle button of his shirt with her fingernail and gave it a flip. "Button your shirt, Robinson Crusoe, and let's go have dinner. You can help me plan my apartment-hunting strategy."

"You're serious?"

"Yes. About dinner and about finding an apartment. After today and the scene with Margaret, it's clear to me that I have to get out of her house. Living with her is not accomplishing what I—'' Dana interrupted herself. "Oops, sorry. Her name just slipped out."

"I didn't hear a thing. Give me about ten minutes to change clothes."

Dana nodded. "Point me toward the powder room, please. I need about ten minutes to change my attitude."

His finger stroked her cheek, then moved guiltily away. "There's nothing wrong with your attitude. You've just been through an emotional upheaval today. Chalk it up to clearing the air and you'll feel better."

Dana didn't think so. Getting an apartment would help ease the situation with her mother. Independence was a great equalizer and Dana wished she hadn't moved into Margaret's home in the first place. But an apartment, independence, wouldn't change the more-than-friends, less-than-lovers nature of her relationship with Rick. He was determined to be her friend, but she sensed the powerful emotions operating beneath the surface. It would never work.

And why should it? Dana questioned a few minutes later as she stood in front of the bathroom mirror. Neither of them really wanted to be just friends. Rick might not admit it, but his kiss had told her as much and the quickening response of her body to his every touch spoke to her of feelings much deeper than friendship. So why was he adamant?

Ethics was only a small part of it. The lawsuit itself wasn't ethical, it was a quarrel. Pure and simple. And it wasn't even hers and Rick's quarrel. She respected Rick for respecting Ki's feelings, but in this case, it was an excuse to keep the relationship from becoming too involved, too personal. She was ninety-nine percent sure of that.

Dana found a brush and began combing the day's tangles from her long hair. It curled around her shoulders like shiny satin. Brown eyes stared back from her reflection with a touch of sadness, a glimmer of challenge. Rick was afraid she'd hurt him again. It was the only answer. He'd mentioned the past, her running away, so it must still bother him. But she had been honest this time. He knew she'd be leaving. She'd told him up front about the job in Philadelphia. But that was months away. And in between were a lot of days . . . and nights.

With a frown, Dana leaned closer to the mirror and examined her reasoning. She did love Rick. It might be just the memory of their fateful summer together and her need for an anchor at this time in her life. It might be something much deeper. But how was she to find out? How could she convince Rick that a relationship didn't have to last forever to be of value?

It presented a problem, Dana admitted. But if she could learn the business of candy making, if she could change her mother's mind about her role as a parent, if she could establish some independence on Margaret's private territory . . . well, then getting around Rick's stubbornness ought to be a simple enough project. One that she could approach with logic and enthusiasm. Not tonight, perhaps, while her emotions were still wounded by his rejection. But in a few days, when she felt stronger and more confident.

Dana nodded, satisfied that at least she had a plan. She'd bring Rick around. He didn't stand a chance.

Chapter Eleven

During the next two weeks, it occurred to Rick that Dana was trying to seduce him. It wasn't anything she said, although her mood was often flirtatious, and it wasn't any particular thing she did. It was just a look in her eyes, a slightly coquettish tilt in her smile, and a subtle enticement in her movements. Rick found the thought fascinating and he spent a lot of time analyzing the possibility.

But it wasn't until one evening, at one of the supper clubs where he'd invited Dana to dance, that he was sure of her intentions. He was flattered, a bit confused, and quite a bit irritated that she should make up her mind to win his heart just when he'd made up his mind not to be won. Still, the prospect of being wooed was entertaining. He couldn't help but wonder to what extent she'd carry the game and how far he'd let it go.

It was so characteristic of Dana to pursue him when she thought he was beyond reach. Rick decided if he'd been a little wiser in the ways of courtship ten years before, he'd have played hard to get and forced Dana to run after him. But he hadn't been wise. He'd been hers for the asking and she'd known it. There was probably an element of egotism in her flirting even now. She'd never, he was certain, entertained any idea that he might not always be hers for the asking. And it wouldn't do her any harm to learn that she couldn't manipulate his actions or his emotions.

"Thank you," she said during one of the brief lulls in between songs. "I never realized before what a wonderful dance partner you are, Rick."

He smiled modestly. "I've had a lot of practice."

"Have you? I'm not surprised. I'll bet you're the number one heartthrob of Taney County." Her voice inflection flirted with him, the expression in her eyes teased and tempted him.

Rick was ashamed of himself for feeling so pleased by her effort. "I might have been before Ki came home, but now... I'm sure he'll take over the number one spot."

"Don't worry, Rick. I'll console you." Dana's lips curved with soft amusement as the music began and she melted into his arms again. "After all, what are friends for?"

Rick had a fair idea at that moment that his days were numbered, but he pulled her close and let the sweet fragrance of her perfume tangle into his senses. The "Heartthrob of Taney County" was about to be taken out of circulation. At least for the next several months. His heart wasn't going to stay cool and unattached. He could already feel it drifting her way and he'd be damned if he could stop it. There was some consolation, he supposed, in knowing that this time, at least, he'd go down fighting.

AT THE END OF AUGUST, Dana decided that if she ever wrote her autobiography, she would devote an entire chapter to "The Great Apartment Search" and she would subtitle it, "Frustration City." It wasn't as if she had an abundance of choices. For all the influx of summer tourists, Branson was a small town and although it overflowed with motel rooms, apartments seemed to be an endangered species. Dana looked at several, but the better ones didn't fit her budget and the others... well, she wasn't going to move into just any old place.

Margaret viewed the search as another rebellion, a childish retaliation against imagined grievances, and she missed few opportunities to chide Dana about it. Charity felt personally responsible for Dana's decision to leave and went to great lengths to make her point. Rick, on the other hand, seemed eager for Dana to be out on her own and made lists of possibilities for her to look into. He teased her about her pickiness, bought housewarming gifts for her, and offered to teach her how to make a bed.

For the first week or so, Dana took it all with a grain of salt. She didn't have a lot of time to spend on apartment hunting, anyway, and she certainly didn't care what Margaret did or didn't think of the plan. Rick's teasing was turned away with a laugh and a promise to get even.

But as the days wore on, Dana found it harder to ignore the subtle pressures. She wasn't about to tell Rick that her budget was scrunched by her college loans and she wasn't about to ask Margaret for a raise, either. Her responsibilities at the confectionery continued to increase and her time for apartment hunting narrowed until it all but disappeared. August was hot. Tempers were short. And Dana finally resigned herself to staying with Margaret. At least until the tourist season ended and affordable housing became a reasonable possibility again.

"There's just nothing available, Rick," she told him one early September evening as they ate dinner in a local café. "Maybe in a couple of months I'll be able to find something, but I just don't have the time to hunt for an apartment right now."

He studied her over a glass of iced tea. "What about Springfield? You could commute."

Dana had already thought of that and discarded the option as time-consuming and too expensive. "I'd have to get up too early in the mornings."

"I wouldn't think thirty minutes of sleep would be worth what you have to put up with."

"It's not so bad. Really. Ever since that last quarrel, Margaret's been cranky, but relatively quiet. I'm not saying the situation is great, but it could be worse."

"I thought you said every one of the employees is tip-toeing around the plant like mice scurrying to keep out of the cat's path."

"That's still an apt description." Dana grinned and speared a bite of salad. "You should see Will Burton looking for someplace to hide when Margaret makes her daily trip through the factory. And just when I thought he was beginning to show signs of real character, too. I don't know why he's suddenly so nervous. She doesn't say that much to him. Not when I'm around anyway."

"Do you accompany Margaret on the daily tour?"

"Not lately. She's still mad at me."

"Because of the apartment business? Or because you're still seeing me?"

Dana shrugged. "A little of both, I imagine. But whatever her reasons, at least she's backed off some, and staying at the house isn't as uncomfortable as it was before. We pretty much avoid each other and that works as well as anything. Charity says we're as sulky as two cats sharing the same sleeping quarters, but I don't think that's such a bad arrangement."

"So you're definitely giving up on finding an apartment?"

Dana set down her fork and frowned across the table at him. "Why does that bother you, Rick? Why does it make any difference to you where I live?"

He couldn't tell her. Rick wasn't quite sure of his reasoning himself. But it had seemed like a symbol, Dana's declaration of independence from her mother's control, and he'd wanted to see it happen. He'd wanted it for her sake and for his own. "I thought it was what you wanted, Dana. I was only trying to help."

She reached over and touched the back of his hand. "I appreciate it, Rick. Really. But for now, I'll just have to stay where I am."

He almost, *almost* offered to let her use the spare room that Ki had used before he moved out. But Rick knew the suggestion would only open a Pandora's box of problems, for his ethics as well as his heart. So he changed the subject. "Do you suppose we could get Ki and Margaret to agree to a settlement if we locked them into a room together? Then they'd have to argue it out and we wouldn't have to go to court."

"They'd just argue until they were both little balls of goo."

"No, Dana. They'd wind up as one giant Peppermint Kiss."

Dana gave in to the tickle at her funny bone. These times with Rick were about the only time she really laughed. She often met him for lunch or dinner, sometimes both, and Dana knew he enjoyed it as much as she did. She'd tried, with little success, to move the relationship beyond platonic, but Rick remained frustratingly friendly. It wasn't that he'd stopped touching her or kissing her, but he just didn't let her get too close. She was aware of the distance, but oddly, was not offended by it.

Their "dates" consisted of long talks, long walks and short, refreshing bursts of laughter. All in public places with plenty of people around. They shared anecdotes of their separate college days, compared opinions on philosophy and argued points of law. At some moments Dana felt she was getting to know someone completely new; at others she felt Rick was someone she'd known forever. And just as she'd conclude he was right and they should stick to uncomplicated friendship, he'd kiss her long and lingeringly and she'd spend the night with restless dreams. It was not, Dana often told herself, the way she'd planned to spend the summer.

DANA TAPPED on the half-closed door of Margaret's office and walked inside. There was an odd smell in the room and she sniffed the air.

"For heaven's sake, Dana, anyone would think you were part bird dog." Margaret folded her arms on top of her desk and indicated a chair with a glance. "What are you sniffing at?"

Dana sat. "There's the strangest odor in here. It smells like...pickles. Dill pickles."

Margaret lifted a bowl and extended it across the desk. "Want one?"

"No. What are you doing with pickles?"

"I'm eating them." Margaret set the bowl back where it had been and picked up a slice, which she popped into her mouth. "The doctor suggested I substitute the sour taste of pickles for my craving for nicotine."

It took considerable effort for Dana to process the information. "You've quit smoking?" she said in utter disbelief. "I don't believe it."

"Neither do I. It's the worst idea I've ever had."

"No. Oh, no. It's great. You know I've wanted you to quit for—"

"Save the enthusiasm, Dana. This is only the second day."

Dana eyed the bowl. "How many pickles have you eaten?"

"A quart, give or take a few."

"And how many cigarettes have you had today?"

"Two." Margaret swept a hand through her short curls. "All right, five, but yesterday I'd had eight by this time, so we're not counting. All right?"

"Fine." Dana kept staring at her mother, trying to probe beneath the surface to what had prompted her to stop smoking, something Dana had been begging her to do for years. "Why did you decide to quit now? I'm glad, you understand. But curious."

"Stay curious, dear. Eating these pickles is bad enough. I refuse to hold a postmortem on my motivation." Margaret reached for the bowl and another pickle. "Did you have some reason for coming in here, Dana, or did you just follow your nose?"

"I was looking for Will. He was supposed to bring me last month's vacation report for the factory personnel. Today's Friday and I have to get the payroll sheets to accounting by Wednesday of next week. I need those figures."

Margaret returned her attention to her own paperwork. "Try the lunchroom. Will spends half of his time there, courting Rachael. Love ruins productivity. There ought to be a law regulating it."

Dana wasn't about to touch that subject. With a murmured thanks, she turned to leave. "I hope the pickles work," she said from the doorway. "I'd like for you to live to a ripe old age."

"I'm not sure it's worth it. I hate pickles."

Dana smiled and left the office.

When she entered the lunchroom, the chatter dropped to a low hum. She was used to that response. After all, she was the boss's daughter, not just one of the employees. However, over the past few weeks, she'd taken to having her breaks with the workers. For one thing, Dana wanted to meet the people who worked in the confectionery and for another, she sensed a growing unease among the employees. Gossip seemed to be bouncing around the factory like a Ping-Pong ball. Dana never quite caught all of a rumor, but she heard enough to realize that most everyone believed the Ausbrook Confectionery was up for sale.

No one said it directly to her, but she knew enough about people to realize something was bubbling beneath the surface and that had to mean there was a fire somewhere nearby. In her own way, Dana set about to put the fire out.

After getting a soda from the machine, Dana spied Will and Rachael sitting in a corner of the room. She didn't wait for an invitation to join them. "Hi, Will." Dana drew up a chair. "I was looking for you."

Will's blue eyes went wide with surprise as he spun around in the chair. "What for?"

"Vacation reports." Dana leaned forward to see around Will to Rachael's slight form. "Hi, Rachael."

The girl's dark hair swung forward, covering a shy and pretty face. "Hi."

"They're on my desk," Will said. "I'll bring them to you after I finish my break. Anything else?"

Dana popped the tab of the cola can. She didn't much like his attitude, but decided it wasn't worth mentioning. "That ought to do it." A glance around the room changed her mind. As she sipped her cola, she phrased another question. "You know, Will, I overheard a conversation the other day. Some of the employees apparently think the confectionery is going to be sold. And they seemed to think it had something to do with the Peppermint Kiss recipe. Has anyone mentioned that to you?"

Will's hand moved to close over Rachael's fidgety fingers. Her glance darted to his, then away. Dana noted the reaction and wondered if it meant anything or was simply a means of connection between the couple. Will continued to hold Rachael's hand as he answered. "I've heard the rumors, Dana. But I don't know what you're going to do about it. People are going to think what they want to think. And I'll tell you right now, that lawsuit is not doing the confectionery any good."

"I wouldn't have thought many people would know much about the lawsuit, Will."

A mirthless chuckle escaped his lips. "That's because you're a big-city girl, Dana. You don't know much about small towns. Anything that affects the Ausbrook Confectionery, affects the people who work here."

"I'm aware of that, Will. What I don't understand is how the rumors about selling the confectionery got started."

He lifted a wide shoulder in a careless shrug. "Rumors come and go. It'll pass. You'll see."

"After the lawsuit is concluded, you mean?"

Will smiled and released Rachael's fingers. "When your mother stops acting like a fool."

A sharp, quick annoyance rose inside her and Dana didn't try to hide it. It was one thing to establish a basis for communication with the employees. It was quite another thing to let such blatant disrespect pass without comment. "Margaret is your employer, Will. You need to remember that when you talk about her."

"Hey, I'm never allowed to forget it." Will's face flushed pink as he pushed his chair away from the table. "I was hired to be part of the management team, you know. No one seems to remember that."

"You take it too seriously, Will." Dana tried to soothe his injured ego.

"And you don't care, Dana. All you want to do is sit in your office and hope no one asks you to make any decisions. Everyone knows you hate the confectionery. It's a big joke, you being named vice president. So drop the pretense of being interested in what goes on around here. I'm on to you, even if no one else has figured out that you're just spying for Margaret."

Dana was thunderstruck. She watched Will stalk out of the lunchroom with Rachael at his heels and wondered if her cousin, no matter how many times removed, was more of a Burton than she'd ever given him credit for being. He'd just displayed signs of the infamous temper. But as to why, Dana didn't have a clue. He obviously resented her position in the company, but to accuse her of spying for Margaret...

Was she? Dana touched her finger to a droplet of cola on the rim of the can and considered the idea. No. She was searching for answers, that was all. Her loyalty did lie with Margaret, but that hardly meant she was disloyal to the employees. She liked them, the ones with whom she'd had a chance to become acquainted, anyway. She liked the camaraderie that existed among the workers, even though she knew she could never really have a part in it. That was the price of her position. But Will resented her position. He'd just made that clear.

Had he expected to be named vice president? Had she somehow usurped his place in the company structure?

It seemed preposterous when she considered his youth and lack of charisma. On the other hand, Will loved the business and knew far more about the everyday details of running it than she did. Had Margaret promised him position and power and then handed it over to Dana instead? Was that the source of resentment and unrest stirring in the ranks of the employees?

With a sigh, Dana rose and dropped the can of soda in the trash receptacle. She should have taken more management courses in college. Then maybe she'd know how to handle the problem on her own. But as it stood, she had little choice except to discuss it with Margaret.

As she walked out the door, though, Dana took a detour in the direction of the experimental kitchen. It was possible that Rachael might shed some light on Will's motivations, providing that he wasn't around to squeeze her fingers and interrupt whatever she started to say. Intrigued by the thought, Dana approached the shiny, stainless-steel doors and signed in before entering the test kitchen.

The gleaming efficiency of the room always pleased her, even though it was smaller than it had seemed when she was a child. Developing and testing recipes wasn't as high a priority as it had been in the early days of the confectionery, before a solid product line was established. The kitchen was still important, but now, there was often only one employee working on a single project whereas the staff had once been three and four times that size. Rachael was the only employee in the kitchen when Dana entered.

"Hello again, Rachael. Just thought I'd stop in and see how things are progressing," Dana said to open the conversation. "Will told me you were doing very well here."

Rachael had pinned up her hair, knotted it in a cute style on top of her head, and without its sheltering veil, her face was heart shaped and pale. "I like the work," she said. "Gram laughs 'cause she never thought I'd be good in the kitchen."

"That just goes to show what grandmothers know, doesn't it?"

"Gram does have strange ideas," Rachael confided as she rinsed utensils in the sink. "She thinks Will's too old for me, but there was eight years difference between her and Grandpa. And four between my mama and daddy."

"I guess Charity worries because you're only eighteen."

"Old enough to work." Rachael turned off the faucet and began loading the dishwasher. "Old enough to know what I want."

"Have you thought about attending college?"

"Not much. Will has a degree, you know. From the junior college. He's really smart."

Dana nodded, only because of Rachael's expectant look. "He certainly was upset back in the break room."

"He ought to be vice president. He has real good ideas, but your mother doesn't listen."

"Oh, she pays more attention to what he says than he thinks she does."

Rachael shook her head. "If she did, he wouldn't . . ." The sentence trailed into silence. "I better get busy, Dana. Will doesn't like for anyone to stand around talking when there's work to do."

Dana wished Rachael had finished what she'd started to say, but she could hardly press for an answer without creating an issue. "You're right, Rachael. I have quite a lot to do myself." She waited until Rachael walked over to the long metal table in the center of the room and then followed. "What are you working on today?" she asked.

"It's the new project," Rachael said with obvious pride. "Will fixed it with your mother so I could work on it. Get hands-on experience, you know."

"Oh, that's good. What is the project?"

Rachael glanced at her in surprise. "Don't you know?"

"I don't think so. What is it?"

Rachael frowned. "It's the Recipe. You know. The one you were talking about to Will."

"The Peppermint Kisses?" Dana's voice rose and she had to force it to a lower tone. "Is that the project?"

Rachael nodded, her expression suddenly cautious. "I'm not supposed to talk about it to anyone, but I thought you knew, Dana. I mean, you're Margaret's daughter."

"Margaret knows about this?"

Rachael dropped a slotted spoon and it clanked against the table. "Well ... yeah."

So Will had been right, Dana thought with increasing agitation. Her mother was acting very foolishly, indeed. She knew better than to use that recipe. She had to be aware of the risks she was taking.

"Thanks, Rachael. I'll find out why no one told me about the project." Dana spun on her heel, an equal mix of frustration and aggravation carrying her out of the kitchen and up the stairs to Margaret's office.

This time she didn't bother to knock or to wait for Margaret's acknowledgment. "I need to talk to you." She plunged into the words like a swimmer in a relay. "I was just in the experimental kitchen talking to Rachael and she said a very interesting thing.''

"That's hard to believe.'' Margaret continued writing on a legal pad. "Rachael usually has nothing of any interest to say. Girls at her age act so silly. Even you did, Dana.''

Crossing her arms low at her waist, Dana let her own Burton temperament rise to the surface. "Age obviously has no monopoly on silliness, Margaret. The new project Rachael's working on is a shining example of that.''

A scowl cut across Margaret's face as she looked up. "I'm trying to stop smoking, Dana. If you have something to say, spit it out and don't irritate me with rhetoric.''

"The Recipe, Margaret.'' Dana stepped forward. "I'm talking about the chocolate-peppermint recipe.''

"What about it?''

"Don't play innocent. You know that recipe is being tested right now in our kitchen.'' Dana slapped her hand against a pile of paperwork on her mother's desk. "Do you realize what will happen if anyone finds out what you've done? You could go to jail. The confectionery could be closed. Lock, stock and barrel. Everything. And you won't have so much as a threadbare defense to present in court.''

"I don't know what you're talking about, Dana. The Peppermint Kiss recipe was stolen. My half of it, anyway. How could we be testing it in the kitchen?''

"Rachael just told me she's working on it.''

"You must have misunderstood.''

"Come on, Margaret. Why would Rachael say something like that if it wasn't true? How would she even know anything about the Recipe if she wasn't working on it?''

"Well, she can't be and that's all there is to it. I don't care what she told you. My recipe is gone. Ki stole it."

Dana brushed at a stray wisp of hair on her cheek. "You've had that recipe for forty years, Margaret. Don't tell me you couldn't duplicate it by memory. All of it. Your half. Ki's half. The whole thing."

"If you're accusing me of disobeying the restraining order and going ahead with the development of that recipe, Dana, you'd better have more evidence than a statement made by a silly child."

Dana's heart began to pound. She hated these confrontations with her mother. How did she always manage to end up on the opposite side of any issue? "You've been telling me for months to think like a businesswoman, so don't turn this into a personal vendetta. I just told you what *I* was told. Now if putting two and two together brings me to a conclusion that offends you, I'm sorry. But that doesn't change what I was told or the fact that you're the only person who knows what goes into that recipe."

"Not the only person," Margaret stated crisply. "Ki knows."

"Oh, well, of course." Dana sat in one of the chairs, angry that this couldn't be discussed in a rational manner. "Let's figure out some way to blame Hezekiah Brown for what's going on in our experimental kitchen. He probably broke into the confectionery in the dead of night and left the Recipe for Rachael to test."

"I don't like your attitude, Dana."

"Oh, really? Perhaps my attitude would be more to your liking if I just ignored the evidence and let you face a contempt of court charge."

"There isn't any evidence, Dana. There can't be. I don't care what Rachael said to you."

"I suggest you get Rachael up here and ask her," Dana stated. "Since it's obvious you can't trust me to tell you the truth."

"Oh, and I suppose your bursting in here to accuse me of flaunting the law shows your enormous faith in me?" Margaret opened a drawer and pulled out a pack of cigarettes. "I don't know why you have to make everything so personal, Dana. Lord knows we have enough trouble being mother and daughter without arguing over the business, too."

Dana sat forward, hands clenched, arms trembling with the effort, hurt warring with anger inside her. "I can fix that. You'll have my resignation within the hour."

Margaret's gaze tangled with Dana's. "Please, Dana," she said on an exasperated sigh. "Let's not bring in emotional blackmail on top of everything else. If you want to resign, then resign. But for heaven's sake, don't do it because you're angry with me. I don't appreciate your threatening to quit every time you disagree with something I've said."

Emotional blackmail worked both ways, Dana thought. If she resigned now, Margaret would call her a quitter. Will would say it only proved his point, that she didn't care about the confectionery. A month ago she would have taken any legitimate excuse to resign. Maybe even as little as an hour ago, it wouldn't have mattered to her what anyone thought. But something was wrong, and Dana couldn't just walk away. No matter how angry she was.

Margaret finished lighting the cigarette and put it to her lips for a long drag. "Now tell me what Rachael said that made you think she was working on the stolen recipe. And keep this unemotional, all right?"

Dana fought down a rebellious impulse to argue further. She was an adult, she reminded herself, regardless of how often Margaret treated her like a child. With a conscious effort, she straightened her posture, lifted her chin and recited the gist of her conversation with first Will, then Rachael. Margaret sat with a meditative frown for several minutes. Then she pressed the Intercom switch on her phone.

"Page Will Burton and tell him I want to see him in my office," she said and broke the connection. "I wasn't aware there was any unrest going on among the workers, Dana. How did you happen to pick up on it?"

"I'm observant. I listen. I couldn't help but overhear some of the comments the employees were making." Dana rubbed the curve of her eyebrow with a restless fingertip and told herself she would not give in to the threat of a headache. "You've been preoccupied with the lawsuit. Apparently we haven't kept it as quiet as we thought we did. For the most part the rumors going around have to do with the sale of Ausbrook Confectionery."

"Why wasn't I informed? I told Will to keep an ear out for that sort of thing."

"I don't know why Will didn't tell you, Margaret, but I didn't say anything because . . . well, because you and I haven't been talking much lately. And I thought I'd see what I could find out first, before I came to you."

"And?" Margaret's frown was impatient.

"I found out that most of the employees believe the confectionery will be sold."

Margaret tapped a pencil lead against the desk. "I'll bet Ki is behind that."

Dana offered her mother a skeptical look and won a grudging admission. "Maybe not, but he's being too quiet, Dana. I know that man and he's up to no good."

"Well, if he gets wind of what's going on downstairs, he'll be perfectly justified in taking decisive steps to stop it."

"That's why I have a lawyer, isn't it? To keep him from taking those steps?"

Dana sighed. "I can't work miracles, Margaret. You'll have to take the responsibility for violating the court order."

"I didn't violate it, Dana." Margaret stubbed out her cigarette and reached for another. Then she shoved the pack aside and reached for a pickle, instead. "This is not a good time for this to happen. How can I quit smoking with a labor dispute and a lawsuit hanging over my head?"

"A labor dispute is the least of your worries, Margaret." She glanced toward the door to make sure Will wasn't there yet. "Did you ever promise Will a position as vice president?"

"I don't think I've ever discussed that with him. Why? Are you planning to bequeath your job to him when you resign?"

That wasn't fair, but Dana didn't say so. "He seems to think if it wasn't for me, he'd be vice president."

"Nonsense. I've given Will a great deal of freedom and responsibility in supervising the confectionery, but he doesn't have enough life experience to step into your office."

"Wait." Dana pinned her mother with an inquisitive gaze. "Was I imagining it or did you just compliment me, in a back-handed sort of way, for having the necessary experience to handle my job?"

"Don't bait me, Dana. You know I think you're eminently qualified to do anything you want. But I'm not in the mood to pass out pats on the back. Not today."

All Dana wanted was one. One pat. One small sign of her mother's approval. But she didn't say that, either.

"You wanted to see me?" Will entered and waited just inside the door. "Is there something—" He saw Dana and stopped. For a second his gaze became shadowed and wary, then he turned his full attention to Margaret. "What can I do for you?" he asked, his tone easy and uncomplicated.

Dana watched him closely as Margaret sketched out the facts. When she put the question to Will about the new project being developed in the kitchen, his expression went round with surprise. "Margaret, you know all about that. It's the Peppermint Kisses. You told us to start working on it a month or so ago."

"I don't recall saying anything like that. Besides, we don't have a recipe for the chocolate peppermints."

"We didn't have a recipe for the caramel creams, either, but we developed one." Will glanced at Dana, as if he was confused by the conversation, as if he were saying, *See? I told you she was acting strange.* "That's why we have the experimental kitchen. To develop new recipes."

"Even if I did initially okay the testing," Margaret said. "Why did it continue after the lawsuit was filed?"

Will's hand swung outward in an innocent gesture. "Dana said the restraining order didn't affect any project already in progress in the kitchen. I assumed she knew what she was talking about."

Dana felt the stab of his animosity. "Will, you read the order. You knew it referred to the recipe for the Chocolate Peppermint Kisses. How could you think it would be

all right to continue testing any candy recipe even re-
motely similar to it?''

His smile was far from pleasant. "I don't get paid to
think, Dana. I follow orders. Margaret's orders."

"Then here's a new order for you, Will." Margaret
stood behind her desk, her small stature taking prece-
dence over Will's larger form. "You'll go immediately
downstairs to the kitchen and suspend any and all activity on that project. It must be stopped now. Then I'd like
to see you back here in my office. There seem to be a few
matters I need to clarify for you."

"Certainly." Will dipped his head in a nod, but Dana
saw the flash of annoyance in his eyes, caught the stiff set
of his shoulders. "If you don't mind, Margaret, I'd prefer you not pull Rachael in on this." His gaze flicked to
Dana with a moment's recrimination. "She's only following instructions and I hate to see her take the blame
for someone else's mistake."

"And whose mistake do you think it was, Will?" Dana
moved to the edge of her chair, intent upon his answer.

His expression cleared as suddenly as it had clouded.
"I wouldn't presume to make that determination, Dana.
It isn't my responsibility."

He left the room at an easy pace, and Dana watched
him go with some confusion. She assumed he'd figured
out that Rachael had mentioned the Recipe and that she,
Dana, had come straight to Margaret, which was of
course what had happened. But why was he angry about
it? He had to know that the "new project" represented a
grave risk to the confectionery's future. Why hadn't he
taken steps to stop it before now? Unless...

Dana did not like the idea that occurred to her. She
didn't like it one bit. "You ordered the testing, didn't
you?"

"What?" Margaret frowned at Dana as she lowered herself into the big executive chair that all but dwarfed her slender body. "You heard what was said, Dana. I don't recall telling Will to proceed with developing the Recipe. On the other hand, I know I did discuss it with him." Margaret idly tapped a fingernail against a crystal paperweight. "Of course, I'll take responsibility for the mistake, and we'll hope to high heaven that Ki doesn't get wind of it."

Margaret seemed oddly vague, as if she were contemplating something in one part of her mind while talking about something entirely different. Dana's stomach twisted with sick frustration. She knew suddenly that Margaret had intentionally disobeyed the court order and gone ahead with developing the Recipe to spite Ki. She'd defied Dana's legal advice, scorned Dana's continued efforts to protect the case from any question of ethics and disregarded Dana's personal sacrifice. And representing Margaret in the lawsuit *had* demanded a personal price from Dana, not only in her relationship with her mother, but in her relationship with Rick as well.

How could Margaret have done it? Dana shifted uncomfortably in her seat, watching her mother stare at the desk. And yet Dana knew she had. Who else could have done it? Margaret *owned* the confectionery. She was *in charge*. She alone had the authority to initiate a new project in the experimental kitchen. Even if she'd originally given the okay before the restraining order was filed, Dana couldn't conceive of a reason not to have made sure the project stopped once the lawsuit had begun. Margaret was undeniably a risk taker, but Dana had never known her to take foolish chances. Not before Hezekiah Brown had entered the picture, anyway.

Dana stood abruptly. She couldn't continue to sit here and stew over Margaret's apparent duplicity. It was upsetting, to say the least. And confusing. And ironic, Dana supposed, that she'd come home to spend time with her mother, only to discover she was more of a stranger than ever.

"Where are you going?" Margaret glanced up, but it was obvious her thoughts were still someplace else.

"I don't know. I need some time to think."

"You're not going to rush out and tell Rick about this, are you?"

A chill of hurt and anger stiffened Dana's spine. "It would serve you right if I did."

Margaret's eyes glistened, but Dana didn't care if it was with anger or tears. "You don't trust me, do you, Dana?"

For a long moment, Dana faced her mother in silence. "No, Margaret, I guess I don't. Lack of trust seems to be a family failing."

Dana turned to leave, but just as she reached the door, Margaret called to her. "Dana? Are you going to resign?"

A lump the size of her disappointment rose in her throat and Dana forced herself to swallow it. "I'll let you know," she said and walked quickly from the room.

Chapter Twelve

Rick noticed Dana's car as soon as he turned into the driveway, and a smile tipped one side of his mouth. He'd picked up the phone at one point during the day to call her and ask if she'd like to meet him somewhere after work, but an incoming call had interrupted and he hadn't had another opportunity. To imagine that Dana had picked up on the thought anyway pleased him.

He parked his truck and followed a hunch to the backyard, where he found her. She stood on the back deck, a couple of feet above his head, and he paused to observe her. With her hands pressed on the railing and the breeze off the hills teasing her hair, she looked like a Monet painting, all soft color and subtle outline. The dress she wore was pale blue and folded gently around her body; the skirt alternately sculpted her thighs and drifted in gentle circles around her calves at the discretion of the light wind. Rick admired the curve of her legs, the slender hips that tapered to a narrow waist, the soft fullness of her breasts.

She was, had always been, beautiful in his mind. He had touched her, loved her a thousand different ways in his daydreams. In midnight's silence, he had whispered the soft promises of a lover and awakened alone. In broad daylight, on a crowded street, he'd caught a glimpse of copper-colored hair and his pulse had quickened at the thought of her.

And until this moment, he'd pretended the woman of his fantasies was nameless.

"Dana." He called to her and she leaned over the rail.

Her hair swung forward and she brushed it back, behind her ear. "Hi," she said. "I've been waiting for you. I hope you don't mind."

"No." He shook his head. Didn't she realize how much he liked coming home and finding her waiting? Not that she did it so often he was accustomed to it. He couldn't afford that, not when he knew it would end soon. "Have you been here long?"

"A couple of hours, I guess. I didn't want to interrupt you at your office, so I've just been enjoying your view."

"You could have gone inside."

"You never gave me a key."

Rick made no comment on that. His heart was pounding fast, as if he'd been running, and he felt warm and cold at the same time. He jogged up the steps, but the physical distress didn't subside with movement. It merely increased as he came close to Dana. He fiddled with the lock on the glass-paneled back door, unable to control the nervous agitation of his fingers. Finally it was open and he stepped inside, holding the door for her. She moved past him, and his breath went with her. The wild-flower scent of the Ozark Mountains lingered on her and meshed with a fragrance that was uniquely hers. It made him think of sunlight and sheets that had been hung outside to dry before being laid upon his bed.

He experienced a flash of fantasy in which he swept Dana into his arms and laid her upon his bed. He buried his face in the satin spill of her fiery hair and immersed himself in the silky contours of her body. He made long and passionate love to her, heard the murmurs of her surrender, and finally consummated a desire that had haunted him through too many lonely nights.

Rick tossed his car keys on a low table and tried to banish the seductive imagery. He couldn't afford to dwell on such thoughts. He'd been so careful to be her friend, so diplomatic about their "platonic" relationship. He'd vowed to protect his heart from her at all costs and he had. Until now. Until he'd looked up a moment ago and gotten tangled in feelings he'd hidden so well he'd almost forgotten they were there. And suddenly he'd known all his effort was for naught. He'd never been in danger of losing his heart to her. Oh, no. His heart had belonged to her all along.

With a start, Rick realized Dana was speaking to him and he hadn't heard a word. He concentrated, trying to catch up with her meaning.

"—and I had to get out of there before I said something I'd really regret." She smoothed her palm against the top of the sofa. "So I came here."

"So I see." It wasn't hard to pinpoint her problem and Rick decided there were worse topics to divert his thoughts. "When are you going to stop letting Margaret get to you, Dana? You shouldn't allow her to upset you."

"I can't seem to help it, Rick. Especially when she—" Dana turned to the window, crossed her arms and stared outside.

He restrained a sigh. She needed to talk and it was his responsibility, as the *friend* he'd worked so hard to become, to let her do so. "Especially when she what?" he asked.

"I can't tell you."

"You can talk to me about anything, Dana. You know that."

She said nothing and he moved to stand behind her, forcing his voice past a thick longing to find a light, teasing tone. "Nothing your mother has said is going to hurt my feelings, Dana. What can she do? Take away my birthday?"

"It's not like that." Dana made a half turn and Rick fought the impulse to draw her into his arms. "It's—" She paused, frowned and finally sighed. "I did come here to talk it out. But I realized before you got home that I couldn't."

A surge of resentment went through him. Had he worked so hard at winning Dana's trust only to be shut out by some nasty remark Margaret had made in a moment of anger? Had nothing changed except his own realization that he wanted Dana, her heart and soul, her fears and dreams, even if it meant taking on her problems with her mother? He moved away from her. "If you don't want to talk, we won't talk."

"Rick, please. I shouldn't have said anything. I just—" The emotion in her voice brought his gaze to hers and the resentment faded as quickly as it had come.

"It's all right, Dana," he said, even though nothing felt right to him at the moment. "I understand. I'm your friend, remember?"

"Yes. You're a good friend, Rick. Probably the best friend I've ever had. And I'm trying to be satisfied with friendship. Really, I am. But I can't help wishing—" Her voice faltered there, and Rick could hardly hear for the hard, fast beat of his heart. Their gazes locked, sharing the memory of a long-ago intimacy that had never reached fulfillment; communicating ten years of wondering "what if" and "why"; declaring a desire sharpened by restraint.

Rick had been so sure that friendship was the best, the only relationship he and Dana could share. He'd thought he could handle that without getting in over his head, without falling in love. But he was more deeply in love than he'd ever been. Maybe Ki had been right. Maybe it was time to trade his dread at losing her again for the memories that could be packed into the next several months. Maybe this moment was one of Life's rainbows that he needed to catch and hold until it faded from his grasp. And maybe, just maybe, in the months to come he could change her mind.

Ethical questions melted as he covered the distance in two long strides and pulled Dana, almost roughly, into his arms. His lips found hers a second later and tasted her hunger for his kiss. Her mouth opened beneath his and her tongue invited him to deeper pleasures. Pleasures he could no longer deny himself or her. He felt the smallness of her hand cup against his chest, capturing the fierce, rhythmic pounding of his heart, and he didn't know how he'd kept this moment of passion at bay for so long.

Dana's thoughts spun with the suddenness of Rick's embrace. She hadn't expected it but, oh, how she'd longed for his touch. For years, she'd been reaching for him, in her thoughts, in her dreams. She'd imagined time and again how it would feel to be cradled in his embrace, to explore without restrictions the length and breadth and strength of him, to know at last the mystery of belonging to him and with him. And now, reality blended with fantasy and she surrendered without a murmur of protest.

Rick lifted her, carried her away from the sunlit window to the shaded center of the room. He knelt there, taking his lips from hers as he laid her gently on the plush carpet. With hardly any effort at all, he pushed aside the sofa table and made a space for himself beside her. Braced on his arms, he sought her gaze, and Dana trembled at the need she saw in his emerald eyes.

"Will you be satisfied with this, Dana?" he whispered as he lowered his mouth to the pulsing hollow of her throat. From there he seared her skin with moist kisses that left her weak and aching in places he hadn't begun to touch. "Or this?" He nipped at her earlobe, his tongue made a slow circle beneath her ear. She went tense at the sensual stroke and shivered with intense desire. When he moved, she followed. Her hands found the rich luxury of his hair and moved down to stroke the smooth muscles of his back. And always her lips waited for his return.

Buttons, zippers, belts and snaps became seductive challenges for fingers that obeyed a hidden agenda, a need to explore further without hindrance or impediment. Dana hardly knew when Rick moved to shrug off his shirt or when she sat up to pull the dress up and over her head. She only knew she wanted to make every effort to accommodate him, just as he made it easy, so easy, for her to undress him. Warm, willing flesh met hers and she settled down and down into the feel of his bare arms around her bare shoulders, the sensation of his hair-roughened chest moving across her breasts, the awareness of his lean, muscled body pressing against her with tender demand.

He pulled her onto her side, draped a long, naked leg over her hips and paid homage to the tiny tremor of passion hovering at the corner of her mouth. There was an overpowering intimacy in the provocative kisses he offered for her approval. And she did approve. Oh, yes, she approved. Just as the ache inside her became a burning need, he began to slow the pace of her desire without ever once letting the urgency slacken.

When his hand stroked downward from her shoulder, along the soft underside of her breast, past her midriff to her waist and the curve of her hips, Dana sighed and allowed her hands the freedom to explore him as he explored her. His chest was broad and covered with the texture of wiry chest hairs. She braided her fingers into the wiry clusters, seeking the taut, miniature nipples almost hidden by the curls. A low moan escaped his throat as she found them and his kisses bloomed into full, impassioned entreaties.

He pressed her onto her back as his lips left hers to capture the rosy tip of a breast. She arched into the delightful imprisonment and brought her hands to rest on either side of his face. Her eyes closed as the swirling pleasure made sunbursts of sensation throughout her body and meshed into a single throbbing heat. But again Rick banked the fire, only to let it build again as he covered her body with kisses and the massaging caresses of his hands.

The seduction lasted long past her surrender and Dana drifted on a stormy sea of emotions too long denied and too wondrous to rush through. She thought at one point that she heard Rick whisper, I love you. She thought she answered in the same way, but a fierce yearning spiraled past her consciousness and she wasn't sure that the love words hadn't been an illusion crafted from desire and need.

It didn't matter. Not when he found his place inside her. Not when she enclosed him with the love she'd kept in her heart just for him. Only for him. She loved him and she knew he loved her. Words were unnecessary as their bodies flowed together like two colors that blend into one.

THE TENDER AFTERGLOW of lovemaking lingered far into the night. They spoke, as new lovers do, in gentle voices accompanied by soft touches and intimate smiles. And when they tired of talking, they made love again. It was all, and more, than Dana had imagined it might be and she wanted the night never to end. She told Rick as much and his answer came in a sweetly poignant kiss that touched her heart as no words ever could.

"I'm satisfied, now," Dana said in a drowsy whisper sometime after midnight as she curled against him on the bed.

He pressed his lips to the top of her head and lay awake long after she fell asleep. So Dana was satisfied, he thought and wished he might feel that way, too. But in making love to her, he'd taken an irrevocable step toward being dissatisfied for the rest of his life. He loved her, but he knew she wouldn't change her mind. The feeling would stay with him forever, but in a few months Dana would leave, returning to a life that had no place for him. She would leave, he knew, no matter what he did.

To be fair, he believed she did love him. But he wasn't foolish enough to equate love with commitment. They were two separate things and Dana had demonstrated a lack of sticking power more than once in the time he'd known her. He wasn't even sure she would stick to her original plan of staying until spring. For all he knew, she might pack up and leave tomorrow.

No matter which way he tossed or turned, the doubts went with him and evolved into troubled dreams in which Dana said goodbye again and again. And each time, he was left alone, declaring his love for her, offering her all that he had, and discovering over and over that it wasn't enough.

Rick awoke tired and drained. Her kisses revived him and he took comfort in the caresses she initiated, but he couldn't recapture the sheer enjoyment of her that he'd experienced the night before. In the sharp morning sunshine, it was harder to believe that the memories would be worth the heartache. No matter how much he loved her, he couldn't get past the knowledge that he was going to lose her . . . again.

"I had no idea you'd be grumpy in the mornings." Dana joined him at the breakfast table. "I somehow had the idea that you woke up as cute and cheerful as you are later in the day."

"Cute is never a problem," he said. "But cheerful is another matter."

"It's a good thing you have compensating qualities. I'm not used to cheerful faces at breakfast, anyway. Margaret is usually cranky. Did I tell you that she's trying to quit smoking?"

"No. What brought that on?"

"I have no idea." The corners of Dana's smile turned down. "I have no idea why she does any of the things she does."

"You didn't tell me what happened to upset you yesterday."

Dana brought the glass of juice to her lips, but set it on the table without taking a drink. "No, I didn't."

"Oh, come on, Dana. I told you that nothing your mother has to say will bother me. I can handle Margaret."

"It's not something she's said, Rick. It's something she's done and, as much as I want to talk it over with you, I can't."

Rick frowned. "If it has to do with the lawsuit, I think, under the circumstances, you could forget that I'm Ki's lawyer."

It was tempting. Dana wanted to confide in him, she wanted someone else to know what Margaret had done and to understand why she, Dana, was so angry. And there was an element of self-righteousness involved, Dana realized. She had done what she had promised to do. She'd taken the proper legal steps to represent Margaret in court, even though the suit was so obviously a nuisance case. She'd listened to unfair accusations about Rick, argued to no avail and put aside her own judgments, in order to keep the peace between herself and her mother. And all the time, Margaret had been developing the candy with no regard or consideration for Dana's principles or sense of honor. It wasn't fair. It simply wasn't fair.

But that didn't relieve her, or Rick, of their separate obligations. She couldn't tell him without breaching her personal code of ethics. And no amount of sympathy was worth that. "I'll tell you this much. I've decided to resign as soon as the hearing is over. I . . . have to."

Rick's mouth went taut and his eyes darkened to a stormy green. "So you're going back to Philadelphia?"

It didn't sound like a question, but Dana answered. "I won't have a choice. Without a job or a place to live . . ." She paused, allowing him a chance to offer her an alternative. If he'd only ask her to stay . . .

"I can't say I'm surprised." Rick got up from the table and carried his plate to the sink. "I didn't believe you'd make it a full year. I didn't really think you'd stick to the job as long as you have."

"Well, thanks for the vote of confidence, Rick." Dana pushed away from the table. "It's nice to know you—" The words choked her. It wasn't nice to know. He'd expected her to quit. Even after what they'd shared last night and during the past few weeks, he couldn't give her the benefit of the doubt. He certainly would never believe she was resigning her job at the confectionery as a matter of principle.

"There's no need to be defensive, Dana. Not with me."

"Then what should I do, Rick? Thank you for bed and breakfast and be on my merry way?"

"You're the one who set the conditions. Not me."

"Oh, and I suppose you were an innocent victim? I'll bet you're surprised I stuck around long enough to make it a one-night stand."

"You know that isn't true."

"I don't know anything anymore, Rick. Not what you want. Not what my mother wants. I'm not even sure I know what *I* want."

He gave a tight laugh. "You've always known what you wanted, Dana. Success, which in your book equals complete independence and unlimited wealth, remember? You're the princess. You can do whatever you please. What more could you want?"

She stared at him, dismayed and angry. "A friend, maybe? One person who believes I'm an adult and doesn't stand around waiting for me to make a mistake? Someone who cares about who I am rather than what I used to be or what I ought to be?" The silence pulsed with tension, every tiny sound in the kitchen became a litany of accusations and regrets. "I expected better from you, Rick. Acceptance, if nothing else. This must be my year for disappointments."

"There was a time, Dana, when I expected acceptance from you and was disappointed." Rick kept close control over his voice and fought the impulse to apologize and soothe his bitter words with love. But she had already chosen to leave. This time, at least, he would hang on to a piece of his pride. "And as the saying goes, what goes around comes around," he said, hating the hurt that made him say it, hating himself for loving her so long and so futilely. "I guess it's just your turn."

Dana couldn't believe he'd said such a thing to her. It wasn't like him. But then maybe she didn't really know Rick, either. "I guess you're right," she said, refusing to unleash the Burton temper and hurt him because he'd hurt her. Turning, she walked into the bedroom and began gathering her things. She exchanged the shirt she'd borrowed from Rick for her blue dress and the rest of her clothes.

She knew when he came to stand in the doorway. She sensed his regret at having said the hateful words and his frustration in not being able to call them back. And she told herself that she would not now, or at any other time, let him see her cry.

Somehow, Dana didn't know how she managed it, she walked past him, out of his bedroom and out of his house. She shed not a single tear on the drive to Margaret's home. It was only when she reached the solitude of her room that the emotions enveloped her and she gave in to the hurt. But the storm passed quickly and Dana found herself staring out of the bedroom window, going over and over the endless questions in her mind.

At length she decided she had to get away from Branson. She needed time to think and she knew of only one place to go, only one person who could offer any perspective on life in general and her life in particular. The idea of seeing her father was soothing in itself, so after debating her options, Dana made a reservation on a flight leaving Springfield early that afternoon. She phoned Leonard Ausbrook and asked him to meet her at the airport in Philadelphia, then she packed a bag. Lastly, she left a note for Margaret, explaining that she was going to spend the weekend with her father and wouldn't be in the office on Monday. Considering the number of weekends she'd worked, Dana felt she deserved one day of vacation. She was deliberately vague about her return, although she'd made a reservation for a Monday-morning flight back to Springfield. She thought it might do Margaret some good to wonder when and if she'd come back to Branson. She hoped Rick might wonder, too. But she knew in her heart he would never even know she was gone.

Chapter Thirteen

The news broke on Monday morning, but Dana knew nothing about it until she got off the plane in Springfield that afternoon. Even then it was only by chance that she caught the story on the car radio. Her hand was on the dial, ready to switch stations, when she heard the announcer mention Ausbrook Confectionery. Several reports of food poisoning had been traced to Ausbrook candy and the matter was under investigation.

Dana searched the airwaves for more details, running the radio dial through its repertoire of stations again and again, but she found only one other news report. The information there was just as sketchy, and by the time she reached Branson at two o'clock, Dana had imagined a host of scenarios, all centered around a common error. She simply couldn't conceive that the confectionery might have any responsibility in the poisonings. There had to be a mistake.

It was evident by the number of cars in the parking lot that whatever the mistake might turn out to be, it wasn't going to be resolved without some publicity. Dana parked in the employees lot, but didn't escape the attention of Lathan Williams, the local newsman. "Dana," he called. "Can you give us a statement for tonight's news?"

She shook her head and hurried inside the building, only to be surrounded by employees and dozens of anxious questions.

"What's going to happen, Dana?"

"Do you know if it's true?"

"When will the FDA people get here?"

"Is the confectionery going to be sold now?"

Dana offered what reassurances she could, but she had no answers and soon broke away from the cluster of employees and ran up the stairs to Margaret's office. She entered the room to find her mother standing at the window overlooking the confectionery below.

"Margaret?"

"Oh, Dana. I'm glad you're here." Margaret's greeting was warm and welcoming, even though her expression was taut. "I called Leonard this morning, but you'd already left." She paused and when she spoke again her voice was rough with strain. "I wasn't sure you were planning to come back at all."

Dana set down her briefcase and ran a hand through her disheveled hair. "I left you a note saying I wouldn't be in to work today."

"I know. But I was afraid— Well, that's neither here nor there. You're back now." She sank into the big leather chair. "I suppose you've heard the news?"

"Just a sketchy newscast on the radio."

"That's about all there is to know. There have been five reported cases of food poisoning. All of them occurred here in Branson. Four tourists and one of our employees."

"Who?"

"Will Burton, of all people." Margaret rubbed her temples with her index fingers. "No one is critically ill, thank God, but, of course, there could be other cases.

More serious symptoms. We just can't know what will happen at this point.''

"What's been done up until now?" Dana sat down and realized suddenly how very tired she was. "Have you talked with the health department? Did you issue a statement to the press?"

"Whatever the news media report is hearsay. They've talked to some of the victims' families, taken the human-interest angle. The kind of publicity we definitely do *not* need." Margaret's gaze swept the top of her desk blankly. "As to the health-department people, I'm waiting for a telephone call now to confirm their initial findings."

"Is there any chance they'll phone to tell you it's all a mistake?"

Margaret almost managed a smile. "No, Dana, I don't think it will be nearly that simple. It's amazing, really, how the health inspectors are able to trace the sources of food poisonings like this. Unfortunately our candy is the prime suspect."

"I don't see how it can be, Margaret. We have so many safeguards. How could something like this have happened?"

"No system is fail-safe, Dana. When you're dealing with a food product, there's always the possibility of contamination. It could be a tainted ingredient, a fluctuation in temperature, a human error during production. We won't even know what we're dealing with until the lab is through testing. That could take several days."

"But how do they know it's our candy that caused the problem?"

"When Will came down with similar symptoms to the other cases, it narrowed the possibilities simply because he hadn't eaten at any of the restaurants or bought food from any of the vendors in the area. The only common denominator was a chocolate Truffle, a candy we sell a lot of in Branson.''

"Yes, I know the sales figures. Have you recalled the candy?"

Margaret nodded. "I've been very cooperative with the officials, Dana. There isn't much else to be done."

"What about the employees? Have you talked with them, explained the situation?"

"No. I've been in this room all day, trying to figure out how the hell something like this could have happened."

Dana felt the first stirring of sympathy. Margaret looked so lost. "I'm surprised you're not yelling about Hezekiah Brown. He's gotten the blame for everything else that's gone wrong around here."

Margaret wove her fingers into a tight hand clasp, then slowly worked them loose. "I'm a foolish woman, Dana, but I'm not a total fool. Ki might do a lot of things to get what he wants, but endangering lives is not one of them. To accuse him would be the same as saying he sabotaged this confectionery and, regardless of what I've said about him in the past, I know he didn't do that."

Dana considered her next words before she gave them voice. "Dad and I had a long talk about you. And about Ki. And about what happened between you. I think, perhaps, that you never stopped loving Ki, that you've always had some regret because you didn't marry him."

"Regret?" The word was a whisper, but it was full of emotion. "I don't know about that. I suppose I must still care about him or I wouldn't be so upset with him after all these years. But, Dana, I loved your father. I've never known a finer, more decent man. We just couldn't live together. I hope you understand."

Dana nodded, but the lump in her throat wouldn't let her answer. Leonard had helped her come to grips with her feelings about the divorce and Margaret's role in it. He'd helped her more than she could ever say. "I think one of us ought to talk to the employees, Margaret, before this crisis explodes in our hands."

Margaret made no move to get up. "You handle it, Dana. I'm trying to quit smoking."

Dana stood, walked around the desk, put her hands on her mother's shoulders and bent down to kiss her cheek. "I love you, Mom. Hang in there. I'll take care of public relations."

A pin, dropped in the room, would have echoed all the way to Philadelphia, Dana thought as she walked to the door. But a daughter had to begin somewhere.

"Dana?" Margaret said and Dana turned around expectantly. "Would you have someone bring up another jar of pickles, please?"

"Dill?"

"As sour as they make them. And Dana?"

"Yes?"

"I love you, too."

Dana's smile came from the heart. "I know."

FOR THE NEXT HOUR Dana talked to employees, in groups and individually. She did her best to calm their worries and in the process found that she became calmer. As a group the employees offered their support, but Dana knew there were a few who turned a deaf ear to her pleas for loyalty and fairness. She accepted that, just as she accepted the need to present herself as a strong leader with the ability to withstand pressure.

It was somewhat easier to be the vice president of Ausbrook Confectionery, Inc., when she spoke to the newspeople. To their intense questioning, she offered simple replies and made no concessions to those determined to place guilt at the company's door. She was confident, serene and positive and when she finally called an end to the session, she was exhausted. Just as she turned to go upstairs to her office, she looked across the room and saw Rick.

He stood by a display case, tall and straight and as solid as a ship's anchor. He was wearing a suit; a neat, conservative gray suit with a pastel shirt and a splash of tartan plaid vest visible where the jacket fell open. No cowboy hat mussed the dark gold hair, not today, and the habitual mischief in his green eyes had been replaced with a concern that Dana knew was for her. She smiled, forgetting the hurt and confusion of their last meeting, recognizing only a very basic need for his soothing friendship.

When he moved toward her, she saw he was not alone. Hezekiah Brown had dressed for the occasion, too. His suit looked a little tight and the thin necktie looked more than a little uncomfortable, but he seemed to have put on authority with the suit and Dana didn't doubt his ability to handle any crisis.

"Hello," she said as the two men reached her. "Aren't you two dressed up. Were you expecting this to be a funeral?"

Ki shuffled his shoulders beneath his tan jacket. "Hell, no. I came to fight. Just show me where to report for duty."

Dana managed a weary smile. "I appreciate the offer of assistance, gentlemen, but you'd better leave before the general finds out you're here. She could order a firing squad and frankly I'm too tired to protect you."

"Protect us?" Ki gave a gruff chuckle and turned to stare at a young, red-faced reporter who had tiptoed up behind him. "Somethin' I can do for you, young man?" Ki asked.

The kid grinned, partially filling out his thin cheeks. "Just doing my job, Mr. Brown. You *are* Hezekiah Brown, aren't you, sir? The owner of London Country Candies?"

Ki raised his eyebrows and pursed his mouth in a low whistle. "You found me out, boy. Now don't say that too loud. We don't want those other cubs hornin' in on your scoop, do we?" He slung his arm around the reporter's skinny shoulders and began walking with him toward the door.

"You look tired." Rick opened the inner door for Dana and waited for her to step inside. When it closed behind them, she thought he surely could hear the pounding of her heart in the narrow confines of the hallway. "Has it been a long day?"

"Yes," she said simply and started up the stairs. "It's been a very long day, so please, Rick, talk Ki into leaving before Margaret sees him. She's been through a lot today, but she still could throw a tantrum if he tries to talk to her."

"Margaret asked him to come, Dana." Rick quietly followed Dana up the stairs. "I was there when she called."

"What? I knew she was in an odd mood, but... Did she invite you, too?"

"I just tagged along to find out what was going on."

The door below opened and closed with a decisive click. "Head for the hills, young 'uns, before another hotshot reporter gets our scent." Ki took the steps two at a time and caught up with Dana and Rick at the top of the stairs. He took in the hallway and offices with one glance. "Where's Maggie Jane?" he asked.

Dana indicated the first doorway and Ki went through it. Rick glanced at Dana, then waited for her to move into the office ahead of him. Margaret stopped pacing and greeted Ki without a smile. "Thanks for coming," she said. There was nothing in her words or her expression to indicate her feelings, but something had changed.

Dana tried to figure out what it was as she listened to Margaret explain the situation. There was a new energy in the room, an intangible ebullience at odds with the serious nature of the discussion. The idea struck Dana that Margaret and Ki were lovers. Maybe not in a physical sense, but certainly in other ways. She glanced at Rick to see if he'd noticed anything and found herself lost in his eyes. Her lover, she thought. In all ways. For all time. How could she have lived so long without knowing that?

Rick turned away and Dana felt suddenly lonely. There were things that must be said between them. She knew that and wished now was the time. But it wasn't. Her first obligation was to Margaret, her duty lay with the confectionery and the employees. Declaring her love for Rick would have to wait a while longer.

"I'm sorry, Ki," Margaret was saying. "I misjudged you. I thought you stole my half of the Recipe. I thought you were trying to cause problems for me here at the confectionery."

"I can cause you problems, Maggie, without half tryin'. Why would I go to the trouble of working at it?"

Margaret pulled open her top desk drawer, looking for cigarettes, Dana suspected, but she closed the drawer again without taking anything from it. "I realized this morning," Margaret continued, "that there is something very wrong here." A humorless smile flashed across her mouth. "Over and above the fact that the health officials are breathing down our backs at the moment. I think the Ausbrook Confectionery has been sabotaged, Ki. I know that's a serious charge and I haven't even a shred of evidence. It's just a feeling. Intuition, maybe. Anyway, you're in the candy business. You know as much about it as I do. Will you help me get to the bottom of all this?"

Ki didn't hesitate. "All you had to do was ask, Maggie. Now, let's go over everything from the beginning."

Ki walked over to the window and began asking questions about the confectionery. Margaret answered, giving information that, given the opportunity, Dana would have advised her mother not to give to anyone. But no one asked her opinion and after a few minutes, Dana motioned to Rick. They slipped out of the room and down the hall to her office.

"There's a real conflict of interests going on inside me right now." Dana kicked off her shoes and, sitting in her chair, she massaged her feet. "I have this weighty feeling of responsibility that tells me to *do* something. And then I have this contrary little voice saying that it's not my job."

"I'm not sure there's anything else to do, Dana." Rick walked over to the file cabinet and leaned against it. She looked tired, he thought. Her cheeks were flushed with soft color, her hair lay in disheveled red-gold waves around her head, her eyes revealed her weariness and yet held a cinnamon sparkle of energy and strength still untapped. A tender concern rose within him and vied with the not-so-tender questions he wanted to ask her. Maybe it was the wrong time, but he couldn't stop the words from coming. "Did you have a good trip?"

"Yes."

"I'm surprised you came back."

"Why?"

"You said you were resigning your job here. I just thought you—"

"I think we've already established what you think of my capacity to act in a responsible manner, Rick. Let's not go over it again."

He opened his mouth to argue and closed it with a snap. "Perhaps I owe you an apology, Dana. You handled the reporters downstairs like a real businesswoman. I was impressed."

She shot him a skeptical look. "You should have seen me handle the employees."

"I'm sure you did a fine job. Margaret is going to miss you when you leave, whether she realizes it or not."

"Yes, well, she doesn't show much regard for my professional opinion at the moment." Dana settled back in the chair and waved a hand in the general direction of her mother's office. "She's taken a whole new turn. Last week, Ki was her arch rival and worst enemy. Today, she's in there spilling her guts to him about the operation of the confectionery and asking him to help her uncover a sabotage plot. It doesn't make sense."

"Oh, I don't know. I think it's past time for them to stop acting like contestants in a yelling match. They need to settle their past and get on with the present."

"But Rick, Margaret hasn't trusted him from the beginning. She thought he came to Branson to make trouble. She accused him of stealing her recipe. She was sure he was behind the anonymous offer to buy the confectionery. She's blamed him for everything since the day he tossed his hat at her. How can she just suddenly say it was all a mistake?"

"My bet is she's known all along it wasn't true. She's just been fighting her feelings. Ki is an honest man, Dana. And he cares about your mother. You should have seen him when she called. He was...well, I can't describe the look on his face. It made me feel kind of weak in the knees." Rick felt that way now. Because of Dana. Because he wanted more than anything to kiss her, comfort her, make love to her. Like a sleepwalker, lost in elusive dreams, he made a move toward her...and stopped when the phone on her desk awakened him.

Dana punched the button and picked up the receiver. "Yes?"

"There's another one of those health people here," Margaret's voice came across the line sharp and crisp. "Will you talk to him?"

Great, Dana thought. Just what she needed. "Sure. Send him here." With a sigh Dana hung up and frowned at Rick. "Stick around and you can watch me deal with the health department."

Rick did watch and was fascinated by what he saw. Dana handled the inspector, a burly man with a butch haircut and a quiet manner, with finesse and skill. She was completely cooperative, but never once allowed culpability or the innuendo of negligence to enter the conversation. At all times Dana maintained a strict adherence to her role as vice president and legal representative of the Ausbrook Confectionery. She didn't forget it and the inspector wasn't allowed to, either. Rick was proud of her and felt badly that, until now, he hadn't realized how much character she possessed. Perhaps he'd judged her too harshly all the way around.

"You were magnificent," he told her when the man had gone. "I'd be honored to take you out to dinner."

Laying her head back against the headrest, Dana closed her eyes. "I'm not hungry, but thanks, anyway. I'll take a rain check, if you don't mind."

"Would you like for me to take you home?"

"I have my car, thanks." She opened one eye. "But I'd appreciate an escort to the parking lot. I don't think I can handle anyone else tonight."

Rick exaggerated a bow. "Consider me your body-guard."

She smiled, but didn't comment. Dana just gathered her things and walked out of her office and down the hall, pausing to lock up as she went. Voices came from behind Margaret's door, so Dana didn't interrupt, but walked on down the stairs. Rick went outside first, checking for anyone who might delay their journey, and within a very few minutes, unlocked Dana's car door and helped her in. She rolled down the window and he braced himself against the frame.

"Anything else I can do for you?" he asked.

"Yes. Explain to me why Margaret didn't sell this place when she had the chance."

"You know the answer—" A new thought broke the sentence in half. "Wait. Say that again."

"What?"

"You mentioned it before, didn't you? Upstairs, when you were talking about Margaret thinking Ki was behind the anonymous offer to—"

"—buy the confectionery," Dana finished for him. "Do you think he was?"

Rick studied the confectionery buildings and Dana touched his arm to reclaim his attention. "Rick, what's on your mind?"

"The anonymous offer. When was the offer made? And through whom?"

Dana told him. "Do you think Ki or someone else from London Country Candies made the offer?"

"No." Rick tapped a fingertip against the top of the car and reached a decision. "Can you get me some information about that offer? It had to have been made through a third party. Maybe we can find out where the offer came from."

Dana didn't know where he was headed with the idea, but she was eager to help. "I have the papers at home, in Margaret's study. Do you want them tonight?"

"Tomorrow morning is soon enough. I think, if you don't mind, I'll make a few inquiries, do a little research on that offer. It might not do any good, but you never know what we might turn up."

"I'll do all I can," Dana said, although she thought he was following a blind lead. "I'll get those papers to you first thing in the morning."

"Thanks." Rick leaned forward and took her lips in an unscheduled and gently sweet kiss.

Dana came very close to asking if she could go home with him, but she didn't. Sooner or later, Margaret would come home and Dana felt she needed to be there for her mother. "Will you call me?" she asked wistfully.

"Every hour," he said and with a smile, backed away from the car.

Dana started the engine and drove away, her lips warm and tingling from his kiss, her heart full of unspoken promises, her body longing to rest against his. But for now, for tonight and tomorrow and the next few days, she had to put her commitment to Margaret first. She had to handle the myriad problems at the confectionery. Only after she had fulfilled that obligation could she turn her attention to Rick and the relationship that now hung, undecided, but promisingly, in the balance.

THE NEXT TWO DAYS passed in a flurry of activity. Dana handed out diplomacy like candy and divided her time between soothing the anxieties of the employees and working with the health officials. Margaret had little to say and stayed in her office, making an occasional appearance to reassure the employees and general public alike. Ki came and went with an ease that Dana envied simply because she felt tied to the confectionery until the incident of the food poisonings was settled one way or the other. Rick did call to thank her for the information on the anonymous offer, but Dana was out of her office and missed it, receiving only a message that he'd had to go out of town and would be in touch as soon as he got back.

Late Thursday afternoon, Dana finally got a break, which was interrupted just as she settled back in her chair.

"Hi, Dana." Will Burton tapped on her office door and entered without an invitation. "How's everything going?"

"Well, hello, Will. How are you feeling?"

"Fine as four fish in a spring flood. The doctor says I can come back to work on Monday."

He'd lost a little weight, Dana thought, although his cheeks were still round and full. "That's good to hear. I'm sorry you got sick."

"Oh, it wasn't too bad. Kind of like the flu. I did have to stay one night in the hospital, though. That wasn't too pleasant."

"It hasn't been very pleasant around here, either," Dana said. "But we're about to come to the end of the trail, I think. There seems to be light just over the hill."

"Oh?" Will came toward the desk. "Have you found out why the candy went bad?"

"Not yet, but we should know by tomorrow. The tests were supposed to be finished yesterday. Frankly, I'll be glad when this is over. It's been a nightmare."

"I guess sales are down."

For a man who knew the business, that wasn't an overly insightful statement, but Dana let it pass. "We need to weather one crisis at a time, Will. We'll worry about sales figures later."

He nodded, looked around the office and brought his gaze back to Dana. "Do you think she'll sell now?"

"Sell? The confectionery? Don't be silly. Margaret has never had any intention—" Dana straightened in the chair. "Do you *want* her to sell, Will? Is that why you continue to bring up the subject?"

His pudgy hands swept the air with impatience. "The employees are asking, Dana. I'm just trying—"

"The employees are not asking." Dana came to her feet in one motion. "I've just spent three days convincing them that there was never any foundation to the rumor, that the confectionery is not for sale and their jobs are secure. Don't try to tell me what's going on in my business."

A look of surprise crossed his face and he brought his hands to rest at his sides. " *Your* business? And when did it become *your* business, Dana?"

She considered that with some surprise, herself. When had she stopped hating Margaret's confectionery and begun to take pride in the business of making candy? "What difference does it make to you, Will?"

"Yes, Will, what difference does it make to you?" Margaret entered the office with Ki and Rick at her heels. Her glance combed the room, her energy electrified the air. "Why are there never enough chairs in here, Dana?

I always have to stand in your office. There's never a place to sit."

Dana looked to Rick for enlightenment and received his smile instead. Ki settled himself into one of the two chairs. "Nice office, Dana," he said. "I like the seating arrangement."

Will began to back toward the door, despite the fact that his way was blocked from several angles. "I'll be leaving, I guess. You all probably want to discuss—"

"No, no." Margaret hastened to reassure him. "I'm glad you're here, Will. It'll make this whole thing easier. We finally got the official medical report."

Rick moved to stand beside Dana as the room got very still.

"You're not going to believe this, Dana." Margaret extended a piece of paper across the desk. "I was right. Someone sabotaged our chocolate truffles. One batch, anyway. It was laced with an herbal powder that causes stomach irritation when swallowed. Now, how do you suppose that happened?"

"Who would—?" Will stuttered and went pale as everyone turned. "Why're you all looking at me? I was one of the ones who got sick, remember? I ate the candy and it made me sick."

"That wasn't real smart of you, Will," Ki said. "You shouldn't eat poisoned candy."

"I didn't know it was poisoned. Why would I—?"

"That's what we're asking." Margaret faced him with deadly composure. "Why did you do it? Did you think it would force me to sell? Did you believe it would make the offer by Randel Stevens more attractive?"

"Randel Stevens?" Dana blurted out. "That's the candy company you talked to me about, Will. The one you visited last summer."

"I . . . don't know what you're talking about." Will's pale cheeks flushed scarlet with his denial. "I've always had the best interests of this confectionery at heart. I wouldn't . . ." His voice trailed into a miserable silence.

"It's time to cut to the chase, here, Will." Ki shifted, bringing his feet to rest on the base of the empty chair beside him. "Rick's been to the Randel Stevens plant in Connecticut. He talked with the man you've been dealing with and he's not happy about this poisoning business. He says you offered to help swing a sale, that you indicated the Ausbrook Confectionery had a new candy under wraps. A chocolate peppermint. All ready for testing and production. He says you called him up and told him all about it six months ago, Will."

"That's—" Will cleared his throat. "Why, that's ridiculous. I didn't know anything about the peppermint candy until the last couple of months."

"But you told me," Dana interrupted, "that everyone knew about it, Will. The feud over the Recipe has hardly been kept secret."

Will rubbed his jaw with a nervous hand. "So what if I did a bit of bragging when I talked to the guy? That doesn't mean anything. You can't hang a man for bein' proud of his company's products."

"But you sure as hell can hang him if he goes off half-cocked, offerin' to hand the Recipe *and* the company over to a competitor." Ki got to his feet, his own face flushing with anger. "And then, when you couldn't get Maggie to consider selling, you endangered the lives of innocent people to force her hand. That's not polite, Will. That's not even decent. I know your folks raised you better'n that."

Will's guard crumbled. "I didn't mean to hurt anybody. I only wanted to shake things up a bit. Make Margaret regret that she hadn't considered Randel Stevens's offer to buy the confectionery. I could have swung a really good deal for all of us. Margaret would have had plenty of money and I could have stepped into a real management position with the company. A progressive company, not a small-time 'family' operation like this one."

"And for that, you poisoned innocent people?" Ki's voice shook with fury.

"No one was hurt. Not really. I knew that herbal stuff would only make people sick. My grandpa taught me how to make some of the natural medicines. I knew what I was doing."

Dana couldn't comprehend such arrogance, such disregard for the rights of other people. "If he'd known how you were going to abuse that knowledge, Will, he'd never have taught you. There is no excuse for what you've done and the consequences are going to be severe."

Will's pudgy chin quivered, but he didn't drop his gaze. "For me or for the confectionery?"

"Both, unfortunately. But the confectionery will be all right. I don't know what will happen to you."

His eyes glistened with watery tears. "I didn't mean any harm. I didn't think it would turn out like this. What's Rachael going to say?"

"She's going to have some tall explaining to do, herself," Margaret said. "But at least you didn't involve her in your sabotage attempt and she did help us put the missing pieces together. She admitted she took the Recipe from my study and gave it to you."

To his credit, Will rallied to protect Rachael. "She didn't want to do it. I convinced her we were doing the best thing for everyone concerned. Don't blame her. It's my fault. All of it. I wanted to have the Peppermint Kiss recipe all set for production by the time Randel Stevens took over. Then when I realized you wouldn't sell, I figured that if I had the candy I'd have more leverage with you. Especially after I found out about the lawsuit and realized how important the Peppermint Kiss recipe was to you, Margaret. So I had Rachael working on it all the time. Even after you told me to quit. You paid so little attention, Margaret, it was easy to keep it quiet. Until Dana started poking her nose in places it didn't belong.''

"Just doing my job, Will," Dana said.

"Your job. Ha. I should have been the vice president. I deserved that position. You don't even like this place, Dana."

Rick's hand moved to enclose Dana's and she cherished the support he offered so freely.

"You're so impatient, Will." Margaret folded her arms and leaned against the edge of the desk. "You could've been a vice president in a couple of years, if you'd just . . . well, it doesn't matter now. I accept some of the blame for what's happened. I gave you too much responsibility and for the past couple of months I've been distracted and didn't keep a close enough eye on what was going on. I should have known you were having Rachael work on the Recipe. I should have realized how much you resented Dana. But—" Margaret lifted her shoulder in a tiny shrug "—I've found out I'm human, after all, subject to the same pitfalls and emotions as the rest of the world. I'm just sorry you got caught in your own ambition, Will."

Will glanced around the gathering, looking for a way out. But there was none.

"I'm disappointed in you, Will," Margaret said. "Really disappointed."

Ki picked up the phone, dialed a number and spoke with someone on the other end. When he hung up, he pinned Will with a steady gaze. "The health officials want to talk to you, boy. I hope you're feelin' well enough to answer their questions, 'cause they're waiting downstairs. Rick and I will walk down with you."

All of Will's blustery protests fell on deaf ears as he was escorted out of Dana's office and down the hall.

"How did you put all this together?" Dana asked when she and Margaret were alone. "It never would have occurred to me to connect Will with the food poisonings. I was beginning to think he wanted you to sell the confectionery, but I didn't know why."

"Rick thought of it first. He made a few inquiries, found out that Randel Stevens had made the anonymous offer to buy, from there, he contacted the company and finally got in to see the man with whom Will had been dealing. The Randel Stevens representative thought everything was on the up and up, had no idea Will was operating on his own. It was Will's idea that they should make the offer to buy anonymously. I guess he thought that would make it more acceptable to me. Who knows what he thought. But once I got the report on the poisonings and knew the powder could only have been added during the production of the candy, it was pretty simple to pinpoint Will. No one else could have circumvented our security and quality checks."

Dana's stomach churned with remorse. "And I thought you'd ordered Will to work on the Peppermint Kiss recipe. I believed you intentionally defied the court order, went behind my back, and despite my legal advice, planned to throw the Peppermint Kisses in Ki's face. Regardless of the consequences."

Margaret nodded. "I know that's what you thought, Dana, but until I had something more than a suspicion of what Will was up to, I didn't want to say anything. Then you were gone and I didn't know if I'd get a chance to explain."

"I'm sorry, Margaret. I should have had more faith in you. But you've acted so crazy ever since Ki— Well, that's no excuse. I apologize."

"Don't worry about it, dear. I've made a few mis-judgments myself. I should have placed more trust in you and your ability as a lawyer. So I apologize, too."

Dana accepted the apology with a sigh and sat again in her chair, feeling drained now that the answers were in front of her. "And Rachael took the Recipe. What made her confess?"

"Guilt, I suppose. She had a heavy conscience and the minute Ki began questioning her, she told us everything she knew, which wasn't much overall, but enough to implicate Will beyond a reasonable doubt."

"Charity's going to be upset."

"Yes, but at least Rachael's only guilty of using poor judgment. I won't press charges or anything. As long as she gives back my recipe half."

The first smile of the afternoon crept slowly over Dana's face. "Does this mean we don't have to go to court tomorrow for the hearing on the Recipe? Aren't you and Ki—?"

"Ki and I aren't anything," Margaret said crisply, making her way to the door. "The hearing is on and we're going to find out once and for all, who owns the Peppermint Kiss recipe. So, be prepared, Dana. I expect you to be ready to oppose every word that Stafford boy utters in the courtroom. We'll show them a thing or two."

Dana halted Margaret's dramatic exit. "As your attorney, Margaret, I advise you to drop this lawsuit and not make a fool of yourself for a recipe."

Margaret lifted her shoulder in an easy shrug. "I've been a fool for lesser things."

Dana shook her head and wondered if she would ever, *ever* understand her mother.

Chapter Fourteen

"Do you have any idea what we're doing here?" Rick asked as he walked up to Dana.

She was seated on a bench outside the courtroom and she scooted over to make a space for him. "I see you had no more success in talking Hezekiah out of this than I had in convincing Margaret."

Rick set his briefcase on the floor. "I feel like I've been talking to a mule."

"I know how you feel." Dana glanced down the hallway. "I just hope the judge understands that we're only representing these idiots, not agreeing with them."

Rick grinned. "Maybe they won't show up."

"No such luck. Margaret rode in with me. I don't know where she is now, but I know she's here somewhere."

"Ki disappeared as soon as we hit the front door, too. You don't suppose they're somewhere throwing candy and hats at each other, do you?"

Dana smiled at the thought. "We can always hope they'll both be arrested before the case is called."

"Have you found out where we are on the docket?" Rick asked, and when Dana shook her head, he stood and disappeared inside the courtroom doors. He returned a few minutes later. "Ki and Margaret better get here soon. We're less than ten minutes away."

Dana reached for her briefcase and got to her feet. "Let's wait inside. No point in hiding out here in the hall."

A clerk of the court approached them before they could be seated in the courtroom. "Would you come with me, please?" he requested.

Glancing at Rick and receiving a questioning look in return, Dana followed the clerk into the judge's chambers. Margaret and Ki, both wearing smiles as wide as the Mississippi, were standing there. And they were holding hands. Dana felt a mixture of exasperation and relief blended with just a touch of apprehension. "Well, well," she said. "Don't tell me we've managed to reach a settlement?"

"Don't get your hopes up," Rick said. "It could be a competency hearing."

Ki laughed, a deep, rolling, wonderful laugh. "We're as sane as two butterflies in an April wind. Maggie and I are getting married."

"Married?" Rick echoed.

"Married?" Dana repeated and her eyes sought those of her mother. "You're *marrying* him?"

"You don't have to look so shocked," Margaret replied. "You're the one who kept saying you thought I'd never gotten over him."

"Well, yes, but..." Dana grappled with the idea. She'd thought of it before, of course, but she hadn't really *thought* about it before. "Married? Are you sure?"

Margaret took Dana by the shoulders. "Hell, no. But I've waited forty years to decide to marry this man. It's pretty obvious I'm not ever going to be sure." Her expression softened suddenly. "But I do believe I love him, Dana. And I haven't felt this way in…well in a long time.''

For the space of a heartbeat, Dana agonized over the love that couldn't exist between her father and her mother and then she surrendered to the joy of seeing Margaret happy. And she *was* happy. It was easy to see in the blush on her cheeks, the excitement in her eyes. How could Dana not feel glad for her? ''I want you to be happy, Mother.''

Margaret's smile was as warm as sunshine. ''Thank you, dear. Will you stand up with me?''

''Now?'' Dana glanced over her shoulder at Rick who was talking with Ki. ''Here?''

''Is there a better time? Of course, here and now. I mean, for heaven's sake. I quit smoking. I have to do something to celebrate.'' Margaret took her hand, took a step forward, then a step back. ''Oh, I almost forgot to tell you. We're taking a trip, a honeymoon. Ki wants to show me the London Country plant and a few favorite spots on the continent. Will you fill in for me at the confectionery? I know this is a terrible time to leave, but—'' she came close, very close, to giggling ''—I'm leaving. I know you can handle anything that arises and I'd like for you to get started on the Peppermint Kisses now that we have both halves of the Recipe. It will be the first joint venture for London Country and Ausbrook Candies and you're the perfect choice to oversee—you didn't really intend to resign, did you, Dana?''

It was impossible to throw so much as a droplet of water on the happy couple's plans, Dana decided. And she had already changed her mind about resigning anyway, now she knew Margaret hadn't lied to her. ''I'll be happy to take care of the confectionery while you're on your honeymoon. How long do you think you'll be away?''

"I don't know," Margaret said. "But when I get back, Dana, I'd like for us to begin again. I know I haven't been the ideal mother, but I want to build on what we've started and get to know you better. I want you to be happy, too. And if that means that once you return to Philadelphia, we have to make time for more frequent visits, then that's what we'll do. Okay?"

Dana only had time to nod her agreement before the judge called them forward and the ceremony began. It was touching to watch Ki and Margaret exchange vows they'd postponed for forty years. Dana had a lump in her throat and a tear in her eye when it was over, but she banished both with a tremulous smile of happiness and wished Ki and Margaret all the best. Ki bussed her cheek with a sweet kiss and told her he'd always wanted a daughter. When the documents were signed, the ill-begotten lawsuit dropped from the judge's docket and congratulations offered all around, the clerk shooed them from the office, and Dana and Rick saw the newlyweds off with a wave.

"Uh, could you give me a ride home?" Rick asked. "They took my truck."

"You should be more careful with your vehicles, Rick. That's the second one you've had stolen out from under your nose."

"I guess I'm just a sucker for a happy ending."

"I hope this turns out to be a happy ending. I'd certainly hate to have to live with Margaret for the rest of my life."

"Good thing you have other options."

Dana glanced once more at the departing truck before bringing her gaze up to meet Rick's. "It is, isn't it? I guess I'll start packing. I definitely want to be out of that house before the honeymooners return."

"You don't have to be in that big a hurry. Ki just bought a house. He'll want to live there, I'm sure." Rick cupped Dana's elbow with his hand and they stepped from the sun to the shade.

"Margaret would never consider moving. She loves her house."

Rick chuckled. "Feud number two in the making. But you don't have to worry about where they live, Dana. They can spend all their time fighting and you'll never even have to know." He sobered. "That's one good thing about living in Philadelphia, I suppose."

With a slanted glance from the corner of her eye, Dana caught his wry grimace. "There are dozens of good things about living in Philadelphia," she said. "Shall I list them for you?"

A heavy sigh passed his lips as he pushed back the edges of his jacket and put his hands in the pockets of his slacks. "No. I'll just have to discover them for myself."

"Are you planning to go there, Rick?" A tiny smile began pushing at the corners of her mouth. "Anytime, soon?"

"Sooner than I'd like, but..." He turned to her, his eyes dark with promises. "I've reconciled myself to staying there as long as it takes to convince you that you can't live without me."

Her heart sprinted into a double rhythm and her lips edged upward with pleasure, despite her attempt to keep them sternly under control. "That could take a very long time, Rick. Especially since I won't be in Philadelphia. Except for short visits to my father, of course. I'm planning to stay here, in Branson."

Over the space of a moment the lines of his face softened with hope, his eyes took on an emerald gleam. "You're staying?"

"Do you think Margaret could have run off the way she did if she didn't have me to take charge of the confectionery for her?" The look Rick gave her melted any further desire to tease him. "I'm staying, Rick. I decided over the weekend."

"Before the food poisonings? Before Margaret and Ki—?"

She nodded. "Last week I was ready to resign and head for the east. But somehow, the closer the plane got to Philadelphia, the heavier my heart felt. I had some long talks with my dad…you'll like him, Rick, he's great. But I realized early in the visit that I wasn't happy there. I missed you. I missed Margaret. I even missed my job, of all things. And so I—"

He pressed a finger against her lips. "Wait. I want to hear you say that again."

"What? That I missed my job?"

He frowned and Dana conceded. "I missed you, Rick. It has finally occurred to me that I don't want to live without you any longer." A shy, hesitant smile graced her lips. "See? You didn't even have to do anything to convince me."

"The hell I didn't. What have I been doing for the past three months if not trying to convince you to love me? Even when you decided to seduce me, I had to hold out for ethical reasons and hope for a better offer."

"Well, this is your final offer. I want the red chair, that little broom closet and a place to reside."

Rick eyed her speculatively. "But not my truck?"

"You don't have a truck, remember. Ki just took it."

"He'll bring it back. You can have the broom closet, just don't tell me what you plan to use it for—"

"An office, of course. When I'm not being vice president at the Ausbrook Confectionery, I may want to practice small-town law. You won't mind sharing, will you?"

He jingled the change in his pocket, pursed his lips and shook his head. "The broom closet is yours, but I can't just give you the red chair without a fight."

"I'll arm wrestle you for it."

"Done. Now, as to the bedroom you wanted—"

"I never mentioned a bedroom."

"You want one, don't you?"

"Well, yes, but I—"

"Okay, then. I happen to have the perfect residence for you. There's just one catch. You have to have a special license to live there."

"A license? To do what?"

Rick reached for her, unable to wait any longer. "To live with me. To love me. To tell the world that I love you and that I want everyone to know you're my wife." He drew her close and the hot September morning got hotter. "Oh, Dana, I've loved you so long and never thought I'd know the joy of this moment. Will you marry me?"

"Yes."

His lips met hers in a promise as sweet as a new morning. When he pulled back, Dana gazed up at him through eyes misty with happiness. "I love you, Rick. I thought I'd gotten over it, but when I saw you again, I knew I hadn't even done a very good job of pretending."

"I was no better. Trying to label you a princess and accusing you of having no sticking power." His hands tightened on hers. "I hope you'll forgive me for the hateful things I said. I was trying to pretend that when you left...again...I wouldn't be left with a broken heart."

She placed her hand over his chest, as if trying to mend the scars on his heart. "I've learned that success is not measured by wealth or independence, Rick. It's the sense of accomplishment that comes with a job well done. I learned that from working at the confectionery." She made a wry face. "Can you believe I said that? Me, who always hated the smell of chocolate?" Her grimace gave way to a frown. "Wait. You're not marrying me to get your hands on an unlimited supply of sweets, are you?"

His grin cut wide across his mouth. "A man's got to do what a man's got to do. But don't let it bother you, Sweets. I'll always love you more than I love fudge."

"Good. Because I love you more than I could ever love Peppermint Kisses." She grabbed his hand and started walking back into the courthouse. "Let's go find that judge."

"Now? Here?"

"Is there a better time or place?" She tugged on his hand. "Besides this is a day of celebration. My mother finally quit smoking."

Rick stepped ahead and held open the door. "We'll name our first child Peppermint."

Dana killed that idea with a look. "Our children will be given names to live up to."

"Hezekiah and Maggie?"

"I was thinking more of Peace and Quiet."

Rick laughed as he followed her inside the cool building. "Well, whatever we name our children, they'll grow up knowing that their father is crazy-sick in love with their mother."

"And vice versa." Dana gave him her heart wrapped in a smile. "It's our own special recipe, Rick. A recipe for love and commitment and happy-ever-after."

He squeezed her hand and together they walked toward the judge's chambers.

CHRISTMAS IS FOR KIDS

AMERICAN ROMANCE PHOTO CONTEST

At Harlequin American Romance® we believe Christmas is for kids—a special time, a magical time. And we've put together a unique project to celebrate the American Child. Our annual holiday romances will feature children—just like yours—who have their Christmas wishes come true.

A reddish, golden-haired boy. Or a curious, ponytailed girl with glasses. A kid sister. A dark, shy, small boy. A mischievous, freckle-nosed lad. A girl with ash blond braided hair. Or a bright-eyed little girl always head of the class.

Send us a color photo of your child, along with a paragraph describing his or her excitement and anticipation of Christmas morning. If your entry wins, your child will appear on one of the covers of our December 1989 CHRISTMAS IS FOR KIDS special series. Read the Official Rules carefully before you enter.

OFFICIAL RULES

1. Eligibility: Male and female children ages 4 through 12 who are residents of the U.S.A., or Canada, except children of employees of Harlequin Enterprises Ltd., its affiliates, retailers, distributors, agencies, professional photographers and Smiley Promotion, Inc.

2. How to enter: Mail a color slide or photo, not larger than 8½ × 11″, taken no longer than six months ago along with proof of purchase from facing page to:

> American Romance Photo Contest
> Harlequin Books
> 300 East 42nd Street
> 6th Floor
> New York, NY
> 10017.

Professional photographs are not eligible. Only one entry per child allowed. All photos remain the sole property of Harlequin Enterprises Ltd. and will not be returned. A paragraph of not more than 50 words must accompany the photo expressing your child's joy and anticipation of Christmas morning. All entries must be received by March 31, 1989.

3. Judging: Photos will be judged equally on the child's expression, pose, neatness and photo clarity. The written paragraph will be judged on sincerity and relationship to the subject. Judging will be completed within 45 days of contest closing date and winners will be notified in writing and must return an Affidavit of Eligibility and Release within 21 days or an alternate winner will be selected.

4. Prizes: Nine Prizes will be awarded, with each winner's likeness appearing on a cover of our December 1989 CHRISTMAS IS FOR KIDS special series. Winners will also receive an artists signed print of the cover. There is no cash substitution for prizes. Harlequin Enterprises Ltd. reserves the right to use the winner's name and likeness for promotional purposes without any compensation. Any Canadian resident winner or their parent or guardian must correctly answer an arithmetical skill-testing question within a specified time.

5. When submitting an entry, entrants must agree to these rules and the decisions of the judges, under the supervision of Smiley Promotion, Inc., an independent judging organization whose decisions are final. Sponsor reserves the right to substitute prizes of like substance. Contest is subject to all federal, provincial, state and local laws. Void where prohibited, restricted or taxed. For a winner's list, send a stamped self-addressed envelope to American Romance Photo Contest Winners, P.O. Box 554, Bowling Green Station, New York, N.Y. 10274 for receipt by March 31, 1989.

Photo-2

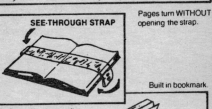